PITKIN COUNTY
library
inspire growth

D0478542

SAUCER

SAVAGE PLANET

ALSO BY STEPHEN COONTS

SAUCER

SAUCER: THE CONQUEST

PIRATE ALLEY

THE DISCIPLE

THE ASSASSIN

THE TRAITOR

LIARS & THIEVES

LIBERTY

AMERICA

HONG KONG

CUBA

FORTUNES OF WAR

THE INTRUDERS

THE RED HORSEMEN

UNDER SIEGE

THE MINOTAUR

FINAL FLIGHT

FLIGHT OF THE INTRUDER

WITH WILLIAM H. KEITH

DEEP BLACK: DEATH WAVE

DEEP BLACK: SEA OF TERROR

DEEP BLACK: ARCTIC GOLD

WITH JIM DeFELICE

DEEP BLACK: CONSPIRACY

DEEP BLACK: JIHAD

DEEP BLACK: PAYBACK

DEEP BLACK: DARK ZONE

DEEP BLACK: BIOWAR

DEEP BLACK

WRITING AS EVE ADAMS

THE GARDEN OF EDEN

NONFICTION

THE CANNIBAL QUEEN

ANTHOLOGIES

THE SEA WITCH

ON GLORIOUS WINGS

VICTORY

COMBAT

WAR IN THE AIR

SAUCER

SAVAGE PLANET

STEPHEN COONTS

ST. MARTIN'S GRIFFIN NEW YORK

This is a work of fiction. All of the characters, organizations, and events portrayed in this novel are either products of the author's imagination or are used fictitiously.

www.stmartins.com

Library of Congress Cataloging-in-Publication Data

Coonts, Stephen, 1946–
Saucer : savage planet / Stephen Coonts.—First Edition.
p. cm.—(Savage Planet ; 3)
ISBN 978-1-250-04200-2 (trade paperback)
ISBN 978-1-250-06198-0 (hardcover)
ISBN 978-1-4668-3921-2 (e-book)
1. Unidentified flying objects—Fiction. 2. Space flight—Fiction. I. Title.
PS3553.O5796S2828 2014
813'.54—dc23

2013046167

St. Martin's Press books may be purchased for educational, business, or promotional use. For information on bulk purchases, please contact Macmillan Corporate and Premium Sales Department at 1-800-221-7945, extension 5442, or write specialmarkets@macmillan.com.

First Edition: April 2014

10 9 8 7 6 5 4 3 2 1

To my grandchildren:
Sophie, Connor, Abby, Logan,
Carson, Hunter and Brenden

On this small planet
Orbiting a nondescript star,
On the edge of a humongous galaxy
Wheeling endlessly in the infinite void,
The river of life flows on and on . . .
Let it flow.

SAUCER

SAVAGE PLANET

1

ADAM SOLO WEDGED HIMSELF INTO THE CHAIR AT THE navigator's table in the small compartment behind the bridge and braced himself against the motion of the ship. Rain beat a tattoo on the roof over his head, and wind moaned around the portholes. Although the seas weren't heavy, the ship rolled, pitched and corkscrewed viciously because she was not under way; she was riding sea anchors, being held in one place, at the mercy of the swells.

Through the rain-smeared porthole windows Solo could see the flood and spotlights of another ship several hundred feet to port. She was also small, only 350 feet long, roughly the size of the ship Solo was aboard, *Atlantic Queen*. She also carried massive cranes fore and aft, was festooned with floodlights that lit the deck and the water between the ships and was bobbing like a cork in a maelstrom.

Through the open door to the bridge Solo occasionally

heard the ringing of the telegraph as the captain signaled the engine room for power to help hold his ship where he wanted her. Johnson was the captain, an overweight, overbearing slob with a sneer engraved on his face and a curse on his lips. He was cursing tonight as he wrestled the helm; Solo ignored the burst of mindless obscenities that reached him during lulls in the wind's song and concentrated on the newspaper before him.

"Possible Alien Starship Found in Australia," the headline screamed. Beneath that headline, in slightly smaller type, the subhead read, "Wreckage buried in coral reef moved ashore for study."

Beside the story was a photo of two men and two women posed in front of a massive pile of unidentifiable junk. Solo studied the wreckage. It was not possible to even determine what the original color might have been. The two men were identified in the caption of the photo as Mr. Rip Cantrell, a young man in his early twenties, and Mr. Arthur "Egg" Cantrell, a rotund, balding man in his fifties. The woman, lean and athletic with her hair in a ponytail, was identified as Charlotte Pine, a former U.S. Air Force test pilot. Beside her stood an Australian archaeologist. Solo studied their faces in the photo, then read the article as rain pounded on the windows and the ship rode the back of the living sea.

The article mentioned that this was not the first spacecraft Rip Cantrell had discovered. About a year before, as a young engineering student on an expedition to the

Sahara, Cantrell had uncovered a perfectly preserved saucer in a sandstone ledge and had even figured out how to make it fly. He almost lost his life when greedy thugs tried to steal the saucer and its valuable technology. Only with the help of former test pilot Charley Pine had he managed to save that saucer and keep it safe. Soon after, a Frenchman named pierre Artois, an evil genius bent on world conquest, had even managed to steal the famous Roswell saucer the air force had kept hidden for decades at Area 51. Once again, Charley Pine had saved the day when she chased the Roswell saucer and it crashed into the ocean as millions watched on TV. Since then, saucer technology had been revolutionizing the world economy. Great leaps forward in alternative fuels, anti-gravity and computer technology, solar power, metal fabrication—all these advances in man's knowledge were leading to new products and improvements in old ones.

Solo was a trim man with short black hair, even features and skin that appeared deeply tanned. He was below average in height, just five and a half feet tall, and weighed about 140 pounds. Tonight he was dressed in jeans, work boots and a dark green Gore-Tex jacket.

He leaned back in the chair and closed his eyes, savoring the movement of the ship.

Ah, once, long ago, he had been out on this ocean in winter, in a vessel much smaller than this one. How the wind had howled in the rigging; spindrift showered the men and women huddled under blankets and skins, trying to stay warm, as cold rain stung and soaked them. Occasionally the rain turned to sleet, and the ship and people were soon covered with a layer of ice.

The motion of this ship brought the memory flooding back. Most of those nights he spent at the steering oar, because he was the best helmsman aboard and he was the captain. In that roaring, wet, absolute darkness the trick was to keep the wind in the same quadrant, keep the unseen sail drawing evenly, feel the way the ship rode the sea, actually become one with the ship. If he held the wind just so and the motion of the ship remained the same, he was steering a straight course. If the sail luffed or the motion of the ship changed, he would hear and feel it.

Without a compass, without the moon or stars, raw seamanship was the only way a course could be sailed. Adam Solo had been good at it then, and after a week of storms and clouds and wind brought them all safely to land.

Solo's chin was on his chest when the door opened and a heavyset man wearing a suit and tie came in. He tossed a foul-weather coat on the desk.

"Doctor," Solo said in greeting.

Dr. Harrison Douglas, the chairman and CEO of World Pharmaceuticals, was so nervous he couldn't hold still. "This is it, Solo," he said as he smacked one fist into a palm. "This flying saucer we are bringing up is the key to wealth and power beyond the wildest dreams of anyone alive." Douglas added, almost as an aside to himself, "If it's still reasonably intact . . ."

"You're sure?"

"If it holds the secrets I think it does, then yes." Douglas braced himself and glanced out the porthole at the heaving sea between the ships. "You still think you can make the computers talk to you?"

Solo nodded. "Yes, but you've never told me what you want from them."

"That's right. I've kept my mouth firmly shut." Douglas took a deep breath, looked around the little room, then fastened his gaze on Solo. "This saucer crashed into the ocean. May be torn all to hell, smashed into bits, but there's a sliver of a chance . . ."

Douglas turned to the porthole and rubbed the moisture from the glass with his sleeve. ". . . A sliver of a chance that one or more of the computers are intact. And if one is, I want you to find the formulas for any drugs that are in the memories."

"Are there formulas for drugs?"

All the experts agreed that interstellar distances were so vast that a starship crew would die before they got to their destination unless their lives were artificially extended. Somehow.

"Yes, there are drugs," said Douglas. "Enough said. You know our deal. I'll pay you ten million cash."

"And make billions."

"I sincerely hope so," Harrison Douglas said. He jammed his hands in his pockets and stared out the porthole into the night with unseeing eyes.

Yes, he did hope to make billions, and if ever there

was a drug to generate that kind of money, a drug that prevented aging was undoubtedly it. Well, Douglas was in the Big Pharma business. If arresting aging involved drugs, by God, World Pharmaceuticals could figure out how to make them. Every man and woman on the planet would like to stop the aging process, or if that proved impossible, at least slow it down, preserve quality of life and extend it free from the diseases that aging causes or enables. An extra ten good years—how much would that be worth to the average Joe? Or twenty? Or thirty? America, Europe, Arabia, India, Japan, China . . . the possibilities were awe-inspiring.

Harrison Douglas twitched with excitement.

Douglas smacked a fist into the palm of his other hand. *Yes, the people of the saucers must have possessed an antiaging drug.*

Douglas was musing on how much money such a drug would make World, and himself, of course, the CEO who made it happen, when he heard Captain Johnson give a shout.

Douglas glanced through the porthole. He saw waves washing over a shape even darker than the night sea.

"It's up!" he said excitedly. With that he grabbed the foul-weather coat and dashed through the door onto the bridge. He went straight through, right by the captain, onto the open wing of the bridge and charged down a ladder to the main deck.

Adam Solo slowly folded the page of the newspaper

that contained the story of the Australian artifact and placed it in his shirt pocket. He pulled on a cap and stepped onto the bridge. Ignoring the captain at the helm, Solo walked to the unprotected wing of the bridge and gazed down into the heaving dark sea as the wind and rain tore at him. The wind threatened to tear his cap from his head, so he removed it. Dr. Douglas was there on the main deck at the rail, holding on with both hands.

Floodlights from both ships lit the area between the ships and the heavy cables that disappeared into the water. From the angle of the cables, it was obvious that what they held was just beneath the surface. Snatches of the commands the chief on deck shouted to the winch operators reached Solo. Gazing intently at the scene before him, he ignored them.

As Solo watched, swells separated the ships slightly, tightening the cables, and something again broke the surface. It was a mound, dark as the black water; swells broke over it.

As quickly as it came into view, the shape disappeared again as the ships rolled toward each other.

Over the next five minutes the deck crews aboard both ships tightened their cables inch by inch, lifting the black shape to the surface again, then higher and higher until finally it was free of the water and hung suspended between the ships. The spotlights played upon it, a black, saucer-shaped object, perfectly round and thickest in the middle. It was not small—the diameter was about ninety feet—and it was heavy; the cables that held it were taut as violin strings, and the ships listed toward it a noticeable amount.

Solo stepped back into the sheltered area of the bridge and wiped the rain from his hair with his hand, then settled the cap onto his head as he listened to the voices on the bridge loudspeaker. The deck chiefs of this ship and the other vessel were talking to each other on handheld radios, coordinating their efforts as the saucer was inched over the deck of this ship. The ship's radio picked up the conversation and piped it here so that the captain could listen in and, if he wished, take part in the conversation.

A moment later Dr. Douglas came in from the bridge wing, pulling the door shut behind him and brushing water from his coat.

"Well, we got it up, Doctor," Captain Johnson said heartily. "And they said it couldn't be done. Ha! You owe us some serious money."

"I will when you have it safely on the dock in Newark," Douglas replied.

"We'll get 'er there, you can bet on that," Johnson said confidently. "The company has big money ridin' on it. They promised every man in the crew a bonus, including me. Gonna be nice money, and I'll be damn glad to get it."

It took twenty minutes for the deck crew to get the dark, ominous ovoid shape deposited onto the waiting timbers on *Atlantic Queen*'s deck and lashed down. The saucer was so large it filled the space between the bridge and the forward crane and protruded over both rails. It seemed to dwarf the ship on which it rode, pushing it deeper into the sea.

When the cables that had lifted the saucer from the sea floor had been released, the sea anchors were brought aboard and the ship got under way. Solo felt the ride improve immediately as the screws bit into the dark water. The other ship, which had helped raise the saucer, had already dissolved into the darkness.

"There you are," Johnson said heartily to Douglas, who had his nose almost against the window, staring at the spaceship. "Your flyin' saucer's settin' like a hen on her nest, safe and sound, and she ain't goin' noplace."

Douglas flashed a grin and dashed for the ladder to the main deck.

Solo went back into the navigator's shack. He emerged seconds later carrying a hard plastic case and descended the bridge wing ladder to the main deck, where the sailors were milling around, inspecting the saucer while they rigged ropes across it and chained the ropes to padeyes in the deck. Several of them were touching the machine . . . and marveling.

As Douglas watched, Solo opened his case, took out a wand and adjusted the switches and knobs within, then donned a headset. Carrying the instrument case, he began a careful inspection of the saucer, all of it that he could see from the deck. He even climbed the mast of the forward crane to get a look at the top of it, then returned to the deck. As he walked and climbed around he glanced occasionally at the gauges in his case, but mostly he concentrated on visually inspecting the surface of the ship. He could see no damage whatsoever.

Douglas asked him a couple of questions, but Solo didn't answer, so eventually he stopped asking. One by one the tired sailors left the deck, heading for their berths. They had been hard at work for almost twenty hours and were exhausted.

Solo crawled under the saucer and lay there studying his instrument. Finally he took off his headset, stowed it back inside the case and closed it.

One of the officers squatted down a few feet away. This was the first mate. "No radiation?" he asked Solo. The sailor was in his early thirties, with unkempt wind-blown hair and acne scars on his face.

"Doesn't seem to be."

"Boy, that's amazing." The mate reached and placed his hand on the cold black surface immediately over his head. "So this is the one that went straight into the ocean like a bullet from over a hundred thousand feet up," said the mate, whose name was DeVries. "Yeah, I heard all about it on TV. Saw all those reruns of the saucers chasin' each other over Manhattan. Bet this thing made one hell of a splash when it hit! I didn't figure we'd find it in one piece, I can tell you. An impact like that . . ."

Solo studied the belly of the saucer as the raw sea wind played with his hair. At least here, under the saucer, he was sheltered from the rain.

"Everything inside is probably torn loose, I figure," DeVries continued, warming to his subject. "Scrambled up inside there like a dozen broken eggs. And that crazy Frenchman flying it must still be inside, squashed flat as a road-killed possum. Couldn't nobody live through a smashup like that. He's gotta be as dead as Napoleon Bonaparte and getting pretty ripe, I'll bet. This thing's been in the water a whole month."

The first mate turned to Douglas and asked, "So, Doctor, how come you're spending all this money raisin' this flyin' saucer off the ocean floor?"

Douglas said matter-of-factly, "Scientific curiosity."

"Eight million bucks is a lot to pay to scratch that itch," DeVries said thoughtfully, a remark Douglas let pass without comment. The salvage operation was going to cost Douglas at least that much.

As those two watched, Adam Solo had placed his hand on the hatch handle and held it there. Now, after ten seconds or so, he pulled down on one end of the handle and turned it sideways. The handle rotated and the hatch opened above his head. Water began dripping out.

Not much, but some. The saucer had been lying in 250 feet of water; if the integrity of the hull had been broken, seawater under pressure would have filled the interior. This might be leakage from the ship's tank, or merely condensation. Solo wiped a drip off the hatch lip and tasted it. He was relieved—it wasn't saltwater.

Now Solo inspected the yawning hole. He stuck the wand inside and studied the panel on his Geiger counter.

"Background radiation," he told Douglas, who smiled in a self-satisfied way and rubbed his hands together, a gesture that Solo had noticed he used often.

Solo turned off the Geiger counter. He carefully wrapped the cord around the wand and stowed it in the plastic case, then shoved the case up into the dark belly of the saucer.

DeVries craned his neck, trying to see inside. "Like, when you going to climb into this thing?"

A smile crossed the face of Adam Solo. "Now," he said. He raised himself through the hatchway into the belly of the ship.

Harrison Douglas bent down and crawled under the ship, then squirmed up through the hatch. Then the hatch closed.

The first mate slowly shook his head. "Glad it was them two and not me," he said conversationally, although there was no one there to hear him. "My momma didn't raise no fools. I wouldn't have crawled into that thing for all the money on Wall Street."

THE FIRST MATE MADE HIS WAY TO THE BRIDGE. CAPtain Johnson was still at the helm. "Well, did you ask him?" the captain demanded.

"Scientific curiosity, Douglas said."

"My ass," the captain said sourly. "Oh, well. As long as we get paid . . ." After a moment the captain continued, "Solo's weird. That accent of his—it isn't much, but it's there. I can't place it. Sometimes I think it's Eastern European of one kind or another, then I think it isn't."

"All I know," DeVries said, "is he ain't from Brooklyn."

The captain didn't respond to that inanity. He said aloud, musing, "He's kinda freaky, but nothin' you can put your finger on. Still, bein' around him gives me goosebumps."

"They got money," DeVries said simply. In his mind, money excused all peculiarities, an ingrained attitude he had acquired long ago because he didn't have any.

"World Pharmaceuticals is gonna have to push a lotta pills to earn back eight million smackers for deep-sea salvage."

"I say it's a good thing," the mate said lightly. "Some of this saucer money is finally trickling all the way down to us."

"Amen," the captain said, and both men laughed.

Then Johnson's mood changed. "Solo is gonna try to fix that thing up and they're gonna fly it," Johnson said darkly. "That's gotta be it."

"You gonna call somebody?"

"After Douglas gets his saucer safely ashore, I don't think he gives a rat's patootie who we tell."

"It'll never fly again," DeVries said with finality. "Bet it's nothing but wreckage inside. Maybe if somebody like Boeing worked on it for a year or two they could get it in shape to fly again, but one guy ain't gonna do it with hand tools."

The captain lit a cigarette one-handed. "Tell you what," he said after his first full puff. "I don't care a whit if it flies or not, or what Douglas hopes to do with it. Guy's got a screw loose."

The mate couldn't take his eyes off the saucer. "Thing's heavy as hell. Like to never got it up. We almost lost it a dozen times."

"Notice how the *Queen*'s ridin? Lot of weight up high. Hope we make harbor before the sea kicks up."

DeVries grunted. After a moment he said with a touch of wonder in his voice, "A real, honest-to-God flying saucer . . . Never believed in 'em, y'know?"

"Yeah," the captain agreed. "Thought it was all bull puckey. Even standing here looking at one of the darn things, I have my doubts."

THE ONLY LIGHT INSIDE THE SAUCER CAME THROUGH the canopy, a dim glow from the salvage vessel's masthead lights. It took several seconds for Solo's eyes to adjust.

As the first mate predicted, the corpse of Jean-Paul Lalouette was there. The force of the impact had caused the seat belt and shoulder harness of the pilot's seat to tear though his body, the major pieces of which were lying on the floor under the instrument panel. There was blood everywhere, but it had congealed and now had the consistency of dry paint.

After a glance, Solo ignored the corpse.

Harrison Douglas thought he ought to do something, so he clasped his hands in front of his ample middle and stood for a moment with head bowed and eyes closed. He stood like that for at least ten seconds. Then he opened his eyes and looked around again like a lucky Kmart shopper. The compartment was round, with a pilot's seat on a pedestal and other seats arranged at floor level along the rear wall. The canopy gave the pilot a view forward and a bit of a look to both sides.

The instrument panel, if that was what it was, consisted of white panels. There were a few knobs. Five of them. There was a control stick for the pilot—at least it looked like a stick—and a lever of some sort on the left side of the pilot's seat. Two pedals where the pilot's feet could reach them. Rudder pedals, maybe.

How it all worked Douglas couldn't imagine. Nor did he care. "Where are the computers?" he asked Solo.

Adam Solo nodded toward the instrument panel.

"Can you get at 'em?"

"I'll try."

"Amazing," Douglas said under his breath, then said it again, louder. Trying not to step in the dry bloodstains, he reached out to touch things.

Solo removed a flashlight from his pocket and snapped it on. He began moving the beam around the interior of the ship, inspecting for damage. There was some. The glass in one of the multifunction displays in front of the pilot was broken.

"Dr. Douglas, I know you've had a long day and have much to think about. My examination of the ship will go much faster if you leave me to work in solitude."

Douglas beamed at Solo. "I didn't think it could be done," he admitted. "When you told me this ship could be salvaged and you could wring out its secrets, I thought you were lying. I want you to know I was wrong. I admit it, here and now."

Solo smiled.

"So this is the saucer they found in Roswell, New Mexico, back in 1947," Douglas said, shaking his head. "And the air force kept it hidden for all these years in Area Fifty-one." He looked at Solo. "Is it what you expected?"

Solo looked around thoughtfully. "Pretty much. I studied everything I could from one of the other saucer's computers. Mr. Cantrell was very generous with access."

This was a lie, but Harrison Douglas swallowed it right down. Egg Cantrell had allowed academics from all over the world access to the contents of the computer removed from the saucer his nephew Rip found in the Sahara. That saucer was a smaller version of this one, everyone said. They were indeed alike in many ways, Solo knew, but there were significant differences. This one was more technologically advanced. He didn't bother to explain these messy facts to his patron, however.

"I leave you to it," Douglas said. "If you will just open that hatch to let me out." He took a last glance at the remains of the French pilot. "He doesn't stink as much as I thought he would," he muttered.

Solo opened the hatch and Douglas carefully climbed through; then Solo closed it again. He stood inside running the beam of his flashlight back and forth, looking carefully at everything. It had been many years since he was inside a saucer; the memories came flooding back. Good memories and bad. He tried to clear his head, to concentrate on his inspection, to look critically at what he saw.

After a moment, Solo opened the access door to the engineering compartment and disappeared inside. He was inside for an hour before he came out. With his flashlight he again inspected every square inch of the cockpit's interior, opened access doors and looked inside, and when he had examined everything he could access, he took stock.

Charley Pine had apparently used the antiproton weapon in the other saucer on this one, attempting to shoot it down. The one-armed corpse on the floor had bled profusely from a cavernous wound in his leg. Solo found the hole in the water tank and repaired it with duct tape.

Fortunately the water tank could function at a very low pressure. If he ensured the pressure stayed low, maybe he would be okay. The reactor provided power to several generators, and they seemed intact. The electrical power was used to separate the water into hydrogen and oxygen—these tanks were highly pressurized and intact—and mixed the gases in the rocket propulsion system. The generators also provided power for the antigravity system. A display on the panel was wrecked, but there were three more, which should be enough. Apparently none of the antiprotons had met a proton in the reactor. If it had, there should be a detectable radiation leak.

Of course, if he powered up the reactor and there was actually was internal damage from antiprotons or the crash into the ocean, Adam Solo and everyone else on this salvage ship would soon be dead.

Solo rubbed his chin as he glanced around one more time.

Well, there was only one way to find out.

Solo retrieved the headband that was still wrapped around the dead Frenchman's head. He wiped it off without emotion and put it on his own head.

"Hello, *Eternal Wanderer.* Let us examine the health of your systems." Before him, the instrument panel exploded into life.

THE FIRST MATE, DEVRIES, STROLLED THE BRIDGE with the helm on autopilot. The rest of the small crew of *Atlantic Queen,* including the captain, were in their bunks asleep. The rain had stopped, and a sliver of moon was peeping through the clouds overhead. The mate had always enjoyed the ethereal beauty of the night and the way the ship rode the restless, living sea. He was soaking in the sensations, occasionally strolling across the bridge from one wing to the other and periodically checking the radar display and compass, when he noticed the glow from the saucer's cockpit.

The spaceship took up so much of the deck that the cockpit canopy was almost even with the bridge windows.

As the mate stared into the cockpit, he saw the figure of Adam Solo. He reached for the bridge binoculars. Turned the focus wheel.

Solo's face appeared, lit by a subdued light source in front of him. The mate assumed that the light came from the instruments—computer presentations—and he was correct. DeVries could see the headband, which looked exactly like the kind the Indians wore in old cowboy movies. Solo's face was expressionless . . . no, that wasn't true, the mate decided. He was concentrating intensely.

Obviously the saucer was more or less intact or it wouldn't have electrical power. Whoever designed that thing sure knew what he was about. He or she. Or it. Whoever that was, wherever that was . . .

Finally the mate's arms tired and he lowered the binoculars.

He snapped the binoculars into their bracket and went back to pacing the bridge. Occasionally he glanced at the saucer's glowing cockpit. The moon, the clouds racing overhead, the ship pitching and rolling monotonously—it seemed as if he were trapped in this moment in time and this was all there had ever been or ever would be. It was a curious feeling . . . almost mystical.

Surprised at his own thoughts, DeVries shook his head and tried to concentrate on his duties.

ADAM SOLO USED THE ONBOARD COMPUTERS TO EXAMine the state of every system in the saucer. The long-range communications equipment refused to come online or self-test. He opened the access plate under the instrument panel and stuck his head in. He found the modules he wanted . . . and found himself staring at one bulged box.

An antiproton exploded in there.

He backed out and closed the panel, then slowly climbed back into the pilot's seat, fighting back his disappointment. Well, there was nothing for it but to play the cards he had.

Thirty minutes later, satisfied that the comm gear and one instrument display were the only casualties, he opened the hatch and dropped to the deck. He closed the hatch behind him, just in case, and went below to his cabin. No one was in the passageways. Nor did he expect to find any of the crew there. He glanced into one of the crew's berthing spaces. The glow of the tiny red lights revealed that every bunk was full, and every man seemed to be snoring.

In his cabin Solo quickly packed his bag. He stripped the sheets and blankets from his bunk and, carrying the lot, went back up on deck. Careful to stay out of sight of the bridge, he stowed his gear in the saucer. Spreading the blankets on the cockpit floor, he carefully laid the remains of the French fighter pilot on the sheet and wrapped them tight. Using a roll of duct tape, he bound the bundle as tightly as he could and eased it through the open hatch.

Adam Solo unfastened one of the chains that bound the saucer to the deck and wrapped it around the bundle. As he dragged it to the rail, he said, "You probably weren't the first man to die in that ship, but I hope you're the last." With that he pushed the bundle over the side. The mortal remains of Jean-Paul Lalouette disappeared with a tiny splash.

A hose lay coiled near a water faucet, one the crew routinely used to wash mud from cables and chains coming aboard. Solo looked at it, then shook his head. The water intake was on top of the saucer; climbing up there would expose him to the man on the bridge, and would be dangerous besides. He had come so far, had waited so long—now would be a bad time to fall overboard, which would doom him to inevitable drowning.

He removed the tie-down chains and restraining straps one by one, lowering them gently to the deck so the sound wouldn't reverberate through the steel ship.

Finally, when he had the last one off, he stood beside the saucer, with it between him and the bridge, and studied the position of the crane and hook, the mast and guy wires. Satisfied, Adam Solo stooped and went under the saucer and up through the hatch.

THE FIRST MATE WAS CHECKING THE GPS POSITION and the recommended course to Sandy Hook when he felt the subtle change in the ship's motion. An old hand at sea, he noticed it immediately and looked around.

The saucer was there, immediately in front of the bridge—but it was higher, the lighted canopy several feet above where it had previously been. He could see Solo's head, now seated in the pilot's chair. The saucer was moving, or seemed to be, rocking back and forth. Actually it was stationary—the ship was moving in the sea way.

DeVries' first impression was that the ship's motion had changed because the saucer's weight was gone, but he was wrong. The antigravity rings in the saucer had pushed it away from the ship, which still supported the entire mass of the machine. The center of gravity was higher, so consequently the ship rolled with more authority.

At that moment Harrison Douglas came up the ladder, moving carefully with a cup of coffee in his hand.

He saw DeVries staring out the bridge windows, transfixed.

Douglas turned to follow DeVries' gaze and found himself looking at Adam Solo's head inside the saucer. Solo was too engrossed in what he was doing to even glance at the bridge. For only a few seconds was the saucer suspended over the deck. As the salvage ship came back to an even keel the saucer moved toward the starboard side, pushing the ship dangerously in that direction. Then the saucer went over the rail and the ship, free of the saucer's weight, rolled port with authority.

"No!" Douglas roared. "Come back here, Solo! It's *mine.* Mine, I tell you, *mine*!" He dropped his coffee cup and strode to the door that led to the wing of the bridge. He flung it open and stepped out. The mate was right behind him. Both men grabbed the rail with both hands as the wind and sea spray tore at them.

The lighted canopy was no longer visible. For a few

seconds Douglas and DeVries could see a glint of moonlight reflecting off the dark upper surface of the spaceship, then they lost it. The saucer disappeared into the night.

"If that doesn't take the cake! *The bastard stole it!*" exclaimed Harrison Douglas, and he shook his fist in the direction in which the saucer had disappeared. "I'll get you, Solo, and I'll get that ship back. So help me God!"

2

RIP CANTRELL, CHARLEY PINE AND RIP'S UNCLE EGG sat on wooden crates staring dejectedly at the objects arranged on the floor of the warehouse. The stuff looked like junk that had been removed from an abandoned chicken coop. Just what the twisted metal and shattered composite material, if that was what it was, might have been before they were destroyed upon entry to the earth's atmosphere and eons of submergence in the sea, no one could say.

Egg turned to the other people there, a man and woman from the Australian Archaeological Commission, and an American archaeologist who was there at Egg's invitation, Deborah Deehring. "It's hopeless," he said. "There's no way to identify the pieces in this condition."

He nodded toward a schematic that was pinned to a wall. "This is what the computer from the Sahara saucer says the starships looked like then. I don't know if the design changed or not." He swept his hand toward the stuff on the warehouse floor. "I can't identify one piece."

Rip was an athletic young man of twenty-three years. His life had taken a hard right turn when, as part of a seismic survey crew, he discovered a flying saucer embedded in a sandstone ledge in the Sahara and dug it out.

Charlotte "Charley" Pine, thirty-one years old, had been a civilian member of an air force UFO team that investigated the Sahara saucer, and she was the one who flew it away when armed thugs tried to confiscate it. A graduate of the U.S. Air Force Academy, she had been a fighter pilot, then a test pilot, before resigning from the service. Rip used to refer to her despairingly as "an older woman." He didn't do that these days.

Egg Cantrell, Rip's uncle, was an engineer and inventor. He was fiftyish and spry, with an ovoid shape, hence his nickname, which he didn't mind. A consummate realist, Egg accepted the world as he found it and tried mightily to understand.

Professor Deborah Deehring was athletic and blond and had huge, intense blue eyes. When she focused those eyes on Egg and smiled, he felt a very curious sensation. He liked the sensation, and Deborah, a lot.

For the past two weeks, Charley, Rip, Uncle Egg and Deborah had stirred through this pile of junk the Australians had found embedded in the Great Barrier Reef. It was, the Australians believed, an ancient starship, perhaps the very one that brought Rip's saucer to this galaxy 140,000 years ago. They reached this conclusion based on an analysis of the metal removed from the reef, and from the geology of the reef construction, which proved the metal had been there for a long, long time.

However, Egg wasn't sure that the Australian scientists were right. If this stuff was originally part of a starship, the metal must have been supercooled in space, heated to astronomical temperatures on its trip into the earth's atmosphere and subjected to a salt bath for over a hundred millennia. Who knows what its original molecular composition might have been? Nor could anyone now recognize the metal. All everyone could agree upon was that it was old and weird. They also agreed that if they were indeed looking at the carcass of a starship, it certainly couldn't be the one that delivered the Roswell saucer, which crashed in New Mexico in 1947 and had ended up in the Atlantic Ocean.

"We just don't know how often earth has been visited by extraterrestrials," Egg said dejectedly. "For all we know, that metal is a million years old. We have no idea how fast saltwater would corrode it."

The Aussie in charge was a woman, Dr. Helen Colt. She was a no-nonsense salt-and-pepper woman who was rarely seen without her clipboard. The assistant, ten years younger than Colt, was a man named Billy Reese. He was smallish in stature, also a PhD, a thoughtful type given to stroking his jaw and saying little.

Just now he eyed the computer on Egg's lap, then scrutinized Rip's and Charley's faces thoughtfully.

"Your opinion, Dr. Reese?" Colt said abruptly.

"I am defeated," he replied. "We have found no shells of computers or reactors or advanced devices of any kind, nothing anyone could point to as evidence that we are looking at an artifact of an advanced civilization. Perhaps it is precisely what it appears to be, a twisted, misshapen structural framework someone built and threw into the sea."

"When?" said Charley Pine. She was a tall, intelligent young woman who looked as if she could handle anything likely to come her way. Today she wore an old air force flight suit and boots, which did nothing to hide her good figure.

"Since we can't identify the metallurgy, we don't know," Reese said slowly, eyeing Charley.

"We really don't know anything," Egg said gruffly. He had spent the last few minutes packing the computer into its travel bag, and now he stood, computer case in one hand and headband in the other. "Glad you invited us Down Under to take a look," he said and tucked the headband under his left armpit so he could shake hands with the two Aussies.

Rip, Charley and Deborah also pumped hands and followed Egg out of the warehouse. Dr. Reese trailed the three of them. He cleared his throat while he was behind Egg, who paused and turned toward him.

"Mr. Cantrell, I can't help noticing that magnificent computer you have," Reese said heartily. "I assume it is from your nephew's saucer?"

"It is," Egg admitted. Actually he had removed it from the Sahara saucer when Rip first brought the saucer to Missouri. That had been a happy accident. Egg mined the computer for technology; the propulsion technology and some of the other major systems were patented and licensed, and much of the rest of the technology that Egg was willing to share—certainly not all—was placed in the public domain. The results were astounding: Industries throughout the world were investing capital in new plants, processes and equipment, and hiring. The world was entering a new era of prosperity.

"It would be a great service to the cause of science if you would allow me and my commission colleagues to examine it for a few weeks," said Dr. Reese. "We can promise to return it to you in an undamaged state."

"Dr. Reese," Egg began, clutching the computer case in his arms, "I am not ready to allow unsupervised access to this computer." In the months after he acquired it he had indeed allowed almost unlimited access to academics, but that was before he fully appreciated the information its memory contained. When he finally realized the implications of extraordinary knowledge in unlearned, unethical hands, he had refused access to all but a trusted few.

Colt had joined them, and now she eyed Egg skeptically. "Knowledge that can be verified should be shared with all mankind," she said. "The only valid ethical position is that scientific knowledge enhances the survival of our species, so the more the better."

"Perhaps," Egg readily agreed, still clutching the computer to his chest, with both arms wrapped around it. "Yet perhaps there is such a thing as too much knowledge, knowledge that the human mind—or the public mind, the humanity of which is debatable—is not yet ready to accept for the simple reason that we don't know enough to give it context."

"How much of the information on that computer is of that variety?" Colt asked, intent on his answer.

"There is much there that baffles me," Egg confessed. "I cannot understand much of it. Better brains than mine might, but I doubt it. I think most of the gold that we can use has already been mined."

Colt and Reese surrendered gracefully. Colt said her good-byes, shook hands and let the Americans retreat. Dr. Reese accompanied them as far as the door; then he too said good-bye.

When the Australians were out of earshot, as they walked toward their rented car, Deborah said to Egg, "You don't really believe that, do you?"

"What?"

"That there are facts we shouldn't know?"

Egg eyed Deborah as Charley unlocked the car. "I could have stated it better. There are things on this computer that our society is not prepared to deal with now. You know some of the stuff I'm talking about."

"He's right, Deb," Charley said as she opened the door and got behind the wheel.

Rip seated himself beside Charley, on the left side of the vehicle, and Egg and Deborah climbed in the back.

"You're thinking about the antiaging drug, aren't you?" Rip murmured.

Egg nodded. "Our civilization doesn't have the moral and ethical framework to deal with something like that."

"Yet," Rip shot back.

"Maybe someday it will, after our scientists take all the baby steps required to discover it for themselves. But not now. And there is the aliens' concept of God. A lot of people would glom onto that like iron filings on a magnet just because they think the aliens knew more than we do."

"Oh boy," Deborah said. "As if religious fanatics aren't causing enough trouble on this rock already."

"Too bad about the starship, if that was what it was," Rip mused. "I would really like to know how old that wreckage was. Was it the ship that delivered the Sahara saucer, or did it come later, perhaps to search for them? Guess we'll never know."

Egg kept a firm grasp on the computer case on his lap. "Yes," he said as he watched the countryside scroll past.

After a bit, Rip added, "I'd like to know if the aliens are ever coming back," then rolled down his window and stuck his elbow out.

"What I'd like to know," Charley replied thoughtfully,

"is what happened to the crew of the Roswell saucer." The government had told the world no alien spacemen were ever found, an assertion that no one had yet proven untrue.

Deborah Deehring rested a hand on top of Egg's. He smiled at her and she returned it. "The computer is a great trust," she said softly. "You must be very careful with it."

"I could use your help exploring its contents," Egg suggested.

"I have to get back to the university. I've been gone too long already. Perhaps in a few weeks I could visit you for a weekend."

They left it there and rode along holding hands. This was a first romance for Egg, a lifelong bachelor, and he was enjoying the sensations. He felt like a teenager.

THE MORNING AFTER THE TRIO ARRIVED BACK IN MISSOURI at Uncle Egg's farm, Charley awoke before dawn and listened to the breeze whisper in the pines outside the window. The window was opened an inch or so to let the night air in, and the wind's gentle song. Rip was still asleep beside her, breathing deeply. Somewhere in the house a telephone was ringing, insistently, urgently. Finally it stopped, then began again.

When she realized there was no more sleep in her, Charley slipped out of bed and pulled on her heavy robe and slippers. She closed the bedroom door behind her and tiptoed down the hall toward the stairs.

She paused there when she heard Uncle Egg moving

around the kitchen. She could also hear the coffeemaker gurgling, the babble of unintelligible voices from the television, and the refrigerator door opening and closing. Egg was busy, busy, busy, as he usually was. The ringing telephone was silent.

Charley Pine smiled. It was good to be home.

Home! Now there was a concept new to her. She continued on down the stairs and around the corner into the kitchen.

"Good morning, Uncle Egg."

"Charley!" Egg said breathlessly. "Sit down, please. I'll get you a cup of coffee." He turned up the volume on the television as Charley hoisted herself onto a counter stool, then turned back to the pot. "Hope the telephone didn't wake you up. I unplugged both of them."

There was a flying saucer on the television screen. She stared, mesmerized, then realized she was watching video taken last month of her chase of Jean-Paul Lalouette in the Roswell saucer over Manhattan. Now the announcer's voice sank in.

"So to recap, the large saucer, the one in front, was raised from the Atlantic three days ago. Everyone presumed it was totally destroyed after it went into the water last month in a vertical dive from an estimated one hundred thousand feet. Destroyed? Apparently not.

"In an interview this morning, just an hour after his ship, *Atlantic Queen,* tied up here in New York, Captain Johnson of Atlantic Salvage stated that after it was raised, the saucer was flown away from the deck of the ship by a passenger named Adam Solo. Other members of the crew confirm this account, including Dr. Harrison Douglas, CEO of World Pharmaceuticals, which funded the salvage."

Dr. Douglas appeared on the screen. He was standing on a pier with the salvage ship moored behind him. He discussed the scientific curiosity that had led him and his company to fund the recovery of the saucer from the sea.

Egg stood beside Charley through all this, sipping coffee himself. When the network began an exposition of everything its reporters had learned about Adam Solo, Egg hit the mute button on the remote control.

"What do you think?" he asked Charley.

"Douglas is smarmy." She took her first experimental sip of coffee, then said, "I am astounded. I thought . . ."

When she stopped speaking, Egg said, "Just before you came in, Douglas said that Lalouette's body was in the saucer when Solo opened it. Blood everywhere." The French pilot had used the Roswell saucer to fight Charley, trying to shoot her down. When he was severely wounded by an antimatter beam from Charley's saucer, he had attacked the Sahara saucer again. He lost, and his saucer went into the Atlantic.

Charley set the cup on the counter and averted her eyes from the television.

"I'm sorry, Charley," Egg said softly, "but I thought you needed to know. Reporters were calling, even though my number is unlisted, trying for a comment or telephone interview."

Charley Pine took a deep breath and said, "Turn off the television and fix me some breakfast, please. Two eggs and bacon would be a treat."

They talked of inconsequential things as Egg busied himself preparing breakfast and the sun crept over the earth's rim. Through the window, Egg examined the clouds critically. "Going to be a good day," he said thoughtfully.

"World Pharmaceuticals," Charley mused.

"The antiaging drug," Egg said, finishing the thought. "I guess a thing like that would be impossible to keep secret."

"So who is Adam Solo?" Charley asked aloud after she had had several bites of egg and munched a bacon strip.

When Rip came downstairs fifteen minutes later, he pecked Charley on the cheek and sat on a stool beside her. Egg used the remote to turn on the television again.

Rip silently absorbed everything Egg and Charley knew about the salvage of the Roswell saucer as he watched a few minutes of the television coverage.

Finally he glanced at Egg, then Charley, and asked, "So who is this Adam Solo?"

"Whoever he is, he's flying a saucer," Charley observed sourly. "Bet we hear more about that before very long."

Rip turned the audio back on. The television reporter finished interviewing Harrison Douglas, turned and looked straight into the camera. "Why did Adam Solo steal the Roswell flying saucer? What does he intend to do with it? Where is it? All the world wonders. We don't know the answers yet, but we intend to find out. When we do, we'll tell you, our viewers. We'll be back, right after this commercial break. Stay with us."

HARRISON DOUGLAS BROKE AWAY FROM THE REPORTers and walked quickly to a waiting limousine. Safely ensconced in his padded-leather sanctuary, he began making calls on the vehicle's encrypted telephone. He was angry, damned angry. The salvage company was demanding their eight million bucks and threatening to sue if he didn't pony up, even though they failed to deliver the saucer to the dock in Newark; Solo had played him for a sucker and robbed him; and the whole world was laughing at him.

Well, that thief Solo wouldn't laugh long, by God! Douglas grew up in Philly, and he still knew some guys. Hadn't talked to them in years, but they knew him too. These were guys you didn't screw with. They ate thieving little bastards like Solo for breakfast.

After three telephone calls, Douglas was tired. He lay back in his seat and closed his eyes.

THE NEWS THAT THE ROSWELL SAUCER WAS NO LONger on the floor of the Atlantic hit the White House like a small bomb. The news that the saucer had been stolen from a deepwater salvage ship and was out there . . . somewhere . . . *flying around* . . . greatly enhanced the explosion.

A horrified P. J. O'Reilly, the chief of staff, rushed into the presidential bedroom with the news. The presidential pooch hastily bestirred itself and shot into the president's closet. O'Reilly ignored the dog, as he did all lesser creatures, which was almost everyone. He found the president eating breakfast at a small table. The morning newspapers were piled beside him, apparently as yet unread.

"What's the matter, O'Reilly? Did the Canadians invade?"

"It's a lot worse than that. That saucer that went into the Atlantic last month was salvaged, raised from the ocean, and someone stole it."

The president felt as if he had taken a punch. He seemed to shrink right where he sat. The color leaked from his face.

"It's out there now, God only knows where," O'Reilly continued, digging in the knife. He enjoyed giving the president bad news, although he pretended he didn't. Now he seized the remote control from the breakfast table and clicked on the television.

The president found he had lost his appetite. Perhaps the fact that he had lived through two saucer crises in the last fourteen months had something to do with his bad humor.

At least, he reflected as he watched the talking heads on CNN, Rip Cantrell and Charley Pine weren't involved in this escapade. Or were they? "Have the FBI find Rip Cantrell and Charlotte Pine," he growled at O'Reilly. "Just tell me where they are." O'Reilly rushed off to make the call.

Charley Pine was a real piece of work, a former fighter

and test pilot who could fly anything, but Rip Cantrell was the one the president worried about. The kid single-handedly took on the world's second-richest man, the president and the U.S. government . . . and beat them all. Just another all-American boy! *Ai yi yi!*

The president decided not to rule out Rip until he saw a photo of Adam Solo.

He opened his bottle of Rolaids and munched a handful. Then he reached for the waiting newspapers.

3

WHEN RIP AND CHARLEY WANDERED OFF TO THE HANgar to work on Rip's airplane, Egg retrieved the computer from Rip's saucer and opened the case reverently. Locked in its memory, he knew, was the scientific knowledge and philosophical framework of the civilization that had built the Sahara saucer, about 140,000 earth years ago, and sent it aboard a starship, the saucer that had reached earth.

Egg carefully donned the headband, ensured it was plugged into the device and said aloud, "Good morning." The computer came to life. Egg marveled again at the computer's ability to read the brain waves of anyone wearing the band, and to respond with images that the user saw in his mind's eye. There was no screen, no keyboard, no other way to communicate, nor was any other method needed. The computer's memory and logic functions reminded Egg of a 3-D or holographic display . . . and the presentation occurred inside his head.

Egg had learned to download information from the saucer's computer onto his own PC and was experimenting with ways to manipulate the data. He hadn't gotten a satisfactory system figured out yet. He had enlisted the help of several computer scientists, who were having a wonderful time but had yet to crack the computer's core code. A linguistics expert was working on the computer's language, if it was language. Still, Egg liked to put on the headband and surf the computer to see what he could find. It was as if he had the Library of Congress in his hands, and yet all he could do was wander through the aisles sampling books.

Even as that thought occurred to him, the computer responded. He saw the organizational outline of the device's memory and sat studying it for a long moment. He had learned that the computer responded to questions, but what if the user didn't know what question to ask?

His mind wandered. Idly, he thought of Rip and his airplane, an Extra 300L, and wondered what Rip and Charley were going to need to do to get it airworthy again.

The computer answered. He saw the damage to the airplane, the bullet holes and bent landing gear, that happened when Rip crashed the plane.

Egg ripped off the headband.

How had the computer learned of the damage?

Egg's mind raced. Well, Rip had worn the headband on several occasions while they were in Australia, idly exploring. So had Charley.

Could it be? Could the computer archive the memory of its user, to add to its database?

Galvanized, he replaced the headband and thought of Rip. What did Rip know about the Extra's condition?

The machine knew.

Rip's childhood, his visits to Egg's Missouri farm. The scenes scrolled past him as if they were on film. Some of the scenes were hazy—perhaps because Rip had forgotten some of them.

The bass—what did Rip remember of the time Egg took him bass fishing? And there it was, a movie filmed from Rip's youthful perspective. There Egg was, baiting the hooks, showing Rip how to cast . . . and there he was holding up a fish, grinning at Rip.

Egg's mind raced on. His trip to the moon? There it was, the French thugs, the obsidian sky full of stars, the weightlessness . . . he could feel the weightlessness and the G forces as the saucer's engines ignited, see the moon, stark and burning brightly in unfiltered sunlight. The experience was right there in his mind's eye and he was reliving it! He even felt the fear that he had experienced then, fear because he knew as he flew the saucer that he was in over his depth.

Now Egg fumbled with the headband, tearing it off his head.

My God!

The computer mined the memories of its users and stored everything they knew.

He sat staring with unseeing eyes at the autumn scene

just beyond the window, trying to get his thoughts in order.

Deborah Deehring had worn the headband. Egg was tempted, for a few seconds, then decided no. Her memories were hers and shouldn't be shared without her permission. Nor should Rip or Charley's.

The ancient spacemen had also worn it; they were long dead, so they had no privacy rights.

WHEN RIP AND CHARLEY CAME BACK TO THE HOUSE for lunch, they found Egg wearing the headband and hunched over in his chair, with his eyes closed. Charley Pine tapped him on the shoulder, which caused him to open his eyes. Reluctantly Egg removed the headband and looked around slowly, trying to come back to this reality.

"Uncle Egg?" Charley said softly.

Egg reached up and took her hand.

He glanced at her and a concerned Rip. "I know now," he said slowly, "why the people who flew your saucer came to earth."

Both Rip and Charley sat down on the couch, side by side, and stared at him.

"Two men and three women were in the saucer. They didn't come to colonize. They came to implant DNA samples in living creatures."

Rip recovered his voice first. "Why?"

"That I don't know. Nor do I know what happened to them. They arrived . . . searched for a suitable place to land and found it beside a stream in a meadow with trees on the surrounding hills. Then the pilot took off the headband." Egg gestured futilely. "That's all I know. Apparently they never returned to the saucer."

"But why would they want to implant DNA samples?" Charley asked with her head cocked quizzically to one side.

Egg threw up his hands. "To create a DNA library? That would be my guess. But I don't know. Yet."

He took a deep breath. "The computer mines the memories of everyone who wears the headband. Your memory is on it, Charley, and yours, Rip. And mine. The computer knows everything we ever learned well enough to recall."

Charley's eyes widened. "Everything?"

"Everything," Egg said with finality, "and it records the emotions you had at the time you had the experience."

Charley turned slightly green. "I am not sure I want my private thoughts on some machine's permanent memory."

"They are there," Egg said. "The good news is that you are a wonderful person."

Charley laughed nervously. She eyed Rip. "Maybe I should put on the headband and check out your head," she told him.

Rip tried to look nonchalant, to hide his embarrassment. "Any time," he said blithely. "But I'm going to have to think long and hard about whether or not I want to use that thing again."

All three of them laughed.

They were eating a lunch of chicken salad sandwiches

when Rip said, "If the saucer people were creating a database here on earth 140,000 years ago, one suspects they returned occasionally."

"A database of living creatures," Egg said thoughtfully, "a database that would be passed along from one generation to the next, a database that would become part of that species' genome. It would be there until that species became extinct."

"No," Rip said. "It would be there as long as there were living descendants of the database creatures, of whatever species."

"Perhaps the Roswell saucer came so the crew could check the library," Charley said between bites. "Look up a reference, or add to the database. And take samples of flora and fauna and rocks and dirt. Just like our astronauts did on the moon. They must have been taking samples of everything they could find."

"It would be amazing if the Roswell visit was the only subsequent visit," Egg observed, glancing at their faces.

"Makes you wonder," Rip agreed thoughtfully. "A hundred forty thousand years is a long, long time."

"Not really," Egg murmured. "And the library could consist of things beside the on-off switches that govern reproduction. The database could consist of computer code that has no effect on the living creature that carries it."

"Isn't eighty percent of most DNA code nonfunctional?" Rip asked with his mouth full.

"Researchers think that the nonfunctional codes are

ancestoral artifacts," Egg suggested. "No doubt some of them are. But what about the rest?"

"I wonder if humans carry a portion of the database," Charley mused.

"You're going to explore that computer some more this afternoon," Rip said to Egg, without even looking at him.

Charley giggled. She didn't do it often, but when she did she brought a wide smile to Rip's face.

Egg tried to shrug off the comment. "Maybe," he acknowledged.

This time Rip and Charley both laughed.

THE PRESIDENT WAS MEETING THAT AFTERNOON WITH the secretary of state and the national security adviser when an aide slipped him a note. This is what it said:

The FBI says the Cantrells and Charley Pine are at Egg Cantrell's farm in Missouri. Their telephones are apparently out of service. Three saucer sightings have been reported to the U.S. Air Force. They are being checked out.

The president read the note, put it facedown on the desk, then picked it up and read it one more time.

He was worried. Saucers flying around again, the media in full cry . . . What in the name of heaven was going on?

He picked up the note again, took a pen and wrote on the bottom, *Why did World Pharmaceuticals pay to salvage the Roswell saucer?* and passed the note back to the waiting aide.

• • •

IT WAS AN HOUR BEFORE DAWN IN THE MOUNTAINS OF western Montana when a large black saucer came drifting down the valley just a hundred feet above the ground. In the meadow near the lake, the saucer came to a stop in a hover and the gear snapped down. The saucer settled gently to the ground.

Adam Solo exited the saucer through the belly door, carrying a backpack in his hand, and duckwalked out from under it. He stood silently, listening and looking as his eyes adjusted to the near-darkness. A chill wind blew from the west, swirling down off the peaks, but the sky was clear. Looking up, Solo saw the Milky Way, a billion stars flung like a ribbon across the sky. The moon was down, so they looked extraordinarily bright.

After a long moment, Solo climbed up on top of the saucer. In seconds it rose gently from the ground and the gear came up. As Solo balanced himself on the sloping deck, the saucer moved slowly out over the lake, then gently submerged itself until only the top was above water.

In seconds the refueling door opened and water began pouring into the saucer's tank. Air came out of the tank in burps and bubbles. The starlight was just sufficient for Solo to monitor the progress of the refilling and to ensure no foreign objects floated into the swirl of water entering the refilling port.

When the water ceased to swirl and all the air bubbles had stopped, the door of the refilling port closed and the saucer rose slowly from the water, inch by inch.

Solo directed it to land again in the meadow. The landing gear snapped down and the saucer came to rest within inches of the spot where it originally landed. Solo carefully climbed from the saucer and stood in the grass with his hand on the curved leading edge.

Without conscious thought, his hand gently caressed the leading edge, running back and forth as his fingertips felt the cool, dark surface while he looked around in all directions, waiting.

Is the water tank full?

Yes.

Finally, satisfied that there were no people about, no witnesses, he slapped the saucer as if it were a horse and said aloud, "Go."

The saucer would be safe in orbit, out of the reach of everyone on earth who wanted it, except, of course, Solo, who could summon it back whenever he wished. If he wished. He wondered if he ever would.

He turned his back on the machine, picked up his backpack and walked away as the saucer rose several feet from the grass. He turned around in time to see the gear coming up as the saucer began to move forward.

In a swirl of dead grass and dirt, it began rising from the earth, accelerating slowly, and turned to an easterly heading. It was several hundred feet high, heading east up the valley, when he lost it in the blackness.

Solo looked around again, then began walking around the lake to the south. There should be a road over there, he thought, and a camping area. Perhaps there were people.

He had just reached the dirt road when far to the east, near the crest of the peaks, the saucer's rocket engines ignited. The light reached him well before the sound. Rising slowly, then faster and faster, the saucer roared into the night sky.

Now the sound washed over him, a deep throaty rumble, impressive with its power.

Solo watched the rising fireball until it disappeared behind the highest peak. He waited for his night vision to return as the thunder of the engines faded.

When the night was again completely silent and dark, he turned and walked on down the road. Ahead of him in the camping area, lights were popping on. Now he heard voices, carried a long way in the crisp autumn night.

They must have heard the saucer too, he thought and walked on, toward the lights and voices.

THE PRESIDENT WAS ON HIS STATIONARY BICYCLE IN the White House gym, pumping the pedals and sweating, when an aide found him. "Mr. President, something, probably a saucer, just went into orbit from western Montana. Space Command tracked it. It achieved a sustainable orbit a few minutes ago."

The president ceased pumping the pedals and sat silently.

"The Cantrells are still in Missouri?"

"The FBI says they are. They have the Cantrell farm under surveillance."

The president sighed and mopped his face with a towel. "Do the networks have this orbit thing?"

"Space Command is issuing a press release."

"I suppose they have to."

"Yes, sir. It would look bad for the air force if someone reported it and Space Command appeared to be caught flatfooted."

"I guess."

It's the media age we live in, the president reflected when he was again alone. He pedaled a few more revolutions, then stopped.

He felt as if he had entered a movie theater with only ten minutes left in the movie, and he had no idea what the plot was.

What in the world is going on?

THAT VERY SAME QUESTION OCCURRED TO DR. HARRISON Douglas of World Pharmaceuticals when he heard the news on the Fox Network. A saucer had gone into orbit—was it *his* saucer? Did that thief Solo fly it into space?

Egg Cantrell out in Missouri. He knew all about flying saucers. Hell, his nephew Rip found one in the Sahara! God only knew where the Sahara saucer was.

Well, he might have lost one saucer, but Douglas knew the name of someone who could probably lay hands on another, if properly stimulated.

As the beautiful young women of Fox gassed about flying saucers and aliens and the state of the universe, Johnny Murkowsky of Murk Corporation, another Big Pharma company, was also thinking about how to get information out of Egg Cantrell. And that young man, Rip. And that test pilot, Charlotte Pine.

The possibilities of human drug information on a flying saucer's computer hadn't previously occurred to Johnny Murkowsky, yet he could add two and two. If that lizard Harrison Douglas had invested eight million smackeroos trying to get at a saucer, there must be something there that could be turned into money. Drug money, which is the kind World Pharmaceuticals and Murk Corporation made. Big money. Really Big Money, or RBM.

Murkowsky didn't have a saucer. Maybe the Cantrells did, maybe they didn't, but they might know something. They would talk. They had to. There was RBM at stake.

A LARGE DOG FOUND ADAM SOLO AS HE APPROACHED the camping area. It came running, barking fiercely, and skidded to a stop just a few feet from Solo, who stood motionless as it approached.

The dog growled and snarled, showing its teeth.

Solo extended his hand and stared the dog in the eyes.

The mongrel ceased to growl. It stood motionless, almost as if it were waiting. Now the upper lip relaxed, covering its fangs.

Solo took two steps toward the dog with his hand extended.

The dog licked his hand, then sat, watching him expectantly.

"Let's go meet your folks," Solo said, and resumed walking toward the camping area, which by now was fully ablaze in lights. Behind him, the sky was beginning to brighten with the coming dawn.

The dog fell in behind Solo and matched his stride.

A man in his sixties standing beside an Airstream trailer hitched to a large pickup truck watched them come. He glanced at Solo, then addressed the dog. "A fine watchdog you are, Pag. You are supposed to be barking, scaring off strangers."

"He did his best," Solo said, gesturing at the dog, "but we talked and became friends."

The man snorted, looking Solo over. "And who are you?"

"Just a traveler," Solo responded. "As we all are. The dog's name?"

"Paganini."

"Ah, you are an aficionado of the violin?"

The man smiled. "Retired from a studio orchestra in Hollywood. By any chance, do you play the violin?"

"As a matter of fact, I do."

"My name's Stephens. What can we do for you this fine autumn morning?"

"I was wondering if I could get a ride into town."

"Did you hear that noise, that rumble like thunder a little while ago?"

"Yes, I did. And there don't seem to be any clouds or

storms around." Solo scanned the dawn sky, looking again at the fading stars.

The man shook his head. "He okay, Pag?"

The dog sat beside Solo and glanced up at his face.

"Well, Pag seems to give you a good bill of health. As it happens, the woman and I are pulling out after breakfast, after we get packed up and police this campsite. Come in and have some breakfast. Then you can ride along."

"Thank you. I'd really appreciate it," Adam Solo said and caressed the dog.

"Damn weather in these mountains is weird as hell," the man said. "We've been here too long anyway. Gonna snow soon, and we sure don't want to be here when it does."

"Yes," Solo replied and followed the man and dog into the trailer.

THERE WERE TWO FBI AGENTS WAITING IN THE OUTER office for Harrison Douglas when he arrived through his private door. The secretary was nervous when she told him about the visitors.

Douglas merely grunted, "Show them in."

They were middle-aged and wore sports coats and cheap ties. After he examined their credentials, Douglas tried to look appropriately mystified. "What is this about?"

"Just a few questions, sir," the agent with the tired eyes said. "We understand you paid for the salvage of the flying saucer from the floor of the Atlantic?"

"I didn't. World Pharmaceuticals did."

"But you authorized the operation, and were there on the salvage ship?"

Douglas acknowledged the truth of that statement with a nod of his head.

"Could you tell us why you wanted the saucer?" the other agent asked.

Harrison Douglas launched into his explanation, the same explanation he had given his board and expounded upon to the press after Solo stole his saucer. The search for scientific knowledge and all that.

"Did you hope the saucer would have secrets that would be marketable?" the first agent pressed.

"Of course."

"What secrets?"

"Well, sir, if I knew that we wouldn't have spent eight million bucks trying to raise the darn thing. We paid for the salvage on speculation. My attorneys assured me that my salvage of that thing was perfectly legal. Said it was abandoned. Sure looked like it to me, sitting down there on the sea floor. Have you people found it, or that thief Solo, who stole it?"

No, they hadn't.

Twenty minutes later they left, knowing no more than Douglas had told the press.

When they were gone, Douglas picked up the telephone on the desk and asked his secretary to ring up a number that belonged to one of the guys he knew in Philadelphia.

• • •

ADAM SOLO AND ABE AND MURIEL STEPHENS RODE along in splendor in the big Ford diesel pickup that Stephens used to tow his camper. Stephens produced a violin from a battered case, and Solo inspected it carefully.

"It appears to be a Jacob Stainer," Solo said, "but it has been altered. The neck angle has been changed."

Stephens took his eyes off the road to inspect Solo again. "What did you say your name was?"

"Traveler. Adam Traveler."

"You know your violins, Traveler. Play us something."

"Ah, it has been a long time. And I haven't practiced." Actually, Solo hadn't played the violin in ten years, but he wasn't going to admit it. "I once played professionally," he did say, "and they say muscle memory can be a great thing."

"Play something," Muriel urged. "Anything."

Solo inspected the violin carefully, then the bow. He quickly tuned the violin, tightening the strings and plucking them until he was satisfied.

Fortunately, he reflected, the suspension on the pickup was more stable than one would expect.

He played a few chords to ensure the violin was in tune, then without ado began.

The music filled the cab of the truck and mesmerized the small audience. Stephens pulled the truck over to the first wide place on the road he saw and stopped. He turned off the engine and closed his eyes.

When Solo had finished and put the instrument on his lap and was again inspecting the bow, Stephens said, "Tchaikovsky's Violin Concerto, Third Movement."

"Yes."

"I have never in my life heard the artificial harmonics played better. Or Tchaikovsky, for that matter."

"This," Solo said, gesturing to the violin, "is a quality instrument. I once played an instrument much like this, a Stainer, for several years. It is a rare privilege to touch one again. To have it in my hands. To play it."

"When? With what orchestra?" Muriel pressed.

"Ah, it was long ago. When I was very young." Solo flipped his fingers dismissively. "Drive on," he said to Abe. "As I told you, I am a traveler."

4

WHEN EGG SAW THE STORY ON FOX NEWS ABOUT THE *Atlantic Queen*'s stolen saucer being in orbit, he mentioned it to Rip and Charley, igniting a freewheeling discussion.

"In orbit?" Rip asked, incredulous.

"Since the day before yesterday. Apparently it's still up there."

"Could Solo be an alien," Charley asked, "waiting for a mother ship?"

Egg shrugged. "Anything's possible," he murmured.

Rip said thoughtfully, "We know the saucer's computer is also an autopilot. What if Solo programmed it to take the saucer into space so it wouldn't be found or confiscated here on earth?"

"You mean he might not even be in it?" Charley suggested.

"I thought about sending the Sahara saucer into space," Rip admitted, "to keep the feds and Roger Hedrick from laying hands upon it. Put it up there for a year or two, then have it programmed to come down in a secret place."

"You have a devious streak I didn't know about," Egg said appreciatively. "Why didn't you do it?"

"Because I didn't know if the saucer could pick up my brain waves while in orbit, so I would have to meet it at the rendezvous point, or else."

"Could Solo have done that?" Charley asked Egg.

"Of course."

"Who is Adam Solo?" Charley asked rhetorically.

"Better question," Rip responded, "*what* is Adam Solo?"

THE NEWS THAT THE STOLEN SAUCER WAS PROBABLY in orbit caused a sensation in the media, but when there was no follow-up, the story went onto the back burner. The Roswell saucer, if that was what it was, was up there circling the earth, but until it came down, the media had column inches and broadcast minutes to fill. Try as they might, enterprising reporters and producers could find nothing on Adam Solo, so he became the Mystery Man. Yet even that angle soon lost its zip. Crime, earthquakes, terrorism, financial shenanigans, sports and politics resumed their normal place in the newspapers and airwaves of the planet.

The FBI report on the interview with Harrison Douglas caused the president more discomfort. World Pharmaceuticals salvaging a flying saucer from the floor of the Atlantic "on speculation"? Douglas used those words to the agents. Obviously, the company was after information that might be in the saucer's computer database—information about drugs.

What secrets could there be? the president wondered, then forgot about the question as he went on dealing with the usual political theater, obstreperous congressmen and senators, and big meetings about serious hot important things that filled his waking moments, all day, every day.

Other people noted the presence of Harrison Douglas and World Pharmaceuticals in the latest saucer crisis and, adding them together, got the same answer that Johnny Murkowsky had. One of them was a fellow named Glenn Beck, a gadfly with a syndicated radio talk show.

"Drugs from an alien civilization, developed after hundreds of thousands of years of research and investment, could be a huge windfall for World Pharmaceuticals, if the company could get the drugs approved by the government," Beck intoned. "Perhaps the drug information in the Roswell saucer's computer could cure the common cold, cure cancer . . ." Here Beck paused dramatically—he was very good at dramatic pauses. "And," he continued, "prevent or cure obesity, prevent aging . . . How about a skinny pill, or a pill to keep you young? Would you take such a drug? If so, how much would you pay to get it?"

After another little pause, because he was a trained broadcaster, Beck added, almost as an afterthought, "Of course, the government had the Roswell saucer under lock and key at Area Fifty-one, a top-secret base in Nevada, since 1947, and apparently did not investigate the database. Or did they? Would they tell *us*?"

So it was that Glenn Beck lit the fuse and tiptoed away, out of our story.

The stolen saucer went right back onto Page One.

The air force denied mining secrets from the Roswell saucer's computer, but no one believed them. Members of Congress demanded an investigation. The AARP filed a Freedom of Information request. Packs of hungry trial lawyers began running ads on television and radio, searching for diseased plaintiffs for lawsuits against the government. The old and the fat also felt better now that they might be victims; class-action lawsuits were filed by the dozens all over the nation.

Watching the frenzy on television, the president asked, "Who is Adam Solo?"

THE FBI SOON FOUND THAT NOTHING WAS HAPPENING on the Cantrell farm in Missouri, except the Cantrells went to the grocery store occasionally. Either Egg or Rip drove Egg's old pickup and came with a list. Once Charley Pine went to the beauty shop for a haircut and 'do. Rip dropped her off, went to the grocery store, and picked her up after she was beautified.

The St. Louis FBI office was up to its eyeballs investigating the usual bank robberies and corrupt politicians, plus a local Yemeni illegal immigrant who wanted to commit an act of jihad that would earn him a ticket to paradise, and two financial advisers who had been running little Ponzi schemes, enriching themselves at the expense of dentists and car dealers who wanted at least a ten percent return on their investments. The special agent in charge of the FBI office was never told that the Cantrell farm surveillance had been ordered by the White House, but even if she had been, the Cantrell surveillance didn't have a case number, and no Justice Department attorney was breathing down her neck about it. So, after reading reports about grocery store and beauty shop visits, she assigned her agents elsewhere.

Consequently, two weeks after the Roswell saucer was stolen from the deck of *Atlantic Queen,* no one was watching when Adam Solo walked up to the gate of the Cantrell farm, climbed over and, with his backpack slung over one shoulder, continued on along the well-worn gravel road toward the house. He was wearing jeans and a set of leather hiking boots, a sweater and, atop the sweater, a jacket.

Solo swung along with a steady, miles-eating gait, one that had carried him along the roads of the earth for a long, long time. Today the earth smelled rich and pungent. The trees still had a few brown leaves remaining on their stark, dark limbs. Squirrels fought for territory amid the fallen leaves on the ground. A high, thin cirrus layer diffusing the sunlight promised a change in the weather.

There had been other trails through the forest, and he and his companions had run along them, free as only wild creatures can be.

One such day he recalled vividly, because it had also been in autumn, after the leaves had fallen and before the snows came. They were after elk, big animals with lots of meat that would keep them through the long, vicious winter when the rivers and streams froze and the forests were choked with snow.

The sky promised snow then too, so they were in a hurry to reach the elk meadows. Consequently they ran into an ambush; two men were dead in as many seconds as arrows filled the air, and war cries, unexpected howls of glee that froze the blood and paralyzed the nervous system for a crucial few seconds. Ah yes, he remembered all of it. The twanging of bows, the sigh arrows made as they flew through the air, the thud of arrowheads striking flesh, the thundering war cries and the whispered death songs . . .

Through the trees, today Solo saw the hangar by the grass runway and walked in that direction. Then he saw the small saucer resting on the stone. It was roughly three feet in diameter, sitting atop the stone on its three landing gear.

He approached it, examined it from a distance of six feet, then got closer. He could even see through the canopy into the miniature cockpit. He found himself staring at the pilot's seat, the controls, the blank instrument panel . . . and he knew.

Here it was! The saucer from the Sahara, the one Rip Cantrell had found. They had discovered how to shrink it.

It was beyond his reach. He had never worn the headband, never communicated with the computers inside this ship, so it would not recognize his brain waves. It would not obey his orders.

He ran his fingers over the surface, feeling the coolness and smoothness.

With his hand on the saucer, he stood looking at the hangar and the house on the hill and the trees. The autumn wind was gentle on his cheek.

He heard voices . . . coming from the hangar. Solo reluctantly abandoned the saucer and walked toward the large wooden building.

The main door was open. He stood in the entrance and found himself looking at an airplane. Two people were working on one of the main wheels, a man and a woman. He recognized them from their published descriptions: Charley Pine and Rip Cantrell.

"Hello," he said.

Rip and Charley both turned to look at him.

"Who are you?" Rip asked.

"Just a traveler."

"This is private property. You're trespassing."

"I suppose so. I climbed over the gate. Hope you don't mind."

Rip looked Solo over carefully. Middle-aged, a small, trim man, clean-shaven. "What did you say your name was?"

"Traveler. Adam Traveler."

Rip went back to greasing the bearings of the wheel that lay on the dirt floor of the hangar and asked, "Know anything about airplanes?"

"A little, yes," the man who called himself Traveler said.

Charley smiled. "I saw a photo of you on television.

You're Adam Solo, the man who stole the Roswell saucer from the *Atlantic Queen*."

Solo grinned ruefully. "And you must be Charley Pine."

Charley gestured toward Rip and pronounced his name.

"Pleased to meet you both," Solo said, and strolled into the hangar.

"The networks are convinced you are in orbit, waiting for a mother ship to pick you up," Rip said wryly.

"Ah, the networks . . ."

"So, do you really know anything about airplanes?"

"As a matter of fact, I once flew them for the British. That was a while back, and the machines were not quite as sophisticated as this, but I am sure the general principles haven't changed."

"Aerodynamics being what it is," Charley suggested.

"Quite."

"And when did you get all this experience?"

Solo eyed her and decided that, for once, perhaps the truth might be best. "During World War I. I flew Camels."

"Indeed," Charley said, intent on Solo's face.

Rip eyed Solo askance, trying to decide if he was lying—and why. "You are the only World War I vet I've ever met," he said. "All the others are dead. Have been for a good long time."

"Good genes," Solo responded.

"Apparently so," Charley said with her eyes narrowed.

"Well, come help us with this wheel," Rip said finally, waving a greasy hand. "Maybe you can help us figure out how to get it back on correctly."

Solo dropped his backpack and waded in.

WHEN THE WHEEL WAS BACK ON THE LANDING GEAR and the jack was removed, so that the plane again sat on its own wheels, Rip said to Solo, "Come on up to the house. I'd like you to meet my Uncle Egg."

"Yes," Solo said thoughtfully and finished wiping the grease from his hands on a red mechanic's rag. Then he picked up his backpack and shouldered it.

They were about to start climbing the hill toward the house when a large SUV raced along the driveway and slid to a stop in the gravel parking area, right beside the rock with the small saucer on top of it. Another SUV was right behind and parked beside the first. Television cameramen and sound techs piled out, complete with cameras and lights and satellite transmission equipment. A sign on the side of one SUV said FOX NEWS.

"Uh-oh," Rip muttered. He raised his voice and shouted, "This is private property. You people must leave. You don't have permission . . ."

His voice trailed off because no one was listening. The cameramen scattered like quail, carrying their equipment. A reporter with a microphone braced Rip and Charley. Behind her stood the last cameraman, looking through his eyepiece.

"This is Rip Cantrell," the reporter said breathlessly into her microphone, "the man who found a flying saucer in the Sahara and flew it to America last year. Mr. Cantrell, what can you tell us about the drug formulas in your saucer's computer?"

"Not a damned thing," Rip snarled into her microphone, which she had thrust toward his face. "Now you people get off this farm, which is private property."

Whether the reporter and cameraman would have left under their own steam will never be known—this was, after all, award-winning television journalism. What happened next was totally unexpected and gave great joy to the producer of this television news show.

Two more SUVs came roaring into the parking lot.

Four men climbed out of each vehicle. Rip recognized the man who climbed from the passenger's seat of the first SUV. Dr. Harrison Douglas of World Pharmaceuticals.

"Well, well, well," Douglas said nastily. Ignoring the television reporter and cameraman, he produced a pistol from his coat pocket. "I thought we would merely have a quiet chat with the Cantrells and Charley Pine, and instead we hit the jackpot and found you here, Solo. You thief! Where in hell is my saucer?"

Solo said nothing. The television cameraman moved so he had a nicely framed face shot of Solo, whom he had ignored up to now.

The men from the SUVs surrounded Rip, Charley and Solo as Douglas waved his shooter around.

"I'm only going to ask you one more time, Solo. *Where is my saucer?*"

Solo ignored everyone except Douglas, whom he regarded calmly.

"Better tell him," Rip whispered. "I think he's a few cards short of a complete deck."

"Up there," Solo said, jerking a thumb skyward. "Don't you watch television?"

"Who is flying it?" Douglas demanded. His face was red; his hand holding the pistol, a semiautomatic, was shaking. The reporter was waving the microphone around, trying to catch every word.

"A friend of mine," Solo replied slowly.

Douglas lowered the pistol and looked at the three of them. Then he put the gun in his pocket. "Let's go up to the house. We'll have a little talk."

Before they could take five steps, another vehicle roared into the parking area and stopped beside the first. A tall man got out, followed by two musclemen and a woman, a brunette with short hair.

"Johnny Murkowsky, you bastard," Douglas exclaimed. "What are you doing here?"

"I came to see what it is you are trying to steal, Douglas."

"I'm not—" Douglas roared but was cut off by Rip.

"Murkowsky? Haven't I heard that name before?" he asked the newcomer.

"Of course you have," Douglas thundered. "Murk Drugs. That's the bastard, right there, along with his masseuse. Never goes anywhere without her. Hey, Heidi, still giving ol' Johnny the happy endings?"

"Let's go up to the house, get acquainted and have a pleasant conversation," Johnny Murkowsky said and began shooing the others up the path. The female reporter for Fox News and her cameraman followed faithfully.

EGG CANTRELL WAS ON THE TELEPHONE WITH DR. Deborah Deehring discussing the latest media speculations on what the government might know about the information on the Roswell saucer's computer. He liked the sound of her voice and the speed with which her mind worked. Although he hadn't said so to anyone and probably never would, Egg thought smart women very attractive. He was thinking about that as he listened to her talk when he glimpsed through a window Rip and Charley and a bunch of other people climbing the hill path toward the house.

"Uh-oh," he told Deborah. "Gotta go. Looks as if the crisis has found us." Even as the words were leaving his mouth, he saw a person at the window aiming a television camera at him. "Turn on your television. I'll try to call you later." He hung up.

He glanced across the hallway at the kitchen. Someone was at the window there too, with a cameraman and microphone.

Before he could sort it out, Rip and Charley came blasting into the house trailed by a small army. “Uncle Egg,” Rip began, then saw the cameras and faces in the windows.

It was Harrison Douglas who first lost his grip on the situation. He pulled his pistol from his pocket, aimed at the nearest window and pulled the trigger.

The report nearly deafened the people in the house. The window exploded outward; cameramen and reporters and sound engineers ran for their lives.

Douglas was so bucked up by the sight of people running that he pointed the pistol at another window and put a bullet through it.

“Stop!” Egg roared. He was an outraged pillar of quivering flesh, such a large amount of quivering flesh that Douglas had second thoughts about the wisdom of shooting at television people through windows. Douglas engaged the safety on his shooter and put the thing away.

“If you want to shoot at them,” Egg told Douglas, “go outside and do it.”

“Maybe later.”

Adam Solo grinned at Charley and went into the kitchen. He opened the refrigerator, snagged a soft drink from the interior, popped the top and took a swig.

THE PRESIDENT WAS SUMMONED FROM AN IMPORTANT Meeting by P. J. O’Reilly to watch the unfolding drama on Fox News.

“These TV people invaded the Cantrell farm, apparently,

just before the drug company moguls arrived. Adam Solo was already there."

The president watched the chaos in silence. He saw Harrison Douglas wave his pistol around, and he heard Solo tell Douglas the saucer was in orbit. Up there.

Inside the Cantrell farmhouse, Douglas and Johnny Murkowsky cornered Egg Cantrell and bombarded him with questions about an antiaging drug.

"Isn't it true that Newton Chadwick found the formula for a Fountain of Youth drug on the Roswell saucer computer," Douglas demanded savagely, "the same saucer that I salvaged from the Atlantic and this son of a bitch, Adam Solo, stole?"

A television camera was back at the window again, the broken one. You must have large gonads to operate one of those.

"You aren't going to give the formula to this bastard Douglas, are you?" Murkowsky demanded of Egg. "Deprive mankind of the benefits of the most important pharmaceutical advance since the invention of antibiotics?"

"I don't have a formula, so I can't give it to anybody," Egg replied, trying to keep his temper.

"What kind of man are you, to make a moral judgment that the American people—hell, everyone on earth—should be deprived of the benefits of antiaging technology?" Murkowsky was belligerent. "Tell us, how is this drug administered? A pill, a cream, an injection?"

"It's a suppository," Egg shot back.

"Then you admit it? The drug does exist?"

"You people get the hell out of my house! *Out! Now!* Rip, call the sheriff! I want all these people out of here or I will prefer charges and the whole damned lot of them can go to jail."

"WELL, THAT'S PLAIN ENOUGH," THE PRESIDENT MUTtered. He liked plain talk, probably because he heard so little of it.

The television picture went blank; the network turned the show over to the hot babes in the studio. The president hit the mute button on his remote.

"What do you think?" he asked P. J. O'Reilly.

The chief of staff rubbed his hands together. "Can you imagine the political windfall that will settle on the party that can deliver a Fountain of Youth drug to the American people? Such a drug might even lead to the demise of the two-party system."

A vision of his political enemies being swept from office passed before the president's eyes. The moment was almost orgasmic. Then reality reared its ugly head.

"Medicare and Social Security will bankrupt the nation," he said bitterly.

"We can raise the retirement age to a hundred," O'Reilly shot back. "Or two hundred."

The president regarded his chief of staff with a jaundiced eye. The man was a fool, no question, but most politicians were. The president wished he had had the good sense all those years ago to join his father in the hardware business.

• • •

WHEN THE DRUG CZARS AND TELEVISION PEOPLE HAD at last disappeared up the driveway, Egg went after Adam Solo, who was still in the kitchen seated on a stool at the counter.

"Who," he asked deliberately, "are *you*?"

"I'm a saucer pilot," Solo answered.

"That phrase has a certain cachet, I must admit," Egg acknowledged. "When did you arrive?"

"I'm not quite sure," Solo replied, the amusement evident in his voice.

"When?" This time it was Rip who asked the question.

"Just a few minutes before I saw you in the hangar."

"No. When did you arrive on earth? The first time."

Solo finished his soft drink, got off the stool and took the can over to the trash bag under the sink.

When he had disposed of the can, Solo turned his back to the kitchen counter and leaned against it. Rip, Charley and Egg were giving him their full attention.

"I am marooned here on this planet, and I need your help."

"No doubt," Rip shot back, "but first you must answer our questions. When did you arrive here on earth?"

Solo took a very deep breath, then exhaled slowly. When the air was gone, he said, "A long time ago."

"So where is your ship?" Charley asked.

Solo shrugged. "Destroyed, probably. One of my colleagues went mad on the voyage here. After he dropped the team, he stole our saucer and took off. We watched him until he was out of sight. I assume that he flew it into the sun. Or tried to fly home, which would have been a physical impossibility in that ship. In any event, he has been gone for a thousand years. He has never returned. I doubt if he ever will."

5

RIP, CHARLEY AND UNCLE EGG EACH SUSPECTED THAT Adam Solo had a very interesting story, but the thousand-year number left them stunned.

As usual, Rip recovered first. "What about the starship that delivered you?"

"It didn't return either."

"If that thousand-year number gets out," Rip said to Solo, "your life won't be worth a paper dollar."

Solo nodded. "They won't believe a word I say; they'll kill me and do an autopsy."

Charley groaned. "Surely not."

"Oh, yes," Egg said grimly.

Solo's lips twisted into a grimace. "I've been in tighter spots. Three hundred and some odd years ago in Massachusetts, Samuel Parris decided I was a male witch. *That* was a close squeak."

Egg seated himself on a stool at the kitchen counter, which he rarely did because the round seat was too small for his fundament. "Convince us you are telling the truth," he said flatly. "Tell us why you are here on this planet."

Solo glanced from face to face, then said, "I am a librarian. This planet is a giant DNA library. My colleagues and I came to check the library, to make deposits and withdrawals, as we do from time to time, and to take DNA samples from plants and animals."

"Roswell, New Mexico, 1947. Were those your colleagues?"

"Yes. Here to look for us, probably. At least I have their ship. Unfortunately someone shot it up with an antimatter weapon and destroyed the communications equipment."

"That would be me," Charley Pine said modestly.

Solo smiled at her, then said, "I need your help. I must use the comm gear in the saucer you have sitting outside on the stone."

"It's a bit small."

"That is a problem. I need it brought back to its full size so that I can get inside and talk to the computers. And talk to my controllers, ask them to send a rescue ship."

"You people haven't been doing so well on this planet," Egg observed. "What makes you think they'll send a rescue mission?"

Solo shrugged. "Who knows if they even can? At least I can report in. The galaxy is a large, hostile place. We are a few tiny blobs of protoplasm, wandering back and forth between the stars. Death could happen at any moment."

"Or you could live for a thousand years."

"Either way, one will eventually be dead forever, which

is indeed a long, long time." Solo smiled. "All that matters is the adventure along the way."

"Do you really believe that?" Uncle Egg asked sharply.

Solo took in a bushel of air and exhaled through his nose. "Well, I used to."

"Let me see if I understand you," Charley Pine said with a toss of her head. "You people have introduced DNA samples into living creatures here on this planet? Is that correct?"

Solo shrugged. "That's essentially correct, but—"

"You are using living creatures here on earth as hosts for alien DNA samples?"

"When you state it that way it sounds bad—"

"Don't you damned aliens have any ethics at all?"

For the first time, Solo's voice hardened. "A few strands of DNA introduced into a host may well be the only way to preserve the information it contains. If the DNA doesn't interfere with the host's life or ability to reproduce, what better way to preserve the information? Everything made by man decays, erodes, eventually returns to dust. Planets come and go, stars burn out, asteroids journey erratically through the solar systems . . . only living creatures have the ability to resist the ravages of time. The bottom line—if your species becomes extinct you've lost your race."

EGG PREPARED DINNER. A LIFELONG BACHELOR WHO appreciated good food, he was an excellent cook. Tonight his heart wasn't in it. He kept glancing out the window into the evening darkness.

"They'll be back," Rip said, reading his uncle's mood. "That's what you are worried about, isn't it?"

Egg whacked a spoon on the counter and glared fiercely. "At times the world is a miserable place. That maniac Douglas shot out my windows. He cares nothing of the consequences if he gets what he wants."

Rip tried to think of something to say and couldn't. John Sutter discovered gold at his mill in California in 1849 and died a pauper. Greedy people took every acre, everything he had. He had faced a human tsunami, and inevitably he lost.

"Sometimes the law breaks down," Rip observed. "Civilization isn't so civilized." He glanced at Charley, who had poured a glass of wine for Solo and one for herself. They were sipping it and chatting.

He glanced at Uncle Egg, who was standing in front of the stove examining his spoon. It was bent double. Apparently Egg had bent it without realizing what he was doing.

They ate dinner in Egg's living room with their plates on their laps as a wood fire in the fireplace threw off heat and cast a cheery glow.

As they ate, the Cantrells and Charley Pine gently questioned Adam Solo. "Tell us about your home, the planet and society in which you grew up," Egg suggested. He had been mining the memories of the Sahara saucer's crew and knew not only where they were from but their life histories and families as they remembered them. He was curious how Solo's history differed.

Solo was reluctant. "It was a long time ago, and I have only fleeting memories. My parents, my brother and sister, the friends I grew up with, my classmates, all gone now. Have been dead for thousands of your years." He shook his head slowly. "For many years I tried to keep their memories fresh, to warm me as I tried to cope with life upon this savage planet. Then I let them go, let them dribble away like sand through my fingers." He paused, cleared his throat, then started playing with the food on his plate. "It is better that way, I think."

The silence that followed was broken by Rip. "Tell us of your adventures here, on earth."

"We landed upon an island. We knew it was an island when we landed. We didn't know what to expect. We hadn't explored much when my colleague stole the saucer, which still contained our portable comm gear, and flew away. We never saw him again." Solo shrugged. "He wasn't a pilot, but perhaps he knew enough to rendezvous with the starship. Probably he told them we were all dead."

"He never returned?"

"Neither him nor anyone from the starship. One can only speculate, and of course we did. Whatever happened, the saucer never returned."

"So you were marooned?"

"On an island on this green planet circling a modest star, on the edge of this humongous galaxy."

They finished dinner as he talked of the natives, the warlords and their armed men, the knights, and the Vikings who raided occasionally. The fire burned low, but no one was willing to break the spell to throw more wood on. Solo's voice was mesmerizing; the adventure came alive in his listeners' imagination.

"It was a difficult time for everyone. The native people's agriculture was barely adequate, they routinely starved in winter, the place was damp and rainy . . . My two companions and I were soon as cold, hungry and dirty as the people around us. To survive, we had to blend in, to become them. We quickly acquired the language while we waited for our saucer to return, or another from the starship. One of my colleagues was killed and the other died soon after."

At last, when the hour was late and the fire sputtered out, Egg announced, "It is time for bed. We will talk more tomorrow. Adam, you will have my guest room."

WHEN CHARLEY AND RIP WERE IN BED, CHARLEY WHISpered, because Solo was in the next room, "Did you believe him tonight?"

"He told us nothing that proves he is what he says he is."

Charley thought about that. "He flew the Roswell saucer."

"*You* flew the one we found in the Sahara, and you are not an alien. The fact is suggestive, but certainly not proof."

Charley persisted. "I thought he was telling the truth," she said.

"Or what he believes to be the truth. It will take more than stories to convince me."

"He didn't look happy tonight as he talked," Charley

observed. "I was watching his eyes. He chose his words carefully."

"Liars often do," Rip observed. "Or the mentally ill."

"Or a man trying to avoid painful memories," Charley shot back. After a bit she mused, "What would it be like to live a thousand years? To stay healthy and active and busy with life?"

"To outlive all the people you loved?" Rip continued the thought. "To watch everyone you care about age and die, one by one? He was never truly one of them. He was a stranger, different in a profound way. Ah, he avoided the disabilities and indignities of old age, so far, but at what cost?"

"If he is telling the truth," Charley said.

"If," Rip agreed.

"Douglas and Murkowsky are greedy men, sociopaths incapable of shame or remorse. They'll be back."

"Sleep, woman. We'll need our strength tomorrow."

STRETCHED OUT IN EGG'S GUEST ROOM, SOLO COULD not sleep. He ran over the events of the day, his impressions of Egg, Rip and Charley, and then his mind began to replay memories of the old days, when he and his colleagues were first marooned. There was much he hadn't told his listeners this evening. He didn't tell them of the battles and the blood, the battle axes and swords, nor of his Viking days. Nor of the cold winters, the miserable little huts, the fleas and lice. People dying of wounds and disease. The struggles, the hopelessness.

Nor did he mention the woman.

He finally fell asleep and dreamed of her.

EGG CANTRELL COULDN'T SLEEP EITHER. HE SAT ON the edge of his bed with the light on, looking at the dark windows and thinking about Douglas and Murkowsky and all those people watching on television, all those people out there in the night who thought a Fountain of Youth pill would be a wonderful thing to have, or who would like to profit from it. He thought those two categories included just about everyone. Maybe he was the only exception alive on this small planet. What was Solo's phrase? "This savage planet."

The computer he had taken from Rip's saucer was in its case beside his bed. The formula was in its memory. No one would believe him if he said it wasn't.

Perhaps he should hide the darn thing.

Yet when Douglas or some other thug put a pistol to Rip or Charley's head, he would tell them where it was. He knew that. They knew that.

He sighed and slowly put his clothes back on, then worked on getting his shoes laced. His ample middle always made shoes a chore.

Dressed, he stood and picked up the computer case. He tiptoed along the hallway and down the stairs. Eased open the front door and closed it softly behind him.

THE PRESIDENT WASN'T HAVING A QUIET EVENING IN the White House; far from it. A delegation from Congress arrived at midnight, threading their way through a mob that had gathered in Lafayette Square, across the street. The mob was unruly, waving signs and chanting about government perfidy.

When P. J. O'Reilly relayed the information about the mob, the president sighed. Life in a free society is often messy.

Yet when O'Reilly told him the congressional delegation was on the way over to see him, the president's mood deteriorated dramatically. "What do those bastards want?"

"Three guesses," O'Reilly answered blithely. Like the president, he too had been watching the media meltdown on every channel on television. People were sure the government knew about the Fountain of Youth drug; the elderly and sick were demanding answers. Politicians were spewing sound bites right and left, promising that they would get to the bottom of the government's cover-up and that if the drugs could be manufactured commercially, they would be. And would be made available to every man and woman on the planet at reasonable prices subsidized by the government and private insurance companies. Eternal life, or its earthly equivalent, was just around the corner.

Consequently, when the two dozen legislators filed into the White House's East Room at midnight, the president was in a foul mood. The congresspeople didn't care. They started talking immediately.

Senator Blohardt spoke louder than the others. "We are

getting enormous pressure from our constituents. They want those drugs and they want 'em now."

"What drugs?"

"Antiaging, for sure," the senator said as his colleagues nodded their concurrence, "and cures for cancer and diabetes, a slimming pill, and a real honest-to-God cure for limp dick. In other words, a cure for every human malady. All of them."

"All."

"Anything and everything anybody ever heard of, including the common cold. Our switchboards are jammed, e-mails have crashed the servers, and the telephones have melted down. Everyone wants some magic drug, and they want the government to stop lying and dithering and get it for them."

"I see," the president said, and indeed, being a career politician, he certainly did see. The elected representatives were facing a tidal wave of unprecedented proportions. Their political careers were on the line. Deliver or else. Well, if their political careers were on the line, so was the president's. He would get nothing from a Congress fighting for political survival.

P. J. O'Reilly stepped in and tried to suavely tell the assembled delegation that the government had not mined the Roswell saucer's computers and didn't know any drug formulas. He was shouted down.

"If we didn't, we should have. What are we going to tell the public? That the U.S. government is incompetent?"

"Why not?" the president muttered. The elected ones said that all the time, twenty times a day. Out loud, so they could all hear, he said, "The fact is the Roswell saucer was put under lock and key in Area Fifty-one because the Truman administration was afraid the public would react badly to flying saucers and aliens from space. Subsequent administrations didn't even know the damn thing was out there in that desert, and even if they had, they wouldn't have had the guts to tell the public flying saucers were real. It was the Cold War, for God's sake—the American people had their plates full confronting Communism and worrying about nuclear war."

"Be that as it may," the Speaker of the House said, "the public believes in flying saucers now, and the people want the benefits of saucer technology. All of them. Cures for diseases, enhancement of human life, all of that."

"All," echoed the president.

"The electorate will not be denied. If this administration and this Congress can't or won't deliver, they'll elect a president and Congress that can. It's that simple."

"If they are willing to wait for the next election," the Senate minority leader said ominously. "From the tone of the messages my office is getting, they might not be willing to wait anywhere near that long. They want it *now*!"

The delegation left shortly thereafter. Despite the lateness of the hour, each and every one of the senators and congressmen and women in attendance held a press conference on the sidewalk in front of the White House. The president watched some of the circus on television. They had told the president, they said. They had delivered the messages from their constituents.

"This is one of those seminal events that will change people's political affiliations for generations," O'Reilly said. "Like the Great Depression. If we don't act, the foundations of America will crack like a rotten egg. *But* if we play this right"—he rubbed his hands and grinned—"we'll take all the marbles."

The president had rarely seen O'Reilly grin, and he wasn't sure he liked it. He felt for his Rolaids bottle. "We'll go to Missouri in the morning," he said. "Tell them to get *Air Force One* ready."

"Should I have the press secretary make an announcement?"

"Hell, no. Let's keep it quiet, like we were going to Baghdad. We don't want this to turn into a media feeding frenzy."

O'Reilly merely raised his eyebrows. The president still didn't get it, he decided. The poor devil.

EGG CANTRELL WAS UP BEFORE DAWN MAKING COFFEE. He hadn't slept more than an hour. He turned on the kitchen television . . . and was astounded to see a picture of his farmhouse.

Egg looked out the unbroken kitchen window and saw the lights from the TV trucks and news sets. Not one, but three . . . four . . . five. Five sets of lights, and cameras, and satellite trucks. He went to the living room and saw another light setup.

The farm was under siege.

Egg raced around ensuring the doors were locked. He put the telephone back on its cradle, then picked it up. Got a dial tone. Called 911.

When the dispatcher picked up, Egg started talking. He gave his name and address. "My property has been invaded by news crews. I need the sheriff, as soon as possible. I'm willing to file trespass charges."

"Are your *really* Egg Cantrell?" the female dispatcher asked, her disbelief evident in her voice.

"I sure am. My house is under siege by reporters and photographers, all of whom are trespassing. I need the sheriff here to enforce the law and get these people off my property."

"Do you have that antiaging drug?"

"No, and—"

"My mother is in a nursing home. She's nearly ninety and senile. I sure could use some of those pills. For her, you understand."

"I am sorry to hear that," Egg said, trying to be patient. "Your mother has had a long life, and I hope a wonderful one, full of good memories and family. I don't have an antiaging drug. Please send the sheriff."

"So you won't help her. Because we don't have enough money? Or because you are willing to let her die? Which is it?"

"I am not God—" Egg began severely but found he was talking to a dead phone. He replaced the instrument on its cradle, and immediately it began to ring. He unplugged the device and added water to the coffeemaker.

"I am not God," he repeated aloud, although there was no one to hear. "I did not make the universe. I am not going to help change it. I am just going to live in it, and when my body wears out, die like everyone else . . . and hope that God has mercy on my soul."

6

ADAM SOLO HAD FINALLY GOTTEN TO SLEEP. HE WAS dreaming. The green, brown and blue planet was below, partially covered with clouds. Clouds in rows, towering thunderstorms, rivers of clouds streaming from the ocean onto the land. The brown deserts were clear, with only wisps of high cirrus.

"Looks inviting," the woman said. She was a biologist, on her first library mission to this galaxy. This was only the second planet they had visited.

"Not much here," Adam Solo replied. "A few cities in the temperate zone, but they haven't advanced to running water and indoor toilets." He was flying the saucer.

The woman shivered. "Let's avoid the natives," she remarked.

"If possible," her fellow scientist remarked. His specialty was paleontology. He was a nice enough guy, into his science.

The fourth team member, a medical doctor, was deeply

depressed. The signs were unmistakable. He was on medication for it and had delusional moments. Solo had argued with the expedition commander that the man should not descend to the planet's surface and had been overruled. The doctor's specialty was airborne bacteria, which might have evolved into deadly strains since the librarians' last visit.

Now he stared through the canopy at the planet, which was overhead since Solo was orbiting upside down. "Savages," he whispered. "We'll never get home."

Solo glanced at the medical man and withheld comment. Every planet they visited was uncivilized, and only a few hosted intelligent life. This one, according to the computer, had been home to manlike hominids for over a million earth years, and to creatures like the saucer crew for a hundred and fifty thousand or so. There was even speculation that the planet's people were descendants of stranded space travelers.

"When was the first mission to this planet?" the biologist asked.

"About then," Solo said distractedly, for she was wearing a headband too and he sensed where she was in the saucer's memory.

The problem of where to land had been addressed aboard the starship, in conjunction with the scientific staff. Prior missions' landing locations were plotted, and natural species dispersion factored in. This mission was supposed to check to see that the introduced DNA data containers were being dispersed as the original plan predicted.

They were going to land on an island that was often under cloud decks that streamed in over a warm sea current that made it a wet, rainy place, and considering the latitude a warm one. Today the island was clear. Well, it was late summer there, so perhaps the weather would hold for a few days, allowing the saucer crew to land, take their samples, then depart.

In his dream Adam Solo relived it again; the landing, the check of airborne and waterborne bacteria and viruses, a quick survey of the area to ensure natives wouldn't attack them while they worked, the erratic behavior of the medical man.

Solo could hear him arguing that they should not open the hatch even though the testing equipment showed the air and water were safe, because he was sure the gear was malfunctioning. Hear his voice, see his face, see the irrational fear. In his dream he reached for him, tried to grab his neck and strangle the fool . . . but the man was just out of reach, just beyond his grasp, moving, babbling and laughing and . . . It hadn't really happened that way, of course, but in Solo's dream the memories and his fears were all jumbled up.

God damn that man.

Then, while the team was outside working, the doctor stole the saucer.

In his dream Solo could see it rising into the night sky on a pillar of fire, hear the earsplitting exhaust roar, feel the helplessness.

He awoke. In a cold sweat.

This room . . . he ran his eyes over it, felt the tangible solidity of the bed, felt the air going in and out of his chest, felt his heart pounding.

He rolled over, put his feet on the floor and sat with his head in his hands while the dream faded.

A knock on the door. "Adam?" The woman's voice. Charley. "If you are awake, you better come downstairs. The house is surrounded."

WHEN RIP ARRIVED IN THE KITCHEN, HE FOUND HIS uncle standing at the window with binoculars, looking out. Egg tersely told him about the news crews and offered him the binoculars for a look. Rip didn't bother with the glasses. He looked, ran to the living room, looked there, then checked the other side and back of the house.

When he returned, he said, "Lots of people out there in back and on the other side, carrying flashlights and lanterns. We're completely surrounded. Call the law."

"I tried. We're on our own."

Rip turned and raced up the stairs to his bedroom. In less than a minute he was back with his old Model 94 Winchester and a box of shells. He dumped the cartridges on the kitchen table and began feeding them into the loading gate of the rifle as he eyed the reporter broadcasting near the hangar. The saucer on the rock was immediately behind the reporter, probably being used as background.

"Rip," Egg said, his voice cracking.

"This is completely out of control, Unc. There's a mob

out there. Someone may get hurt, and it isn't going to be us."

"You once told Charley that you didn't want to shoot anyone over the saucer."

"I don't think I said that to you."

"It's on the computer."

Rip took a deep breath. "The saucer isn't the issue." The rifle's magazine was full. He worked the action, chambering a round, then lowered the hammer to half-cock. "Our safety is. I will shoot any of those people to protect you and Charley and Solo."

Rip gestured toward the television. "Turn up the sound. We might as well listen and get the whole greasy enchilada."

Egg did as requested, just in time to hear the reporter say, "Stay with us. We'll be back after the break." The television began running a Viagra commercial.

"Want some coffee?" Egg asked.

Rip sighed and laid the rifle on the table. "Sure." He pocketed the remainder of the cartridges.

In a few minutes Charley and Solo joined Rip and Egg in the kitchen. Egg poured coffee while he briefed them. They stood at the unbroken window looking out.

The rising sun was lighting up the sky to the east.

"Maybe we'd better get some breakfast before the party begins," Rip suggested. "When the day is completely here the TV people won't need those lights and will be up on the porch pounding on the door and looking in the windows."

Charley sipped her coffee and looked directly at Egg. "You are going to have to give them that computer you took from Rip's saucer," she said. "This is just too big."

"No," Rip shot back.

"What do you think?" Egg asked Solo.

Adam Solo took his time answering. "Sooner or later someone always wondered why I wasn't aging like they were. The trick was to be moving along before that thought turned into action."

"Little late for that now," Rip said curtly.

"Apparently," Solo agreed amiably.

"So?"

"I don't know what is on your computer. And it's your computer. You people will have to decide."

"Everything that was on yours, less a hundred and forty thousand years of research."

"Actually, it doesn't work like that," Solo said, glancing from face to face. "Space and time are warped by gravity. Your Albert Einstein explained it rather well, I thought. If you travel in space, you travel in time. They are essentially one and the same."

"That explains the space maps in the computer," Egg said thoughtfully. "You must chart your course to arrive at your destination at your chosen time."

"That's basically it," Solo said. "The computer contains sailing directions."

"So why didn't your people return for you and your colleagues?" Charley asked.

"They tried, apparently, but going back in time is very

difficult. Think of a ship's course being dictated by the wind. In space we go where black holes and concentrations of matter let us go. Perhaps the Roswell saucer was on a rescue mission. Or perhaps not. Obviously I am still here."

"Stay with us," the television reporter intoned breathlessly. "We'll be here at the Cantrell farm all day reporting events as they unfold. We hope to interview Egg Cantrell and Adam Solo, both of whom are believed to be still in the house." This was followed by an appeal from a Houston law firm for clients who might have been injured by a bad drug. There was apparently lots of money in human suffering.

"Hell," Rip said to Solo, "don't despair. You have a great career ahead of you hawking antiaging pills."

Solo smiled.

Rip glanced out the window. Dawn was well along.

"We may have to give them the computer," Egg muttered. He got busy making breakfast.

AIR FORCE ONE LANDED AT COLUMBIA, MISSOURI. Surrounded by Secret Service agents, the president and P. J. O'Reilly trotted across the mat to a waiting helicopter, which got airborne as soon as the door closed.

An air force major was waiting in the chopper to brief the president. He described the media siege of the Cantrell residence, the traffic jam on the local roads and the estimated four hundred gawkers who surrounded the house. The county sheriff was now on the scene and wringing his hands. "Most of the onlookers are local voters," the major said to the president, quite superfluously.

"All this on television?" O'Reilly asked sharply.

"Every channel. All the broadcast and most of the major cable networks. Even the cooking channel. The producers go back to their studios occasionally to let the talking heads and hot babes have their moments, interview 'experts,' run commercials, that kind of thing. But you, Mr. President, will be on the air worldwide as soon as the helicopter comes into view of the cameras."

"So what's happening this morning?" the president asked.

"Nothing," the major replied. "The Cantrells have stayed in the house. The reporters have knocked on the door, which didn't open. One of the producers was talking to his boss in New York about cutting the electrical and telephone wires to force the Cantrells out. Egg Cantrell could sue them, but they would have their story."

"Is Adam Solo there?"

"The networks believe he is. He was there yesterday and hasn't been seen leaving. I doubt if a field mouse could have gotten out of the house during the last twenty-four hours without being seen."

"The drug moguls, Douglas and Murkowsky?"

"Watching television somewhere, I imagine."

The president looked out a window of the chopper at the rolling Missouri countryside sliding by beneath—at the patches of woodland, the fields that were harvested weeks ago and the neat little farms connected to the paved roads that snaked across the land.

As the major predicted, a live shot of the helo approaching the Cantrell farm hit every major network within seconds. Producers almost melted down in ecstasy when the president of the United States stepped out. Reporters tried to mob him, but the Secret Service agents kept them away, mainly through brute force.

The president pretended the press wasn't there. He set his eyes on the front door of the Cantrell residence and marched up the path, trailed by P. J. O'Reilly and two agents openly carrying submachine guns and wearing headsets with boom mikes.

Rip was already at the door to open it for the president. He had wisely left his rifle in the kitchen, so there was no unpleasantness with the Secret Service agents, who followed O'Reilly, who followed the president.

After the president shook hands with Rip, saying, "Good to see you again," he motioned the security detail to go into the empty living room and asked, "Where's your uncle?"

"In the kitchen." Rip led the way.

Someone had turned off the sound on the TV set, so there was only the video of a reporter gesturing wildly and pointing toward the house as his mouth worked rapidly.

Rip did the introductions. The president held on to Solo's hands while he looked him in the eyes. "You and I need to have a long chat," he said.

Solo nodded.

Charley Pine got a kiss on the cheek from the president—he liked to kiss beautiful women and made no secret of it—but Egg got the full treatment. He found his hand trapped by the president's, and then the president put one arm around his shoulder and hugged him tight.

"Mr. Cantrell—I'll call you Egg. I came from Washington to have a personal talk with you. Is there a place where we can have a private conversation?"

"Rip and Charley and Solo have a right to hear everything that is said. How about a cup of coffee?"

"Sure."

The president started to sit at the kitchen table and found himself staring at Rip's Winchester. "This thing loaded?"

"Yep," Rip said flatly.

The president gingerly eased it to one side of the table and dropped into a chair. O'Reilly remained standing in the doorway. From time to time the chief of staff glanced at the television.

"Folks, we have ourselves a real mess here," the president declared. "The press and the public are convinced that you have a bunch of formulas for some real high-tech drugs on that computer you took out of Rip's saucer."

Egg started to speak, but the president stopped him with an upraised palm.

"We know you have it. Everyone on the planet knows you have it. And the public won't take no for an answer."

"It's private property," Egg pointed out as he handed

the president a cup of black coffee. "I have the law on my side and I have possession. I'm keeping it."

"Is there a formula for an antiaging drug on that thing?"

Egg knew this question was coming, and he still didn't know exactly how to answer it. He stood there blinking while he made up his mind. After a moment he nodded, once. Yes.

"I want the formula."

"No," Egg said forcefully. "You don't." He repeated his arguments about the drug distorting the economy by artificially extending human life, talked about the ecological damage that would result from an ever-increasing human population and explained that the species would become extinct as all those people gobbled up the earth's resources. He finished with the remark, "You and Congress can't even balance the government's budget, and now you want to repeal the law of evolution? The expanding population of hungry people will result in anarchy, here and abroad. The future will become a horrible nightmare for everyone on the planet. Do you want our species to become extinct? Giving mankind this drug will accomplish just that, and in the not too distant future. This drug is the purple Kool-Aid." He took a deep breath. "Maybe the beetles will win after all."

The president let Egg have his say. When Egg fell silent, he said, "I'm inclined to agree with you. On the other hand, America is a democracy. If a significant majority of the voters want this drug, they are going to find a way to get it. Hell, we can't even stop people from using marijuana, heroin and cocaine."

"No," Egg said.

"How about you, Solo? You know the formula for this drug?"

"Mr. President," said Adam Solo, "the networks are turning over every rock, questioning people all over this planet about me. No doubt your FBI and police agencies can and will join the investigation. Sooner or later your investigators will learn enough of the truth to guess at the rest. I was a pilot of a saucer that landed some years ago. I have not aged since then. The conclusion will be inescapable: I know the formula and how to manufacture the drug, and I have extended my life by using it. So I admit it to you, here and now."

"Well," the president said after examining Solo's face and scrutinizing the faces of Rip, Charley and Egg. "Well, well, well." He looked again at Solo. "When did you arrive on earth?"

"About a thousand years ago."

The president's mouth fell open and he stared at Solo.

"Mr. Cantrell is right, and you know it," Solo said forcefully. "The existence of this drug commercially will doom the human species. The desire to acquire and use it, at whatever price, will be irresistible for a great many people. Too many. The economy will crash, the planet will be raped, and humanity will become extinct."

The president took his time answering. When he spoke, he said, "In a democracy the people get to make their own mistakes."

Rip snorted. "When this cat gets out of the bag, no one will ever be able to put it back in. The damage will have been done."

The president smashed his fist on the kitchen table, making his coffee cup and the rifle jump. "You think I am the dictator of the world? I'm just an elected public official, and there's another election coming along—there always is. People are putting excruciating pressure on their senators and congressmen. They are elected officials too."

He waved his arm at the window. "You know what's out there. Four hundred people and television cameras piping signals all over the globe. That's the world we live in. They want it and they're going to get it, one way or the other. Now, your choice, quite simply, is whether you are going to give up the formula willingly or wait a short while to get run over by the train."

Solo looked from face to face, then turned to the president. "I'll write it out for you."

"The hell you will. I take a piece of paper home and give it to the FDA and meanwhile you people boogie. Then the formula turns out to be fiction. You'll make me look like a goddamn fool."

"Which you are," Charley Pine said to his face.

The president ignored her. "I want Egg's computer," he said. "The wizards can get the formula off of that thing, and whatever happens, I won't get covered with crap."

They argued for several more minutes. P. J. O'Reilly weighed in when the president ran out of words, issuing threats. Egg ignored him, helped himself to more coffee and sipped it.

Finally even O'Reilly ran down.

Reluctantly Egg opened the kitchen cupboard and took a computer case from the top shelf.

"No, Uncle," Rip said. "Screw 'em all. Don't give them that thing."

"You shouldn't," Charley said, grasping Egg's arm.

"We don't have a choice," Egg said, resigned. "This fool wants to give the human race a suicide pill, and we don't have any way of preventing it." He stepped toward the president and started to hand him the case, then drew it back.

"You must get all those people the hell off my farm. Go outside, hold a press conference, then have the Secret Service run everyone off. I can't live like this. And I won't."

"They'll be gone before the helicopter is out of sight," the president promised and took the case from Egg's hands.

THE PRESIDENT WAS ALMOST RIGHT. HE HELD HIS press conference, gave the cameras a good look at the case in his arms, then boarded the chopper. The helicopter was over the horizon when the television crews began breaking down their equipment and loading it in their trucks.

"What do you think will happen when the president finds out the computer is smashed?" Rip asked Egg.

"Won't be pretty," Egg said.

Rip went to the back of the house and watched Secret Service agents there herd the crowd away. The men with the submachine guns weren't tolerating lollygagging. The sheriff and his fat deputies got busy directing traffic.

Grabbing a garbage bag from Egg's kitchen stash, Rip tossed in a loaf of bread, a jar of peanut butter, some cold cuts from the refrigerator, two six-packs of bottled water and all the canned soup the bag would hold.

Fifteen minutes after the helicopter departed, the last of the television trucks and vans headed off up the road to the gate. The Secret Service agents rode along with them. The sheriff was the last man to drive away.

"Well, folks, let's get out of Dodge while we still can," Egg said. Solo hoisted his backpack, and Rip, Egg and Charley picked up pillowcases containing clothes. Rip grabbed the black garbage bag full of food and water, then had another thought. He handed his bag to Solo and went back to the kitchen for his rifle.

They gathered on the front porch.

Solo said, "I hope the comm gear in your saucer works and I can send my messages. Then all I must do is wait. Are you sure you want to leave here?"

Egg spoke first. "You've been waiting a thousand years, you said."

"Believe me, I had given up hope of ever living until this day," Solo replied. "A few more weeks or months or even years won't matter much."

Solo seemed reluctant to say more. In the silence that

followed, Charley Pine put the question, "So what do we do now?"

"Canada," Solo said. "There is a place on the southwest shore of Hudson's Bay, with a cave that was used by ancient people. We can put the saucer in the bay."

"If it isn't covered with ice."

"If there is an ice sheet, it will be thin. We'll put the saucer in, then let the ice freeze on top of it."

"We aren't really dressed for the Canadian winter," Egg pointed out.

"Get coats and winter gear. Boots. Sleeping bags if you have them. Blankets. Everything you can carry. And matches. We'll make do." He scrutinized their faces. "I've had some experience with that."

Ten minutes later they gathered again on the porch. Everyone had bundles. Egg locked the door behind them.

They trooped down the hill to the saucer resting on the stone outcropping. As they approached, it lifted off the rock into a hover.

The saucer set out at a walking pace toward the two-acre farm pond on the other side of Egg's runway. The people trailed along toting their bundles.

Egg flew the saucer into the middle of the pond, dipped it once in the water to get it wet and raised it about four inches above the surface.

"Better cover your eyes," he said.

All of them turned their backs and put their hands over their eyes. Still, the flash that followed was so bright they could see it through their eyelids. In seconds the first flash was followed by another as millions of volts coursed from the saucer into the water of the pond, then into the earth. The electrons in the atoms of the saucer were making quantum leaps in their orbits, releasing extraordinary amounts of energy.

Three more flashes followed, then Egg's voice. "That's it, I think."

They turned and looked. The saucer was back to its normal size, about seventy feet in diameter. It looked black and ominous in the diffused morning sunlight.

Egg opened the refueling cap on top of the saucer and submerged it into the pond. The water level rose a few feet, then seemed to subside somewhat as water rushed into the saucer's tank.

When the gurgling stopped and the surface of the pond was once again placid, he lifted the saucer from the water. It looked majestic rising slowly, dark and wet. When it was free of the water, Egg brought it over to the shore and sat it down on the ground a few feet from them. The hatch opened slowly. They all began shoving bundles in.

"Mr. Solo, do you want to fly it?"

"Why not?" Solo said and led the way into the ship. As Egg and Charley stowed their gear, Rip ran into the hangar to grab his fishing rod and tackle. When he returned, he threw it up into the saucer and clambered aboard. Solo was already in the pilot's seat, and the reactor was on, the computer displays dancing vividly across the screens. Rip closed the hatch. Everyone took a seat and strapped in.

The presentations continued to dance across the

screens in front of Solo, as fast as thought as he ran the built-in tests of every system in the ship. Two minutes passed as Rip and Charley and Uncle Egg sat silently, alone with their thoughts.

"Is everyone ready?" Solo asked. He already had the saucer off the ground and the landing gear retracting. He moved out over Egg's runway, accelerating.

The passengers said "Yes" simultaneously. The saucer continued to accelerate on the antigravity system. Then the rocket engines ignited, giving just minimum boost. The acceleration continued, pressing everyone back into their seats.

The nose rose into the sky as the flame from the rockets increased steadily.

Soon the saucer was standing on its tail, pointing straight up, rising atop a pillar of fire.

As the saucer climbed, it shot by two news helicopters. The cameramen beamed their pictures to the satellite. As they received the video feed, television networks broadcast it all over the globe. People in New York and Los Angeles, Chicago and Houston, Minot and Wheeling saw the rising saucer on their television screens. They saw it in London, Paris, Berlin, Cairo, Moscow, Istanbul, Baghdad, Mumbai, Tokyo, Cape Town and Sydney. And everywhere in between.

The saucer rose though the clouds and began tilting toward the northeast. Up, up, up, until it was just a star in the noonday sky and the roar of its rocket engines faded to a whisper.

Then it disappeared from sight. The sound level dropped to a kiss by the breeze; then it too was gone.

Little puffy clouds continued to drift across the Missouri countryside, under that milky sky, just as they had since the world was born, but there was no one at Egg's farm to look at them.

7

HARRISON DOUGLAS AND JOHNNY MURKOWSKY WERE in the lounge of the fixed-base operator at the Columbia airport when the television began airing the video of the saucer rising on a cone of fire through puffy clouds into the heavens. They were waiting for the crews of their respective private jets to complete the preflights and come for them. *Air Force One* had just taken off and retracted its wheels. Heidi, Murkowsky's masseuse, was having a glass of wine in the bar.

Now, as the roar of the saucer's rockets emanating from the speakers of the TV set filled the room, the two moguls stood in front of the idiot box shoulder to shoulder, watching.

When the saucer's exhaust was but a pinpoint of light on the screen, Johnny turned to Douglas. "We should join forces, combine our efforts. That flying plate has to come down somewhere. When it does . . ."

"What is this 'we' shit, Kemo Sabe?" Douglas shot back bitterly. "I spent eight million bucks raising that saucer, or one like it, from the Atlantic. You're a little late to the party, Johnny-boy."

"Late?" Johnny Murkowsky asked incredulously. "Eight million bucks? What a skinflint you are! That kind of money is chicken feed, pocket change. Every single person on this whole round rock, all six or seven billion of 'em, will want a regular supply of those antiaging pills. We'll be richer than Buffett and Gates combined. We're not talking about a nice profit—we're going to get all the money. *All of it.* Every last, dirty, solitary dollar."

Harrison Douglas stared at Murkowsky.

"Man, if we work together and don't try to sabotage each other, you and I can *own* this damn planet," Johnny Murkowsky roared.

The light began to dawn for Harrison Douglas. "You're right," he said softly. After all, somewhere along the way he could always double-cross Johnny Murk, and probably would have to, before Murk did it to him.

"Of course I'm right! All we have to do is cooperate, get that formula one way or another. Any way we can. Then we will have to defend it, keep everyone else from ripping us off. If we can do that, we will have won the game. We'll get all the marbles. *All!*"

Harrison Douglas had the same vision. "It's possible," he said. "A long shot, but possible."

Murkowsky swelled up like a toad as he contemplated

the future. "Maybe we'll change the name of this planet," he said. "Name it after ourselves."

THE PRESIDENT WAS IN HIS PRIVATE COMPARTMENT aboard *Air Force One*, somewhere over Illinois, when he opened the computer case that Egg had given him. He reached in to pull out the computer and realized that his hand was touching bits and pieces. He emptied the computer case onto the bunk.

A pile of junk.

He stirred through the shards as the realization came to him that Egg had somehow smashed the computer before he gave it to the president.

Egg knew all along that he would eventually have to give the computer to someone, so he destroyed it before that moment arrived.

Maybe the wizards could put it all back together and get something out of it.

Even as that thought crossed his tricky mind, the president realized how forlorn that hope was. He cussed a while, really got into it, said every dirty word he knew, which was a staggering lot because he had been in politics for twenty-five years. He smacked the bulkhead with his fist, which made him wince.

Damn and double damn!

When he finally calmed down, he began to survey the size of the mess he was in. What had he said to the television people as he stood in front of Egg's house? He remembered, all right. "I have in my hand a saucer computer that contains a formula for an antiaging drug, a Fountain of Youth drug, some call it."

Well, he didn't have it. That was a hard fact.

He was sitting down, trying to control his breathing, when there was a knock on the door.

"Yes."

The door opened. It was O'Reilly.

"The air force reports that a flying saucer went into orbit from central Missouri ten minutes ago."

The president lowered his face into his hands.

O'Reilly's eyes went to the junk strewn on the blanket of the bunk bed. "What's that?"

The president didn't look up. "That pile of crap is the computer that Egg gave me. The bastard smashed it to bits."

A wave of self-pity swept over O'Reilly. He didn't much care if anyone else got access to the Fountain of Youth drug, but as a very high government official, he knew he was fully entitled to a prescription and had let his hopes soar. Now they came crashing down. He sagged against a bulkhead.

"So what are we going to do?"

The president gestured futilely. "We've got to get our hands on that saucer. Somehow, some way."

O'Reilly had never seen the president so low. He kinda enjoyed that, but he felt pretty low too. "It's gotta come down sometime, somewhere."

"Yeah," the president said. Then he added, "Maybe."

A moment passed; then he asked, "Is that saucer Solo stole from Douglas still up there?"

"Yes."

"Well, Solo isn't in it. He was sitting in Egg's kitchen telling lies. Have the FBI find out if anyone is still at the Cantrell farm. For all we know, there is no one in either saucer."

"That's impossible!"

"And find a tame judge somewhere that will issue arrest warrants for all that bunch: Solo, Egg Cantrell, Rip Cantrell and Charley Pine."

"What's the charge?"

"Hell, I don't care. Make something up. Income tax evasion, bank robbery, treason, sex with farm animals, whatever. Go, O'Reilly. Make the calls."

After his chief of staff closed the door and the president was alone, he began scooping shards of computer back into the case that had held it. He wondered, Was Solo lying?

A thousand years!

Oh, my God!

RIP, EGG AND CHARLEY FLOATED NEAR THE SAUCER'S pilot seat while Adam Solo busied himself with the comm gear. If anyone was out there listening, he didn't say. The three floaters balanced themselves in the weightless environment by using a finger on the back of the pilot's seat or a touch of the overhead or floor or bulkhead. Didn't take much, they discovered.

They watched fascinated by the planet they were spinning around, although it appeared that the planet hanging there in the black void was revolving slowly under them. Above it all, in the inky blackness a billion galaxies wheeled in the eternal sky.

"We are going to need a plan," Egg said. "We can't really stay up here in this saucer very long, not without toilet facilities and more food and water."

"Amen to that," Charley said. She was regretting not making a pit stop before they left.

"WHAT ARE THEY GOING TO DO NOW?" THE PRESIDENT asked the air force chief of staff when his plane landed at Andrews Air Force Base. The general was there to meet him and walked with him to the helo, *Marine One,* that would take the commander in chief back to the White House. The general had so much chest cabbage that it was difficult to see that the front of his suit was blue. The four large silver stars on each shoulder were pretty gaudy too.

"Ah, I dunno, sir," the chief of staff said.

The helicopter pilot was a marine major. The president stuck his head into the cockpit and asked him, "What are Rip and Charley going to do with that saucer?"

"I'm sure I don't know, sir," the major said, so the president took his seat and strapped in.

When the chopper landed on the White House lawn, the president went down the stairs and returned the salute of the enlisted honor guard. The first guy in line was a navy petty officer third class. The president paused and asked, "What do you think the Cantrells are going to do with that saucer?"

"They can't stay up there very long, sir," the petty officer said. "Ain't got a head in that thing, I heard. I kinda figure they'll find a place to hide it and wait."

The president took a good look at the sailor's face. He looked maybe twenty years old and shaved perhaps twice a week. "What do you think they're waiting for?"

"Aliens, sir. A starship."

P. J. O'Reilly nudged the president's elbow, trying to get him to move along. The old man wasn't moving. He looked at the sailor's name tag. Hennessey.

"Thanks, Hennessey. Glad to know that someone around here is thinking about possibilities. Keep it up."

"Yes, sir."

The president walked on into the White House.

THE NEW PARTNERS, HARRISON DOUGLAS AND JOHNNY Murkowski, were wondering too. What would Egg, Rip, Charley and Adam Solo do next? Presumably they were in the Sahara saucer orbiting the earth.

"Are they really?" Murkowsky asked. He was in the left seat of his Citation V, and Douglas was flying copilot. They were in the flight levels, on their way back to Connecticut, where they kept wives, mistresses, extra clothes and Christmas decorations. Their companies were also there.

"I'll admit, seeing Adam Solo at Cantrell's farm was a

shock," Douglas replied. "I checked with a contact in Space Command ten minutes before I drove up to the place. That saucer Solo stole is still in orbit, circling the earth every ninety and one-half minutes."

"And Solo isn't in it?"

"Apparently not."

"Well, who the hell is?"

"Damn if I know. I kinda suspect no one is. That being said, if anyone is in that thing, it's probably somebody we don't know about. *It's* up there going round and round, thinking big thoughts."

"It?"

"It," said Harrison Douglas. "If anybody is flying that thing, it's probably an alien. Some critter from outer space. Hell, I bet Solo is an alien himself. He flew that saucer right off that salvage ship like he knew what he was doing."

"You know, we've got ahold of something that is a lot bigger than it looks," Murkowsky said.

"Who knows how many aliens are out here running around," Douglas mused, "looking like real people, but ready to do something rotten. Something terrible. Conquer the world or blow it up."

Murkowsky was dubious. "Why would an alien civilization launch a starship across the void, at tremendous cost in treasure and perhaps lives, just to blow up stuff, eat kids and scare the crap outta everyone?"

"Man, weird people have been writing stories like that

for a hundred years. The bookstores and movie theaters are full of them. I know it sounds goofy, but maybe it could happen."

"Let's assume, for the sake of argument," said Johnny Murk, "that aliens are rational creatures who have done a ton of research that we would like to have. Research that is going to make us rich."

"Okay."

"Pine and young Cantrell and the fat one may be aliens too. Ever thought of that?"

"Solo couldn't be the only one. They're like snakes."

"Even if they are aliens that live in a sewer and want to conquer the world, what the heck are they going to do with that saucer?"

"I haven't a clue," Harrison Douglas confessed.

ADAM SOLO FELT A STRANGE LASSITUDE AS HE SAT strapped to the pilot seat of a saucer, watching the earth spin slowly by underneath. The stars were there in the obsidian heavens, of course, hard and bright as they can only be when their light isn't diffused by the atmosphere. Yet they were made trivial by the sun. The brilliant energy of the local star swept the saucer's cockpit with every orbit of the planet. The sun rose over the horizon, climbed the sky and then descended, flooding the cockpit with light and heat. When it became too much, Solo merely rolled the saucer until the sun was below the belly.

"Why," Egg asked, "isn't intelligent life more common in the universe? Why aren't we here on earth bombarded with alien radio broadcasts and television shows?"

Solo took his time replying. He had to focus on the question and think about it. "It takes billions of years for life to evolve. Most solid planets within the life zone, which means a significant percentage of the planet has a temperature below the boiling point of water and above the freezing point, are too unstable. Other planets pull them out of orbit, asteroids crash into them, some cosmic catastrophe wipes out budding life."

"Why didn't that happen on earth?"

"The presence of the moon helped enormously. Stabilized the planet's orbit. And this is a quiet little corner of your galaxy."

"We like it," Egg admitted.

"You should. If it were busier, with a nearby nova or supernova, or a neighborhood black hole, or your solar system had a massive planet in an irregular orbit, or a star that was a little bit bigger or smaller, things would be much more exciting and higher life forms wouldn't exist. Wouldn't have had the time to evolve."

"The moon," Egg mused, looking at it.

"It was torn from the planet by an asteroid collision, when the solar system was very young. Reduced the size of the planet by one-seventh and stabilized the earth's orbit, causing it to be more regular. Lucky for you."

"Is this situation rare?"

"Oh, no. There are millions of solid planets with life on them. The universe is a big place, though. A really, really big place. The edges are expanding at a huge fraction of the speed of light. The edges are traveling away from each other at a combined speed that exceeds the speed of light, so light from one side of the universe never reaches the other."

Egg hadn't entirely swallowed Solo's tale of his life and adventures, so he shot back, "We're lucky? You are implying that intelligent life that realizes it is mortal is a good thing. Is it?"

A trace of a smile crossed Solo's face, and he didn't reply.

Egg pressed. "And you, Solo. Let's talk about you. Perhaps everyone on your planet lives for a thousand of our years, but I doubt it. Evolution would slow to a crawl. So is your experience typical of your species?"

"No," Solo said curtly.

LOOKING AT THE PLANET FROM THIS VANTAGE POINT was an emotional experience that hit Solo hard. It had been over a millennium since he had seen this view. Since then he had lived through so many experiences and known so many people, almost all of whom were long dead, and he alone walked on into the unpredictable, unknowable future. A good thing? Wasn't that Egg's question?

Well, is life a good thing or a bad thing? A positive or a negative? Or just a wash?

He had had the good parts, and the bad. And those times when he was unsure if the pain was outweighed somehow by something more.

Like the time . . . oh, it was a winter day, he remembered that. Cold, the naked trees, the wind . . . The weather had been warm for a few days and the snow on the ground had melted, but spring was still a long way off.

The hut was one of a dozen or so near the river, among the big trees. He could never remember seeing trees so large, each over five feet in diameter, as if they had been growing since the earth was born.

Inside the hut was an old, old woman. She lay on a bed of skins and dry leaves that had been gathered earlier in the fall and only now spread to give the bed some softness, some cushioning. Her hair was white, her face lined, her breathing irregular. He sat beside her and held her hand . . . examined the blue veins and tendons that stood out clearly . . . looked at the work-cracked nails, the calluses on the fingers . . .

Said her name.

She opened her eyes. She didn't recognize him, which was perhaps fortunate. The experience was one he wanted, and was for him. Not for her. She wouldn't have understood. She would have been confused, frightened.

He studied her features. Yes, he could see something of her mother in her. Of course, her mother died young, murdered by Hurons. He had taken his vengeance, glutted it, a memory he now regretted. Vengeance does not bring back the dead, does not solace the empty place.

But he was younger then and he didn't really think about it. Just did it. The others expected it of him, and he thought perhaps she would have expected it too. So he had given himself to revenge and blood and slaughter . . . and eventually the Hurons were no more. He and his warriors killed them all. All! Each and every one. Until not a drop of their blood flowed in the veins of any living creature. The arrow, the tomahawk, the knife . . . blood. Red blood, warm, flowing freely . . .

Their daughter knew none of that, of course. She had been an infant, nursed and loved and taught her words by her mother's parents.

Now she was old. Very old. Eighty winters. Most of her teeth were gone, and her heartbeat was irregular—he could feel it in her wrist.

His wife was murdered . . . and eighty years later he sat watching their daughter die of old age.

He couldn't stay, of course; that would have aroused suspicions. So he spent another hour with the old woman, said he had known her sons and grandsons, which was true, and then left long before the shadows turned to darkness.

It had snowed that night. Now, sitting in the saucer pilot's seat, staring at the eternal blue Pacific and the clouds swirling over it, he remembered walking through the forest in the snow crying for his wife, Minnehaha, and their daughter . . . and for himself.

He had lived too long.

He knew it then.

He knew it now.

8

"A STARSHIP WILL ARRIVE IN ORBIT A WEEK FROM now," Adam Solo told his passengers, who were floating about the interior of the saucer.

"I didn't hear you talking on a radio," Charley objected. "Nor did I hear alien voices."

Solo shrugged.

"So how does the comm gear work?"

It reads my thoughts and broadcasts them, emitting a much stronger signal. And it picks up theirs, too faint for me to receive, and rebroadcasts them to me.

With a start, Charley Pine realized that she had heard Solo, yet he hadn't made a sound.

You can read minds? she asked, not voicing the words.

Yes.

"Holy damn," she said aloud, looking at Rip and Egg. "He can read our thoughts."

Egg looked thoughtful. **So that's how he learns languages so quickly,** he thought.

Yes.

Rip wondered, **How many languages does this guy know, anyway?**

All of them, was Solo's reply. **This skill helped me stay alive. I knew what people I met were thinking when they were thinking it, regardless of the language they spoke, regardless of what they said.**

Did you read the president's thoughts? Egg wanted to know.

Oh, yes. Amazingly, he is an honest man. He said precisely what he thought. That kind of honesty is rare in the human species.

"I suppose," Egg said aloud. He wasn't sure he liked hearing Solo's voice in his head when none of the others could hear it. He definitely was uncomfortable with Solo reading his thoughts. "Maybe you'd better stay out of my head," he said aloud and got no reply.

"You're a difficult man to lie to," Rip mused.

It is difficult, but not impossible. A few have done it.

"Tell you what," Egg said. "Since I am kind of old-fashioned, I'll pretend you can't get into my noodle and we'll all just keep saying aloud whatever we want others to know. Deal?"

"Deal," each of his companions said in turn.

"Well, we can't stay up here a week waiting for the cavalry to come riding out of the void," Charley Pine declared. "I need a pit stop within a few hours or it's gonna get messy."

"Canada," Solo said. "We'll start down in a few minutes."

They discussed it and agreed since no one else had a better idea.

"But some starship rescuing you from these people howling for your blood isn't going to do us any good," Rip said to Solo. "You may have a way off this planet, but we are kinda stuck here. While we are alive, anyway. And I don't want to be in any other condition anytime soon."

"I have a plan," Adam Solo replied. "We need a diversion, something for the public to think about besides us. I've given the orbiting saucer instructions."

"I thought its comm gear was *hors de combat*?" Charley said.

"Its long-range communications gear certainly is, but it can receive my brain waves. However, it can not transmit."

"So you didn't get an acknowledgment that it received your order?"

"Life is often uncertain. Let's wait and see what happens."

THICK STRATUS CLOUDS COVERED MOST OF CANADA. The saucer's pilot and passengers could see the cloud cover from space. Solo had the saucer plunging downward toward the white gauze. It was still afternoon here, with the sun low on the western horizon. A sliver of moon was visible in the eastern sky.

The saucer raced downward, drawn by gravity. The

atmosphere below would slow the machine with friction, heating up the leading edge of the saucer to a cherry red glow.

Charley Pine saw it and marveled yet again at the technical achievement of the saucer people, to build such a ship. At least 140,000 years old, it could still perform its mission, carrying people and things up and down from the surface of the planet.

Adam Solo was an alien, and his people were coming back to rescue him. What, she wondered, must the starship be like?

Egg Cantrell was not enjoying the ride. He was fretting about the antiaging drug and the havoc it would cause. Then there was the impact the presence of an alien starship circling the planet would have on the people of earth. Once and for all, irrefutable proof would be flung in the faces of the world's people that they were not alone in the universe.

A good thing or a bad thing?

Or a fact that would have to be faced, and damn the consequences.

Rip's thoughts were about Adam Solo. He believed Solo's tale, he decided . . . and yet he didn't. The ability of the mentally ill to weave complex alternative realities was on his mind. As the first tugs of the atmosphere upon the saucer caused him to grab the back of the pilot's seat, he resolved to keep a wary eye on Solo.

If the guy tried to steal the saucer . . . well, Rip had a

rifle and no qualms. He, Charley and Egg weren't going to freeze to death in the Canadian Arctic if he could help it. Alien or nutcase, if Solo pulled something, he was going to stop some lead.

That's a warning, Solo.

Received.

After a long ride down, the saucer plunged into the top of the stratus layer. "At least everyone on the ground won't see us," Egg remarked.

Rip wondered how many people were this far north as the Canadian winter began to wrap its icy fingers around the land and lakes.

Plunging downward through the clouds, everyone in the saucer watched the computer presentations on the instrument panel. The radar was painting a picture of land and places without return—no doubt frozen lakes. The radar's energy bounded off the ice and didn't return to the antenna.

Solo seemed quite comfortable with the presentations on the screens before him. They changed occasionally, as fast as thought, because he was wearing the headband and had merely to think about the information he would like to have, and the computer presented it to him.

Down, down, down. Toward the surface of the planet. Still doing several times the speed of sound.

Solo leveled finally and let the speed bleed off. He didn't start the rocket engines, didn't change course, merely let the saucer slow, and when he judged the moment right, he raised the lever on his left to activate the antigravity rings and prevent the saucer from impacting the earth.

At last it came out of the clouds, a thousand feet or so above a flat countryside of snow-covered trees and frozen lakes. Solo changed course almost ninety degrees, to the northeast. He let the saucer descend until it was running perhaps a hundred knots just above the treetops in this flat wilderness.

The sun slipped below the horizon and the sky darkened. The saucer ran on in the twilight.

"You do know where you are going?" Rip asked Solo.

"Yes."

"When was the last time you were here?"

"A long time ago."

"How long?"

"Very long."

"How about a straight answer?"

"I lost count of the seasons several times in my life. Nine hundred of your years ago, I think, give or take."

"Who were your shipmates?" Egg asked, although he expected he knew the answer.

"Little men, bearded, tough. Warriors inured to the cold. Vikings."

"You were with them?"

"I was their leader. I pointed out the dangers of the voyage, and they insisted we go anyway. They trusted me. They knew life was short and they would end up in Valhalla, so the adventure drew them on."

"And you?"

"I didn't care if I lived or died."

"Do you care now?" Charley asked.

Solo didn't reply. Ahead in the twilight they could see water. Hudson's Bay.

"IT'S CANADA," JOHNNY MURK TOLD HARRISON DOUGlas. They were sitting in the FBO lounge at the Greenwich, Connecticut, airport. Heidi was massaging Murkowsky's neck. The chairman and CEO of Murk Corporation turned off his cell phone and dropped it into his shirt pocket. "That was a guy with Space Command who wants a job after his military hitch is up. He says the White House is being notified."

"So we are ahead of the government?"

"If we can move fast enough, we are."

Heidi finished Murkowsky's neck with a vigorous short rub. "You need to stay loose, Johnny."

"Yes, dear."

THE CLIFF AT THE EDGE OF THE LAKE WAS ABOUT A hundred feet high and ran parallel to the lakeshore for several miles. It was a geological anomaly in this flat country scoured by glaciers.

Solo cruised just above the water, looking at the cliff. He couldn't seem to find what he was looking for. If he was looking for a cave, it wasn't visible.

"Was the water level lower then?"

"Higher, actually. The world was warmer."

He stopped the saucer and stared through the canopy at a massive round formation that ran right to the water.

"I think there has been an earthquake," he said. "Looks like that formation has slipped toward the water."

"No cave there now."

Solo didn't answer. He flipped on the saucer's landing light and let it drop into the choppy water. It went under and he used the antigravity rings to take it toward the cliff.

In a few seconds the stone formation appeared before them, illuminated by the light.

"No cave there," Rip said flatly.

The saucer went deeper, with the cliff right in front of it. Then it wasn't there. It ended in a shelf. Deeper still Solo took the saucer, then began creeping forward, under the stone roof. The glow of the landing light helped. The floor of the sea bed rose, so Solo coaxed the saucer up. They broke the surface. The landing light revealed that they were in a large cave, surrounded by rock. Ahead of them was a beach, perhaps a hundred yards long. High on the beach, under another stone shelf, sat a ship. A wooden ship, but without a mast. Sweeping prow and stern. Clinker-built.

"A Viking ship," Charley whispered.

"Still there," Solo said with a sigh. "Right where we left it."

"MR. PRESIDENT, ONE OF THE SAUCERS IS COMING OUT of orbit."

"Which one?"

"The one that launched from Missouri."

The aide gave him the projected flight path. Space Command said the saucer descended over Alaska. The projected flight path had it impacting in the northern Canadian wastes.

"Ridiculous," the president said, glancing at the three-foot globe mounted on a stand in the corner. He stepped over to it and gave it a spin.

"They'll refuel it in a lake somewhere," O'Reilly suggested. He was, the president thought, a master of the obvious.

"The United States government had better find out which lake before anyone else does," the president said pointedly, frowning at O'Reilly.

The president was worried. Petty Officer Hennessey's comment about waiting for aliens had planted a seed. This situation was out of control, with everyone in an uproar over an antiaging drug. Yet if there was any truth to Hennessey's comment, things could get worse. *A lot worse!* Aliens!

A painting on the wall caught his eye. It was an original, on loan from the Smithsonian. A group of almost naked Indians with a few feathers in their hair stood on a beach watching Christopher Columbus' three ships approach.

Things hadn't worked out so well for the Indians after Columbus' arrival. Would the arrival of people—or creatures—from another planet start a similar collapse of the current civilization?

The president rooted in his drawer for his Rolaids bottle and helped himself to a handful.

SOLO LANDED THE SAUCER ON THE ROCK-STREWN beach beside the Viking ship. When he turned off the landing light the darkness was total. The four people in the cockpit looked at each other in the glow of the instrument lights, but no one spoke.

"I brought a flashlight," Egg said finally.

"Let's get out," Rip suggested, "see if we can find some wood to use for a fire."

"We can always burn the ship," Charley noted.

"If we spend the winter here, we'll have to."

They opened the hatch and Rip dropped through. Then Charley, Adam Solo and Uncle Egg.

Indeed, there was ancient dry wood in a crevice near the ship. Slivers cut with Rip's pocketknife provided the kindling. In minutes a small fire was burning, and its light illuminated the ship's hull. Charley came to the fire straightening her clothes. "Are we going to get asphyxiated in here?" she asked.

"I feel air moving," Rip said. "I think we're okay."

"You guys need to put toilets in those flying plates," she told Solo.

After answering nature's call, Solo inspected the sides of the Viking ship, then clambered aboard.

Charley joined him. The flashlight beam illuminated seats, some shields, spears . . . short swords. Helmets. Bones in one corner. "Caribou," Solo said.

A large slab of stone that had apparently fallen from the roof lay on a portion of the stern, which was wrecked when it fell.

"After all these years . . ." Charley mused.

"The wood is deteriorated but not dust. The cold air preserved it, I guess. The thing wouldn't even float now, even if that rock hadn't fallen on it. But back then she was a good ship. Rode the back of the seas, didn't leak much, sailed well downwind . . . a good ship."

He climbed over the side and boosted Egg up.

They heard a shout from Rip. "Hey, over here. There is a breeze coming in from the outside."

After scrambling over the rock, he found the opening, a crack that led to the outside. Rip took the flashlight and, turning sideways, slipped through. In a moment he was back. "Goes all the way outside. Cold out there."

"Must have opened in the landslide that dropped the roof," Solo said.

"Let's get the rest of our stuff on the beach and build a bigger fire. We'll need it tonight."

Rip went back to the saucer and climbed inside. He grabbed bundles and pushed them through the hatch. Solo and Charley took them and headed toward the fire, where Egg unpacked and arranged things. When all the duffel was out the hatch, Rip climbed down. He picked up two sleeping bags and the sack of food and trailed along toward the fire.

"What do you think of the Viking ship?" Rip asked softly, so only Egg could hear.

"It's real, all right." Egg sighed. "Every museum on the planet would love to have it. The wood has deteriorated, but still . . . Rip, it's as if they pulled it up on the beach, climbed down and walked away, intending to come back, but they never did. Or when they returned a slab had fallen from the rock roof, or perhaps the whole mountain had shifted and they couldn't get their ship out of what had become a cave."

Egg warmed his hands at the fire and finally began inspecting the interior of the cave, what he could see. The only illumination was from the fire, so it was difficult. The ceiling appeared to be about eighty feet high.

"Smoke is rising nicely," Rip observed. "There might be a hole or crack in the roof."

Using the flashlight, Egg inspected the rear wall of the cave. He found a Celtic rune hacked into the stone. He cast the beam around to see what else might be there, then studied the rune by flashlight.

Solo joined him. "I buried a man here," he said. "Scurvy, starvation, and a respiratory infection. He didn't last long."

"To die here in this wilderness . . ." Egg looked around again with the flashlight's beam.

"We all have to die someplace, sometime," Solo said curtly. "He died among friends, and this is as good a place as any."

"How would you know? You're the man who doesn't die."

"Oh no, Egg Cantrell. You have that wrong. I am just a man who is living a little longer. But my time will come. Rest assured of that."

The night could have been worse, Charley Pine reflected. The fire burned well, fed by dry wood that burned quickly, the cave was reasonably warm, and the sleeping bags were comfy. Before she drifted off, she checked her companions, who were all snuggled up in their bags. Uncle Egg snored softly.

On the far wall of the cave, in the dim reflected firelight, beyond the dark, ovoid shape of the saucer sitting on its landing gear, she could just see the outline of the Viking ship.

She was studying its shadow on the cave wall when she drifted off to sleep.

PETTY OFFICER HENNESSEY WASN'T THE ONLY PERSON on the planet to connect two orbiting saucers with the possible arrival of a mother ship. People tweeted about the possibility; then it went viral on Facebook and the other social networking sites. Within minutes, the possibility became a certainty and everyone everywhere knew everything about it and was absolutely sure. After all, we're wired up now.

The world's population was a bit nervous. As the minutes ticked by, they became more nervous. Visions of alien space fighters zapping everything, ten-foot-tall green predators with spiderlike mandibles catching and gobbling folks, starvation, anarchy, chaos and civilization in ashes flashed through the collective mind. The possibilities went from the triple-digit cable channels to the network news shows and the world's front pages as fast as fingers could type, which was almost at the speed of light.

The networks' babes and commentators talked about these sci-fi fantasy possibilities with straight faces. The reaction of the viewing public was predictable: Teenagers the world over began screwing like rabbits, unhappy spouses abandoned their families, people maxed out their credit cards in restaurants and jewelry stores, and survivalists took to the hills to fort up.

A tidal wave of people headed for Las Vegas, which for the first time in the history of the world had to declare itself full—closed to new visitors. Police turned away all traffic into town, and the FAA would allow only empty airplanes to land at McCarran. The casinos were packed wall to wall; strippers wriggled and writhed around the clock; hookers doubled, then tripled, and finally quadrupled their prices. Every woman in town with fake tits ordered a new car; Corvettes and Porsches seemed to be the most popular.

In cities and towns across America some people even went to church. Collection plates filled to overflowing as thousands of preachers dusted off their best sermon on "Where Will You Spend Eternity?," mounted their pulpits and spurred the choirs.

Inevitably the politicians wanted their constituents to see them molding and shaping events. Hordes of them descended on the White House, where the president was forced to admit them in waves of fifty each.

From Congress and statehouses and city halls all over America, the politicos demanded action. They wanted the government to protect everyone, to negotiate with the alien space monsters and remind them of the glories of diversity, and if that failed, to send them all straight to hell. Or to somewhere politically correct, if by chance the monsters didn't believe in hell. A few pacifists and left-wing dingbats counseled nonviolence and turning the other cheek, but they were howled down or ignored.

"Find that saucer!" the president told P. J. O'Reilly every time he saw him. "Space Command said it came down in Canada, which is a very large place."

"It might not even be in Canada," O'Reilly protested. "Just because it came down headed for Canada doesn't mean—"

"Find it."

"Mr. President, that saucer could be anywhere. It might even be on the bottom of Lake Mead. Solo and the Cantrells might be partying in Vegas."

"Find it!"

Being human, the president wondered how it would go down if aliens arrived to fight or parley. He had sweated all that during the first saucer crisis just over a year ago. The memory of those days gave him the shivers. He recalled that his political adviser then had told him to look presidential and not to give away the country or pee his pants. Sound advice that, he reflected.

Pulling off those three feats was going to be a real trick, however.

He glanced at his watch. He had five minutes before the next herd of politicians was due to storm the East Room. He asked the honor guard aide to send for Petty Officer Hennessey. They met in the hall outside the East Room. Through the closed door, the president could hear the herd shuffling in.

"These aliens," the president began. "If they show up . . . Got any thoughts on that?"

"They'll want something," Hennessey said. "Wouldn't have bothered to come all the way from wherever to here if they didn't."

The president nodded. Sure. He saw that.

"They'll want to talk to the head dude. That'll be you. You just gotta take charge, get what you want in return for what they want."

"So what do I want?" the president asked aloud, staring at the wall.

"I dunno, sir," the petty officer said. "Maybe them Fountain of Youth pills, which don't sound too smart to me, or a cure for cancer. Give something, get something."

"Yes. Yes." The president straightened his shoulders and adjusted his tie. He could handle negotiations.

Hennessey thought so too. "You're our guy, sir," he said and saluted.

The Secret Service agent opened the door to the East Room, and the president strode in.

THE PRESIDENT WAS TAKING A MAKEUP AND POTTY break between delegations when O'Reilly came rushing in with a message. He handed the sheet of paper to the president while he told him what it said. "The NRO has tracked the saucer. It's in Manitoba."

The president shooed out the makeup artist, a cute twenty-something female with a theater degree from a little college in New England. She was doing this gig powdering the presidential nose until something on or off Broadway opened up. The president watched her hips as she walked out.

"Manitoba, like in Canada?"

"Yes, sir," said P. J. O'Reilly. "Near Hudson's Bay. Or in Hudson's Bay."

"You know I don't know all those damn initial agencies."

"The National Reconnaissance Office. The spy satellite people."

The president folded the paper into a little square and handed it back to O'Reilly. "Well, who are you going to send after them?"

"There's this little problem, Mr. President, and State is working it. Canada is a foreign country, so we can't just send a squad of U.S. Marshals or Marines up there to arrest them without the Canadian government's permission."

"Get it. Bet the people in the saucer didn't go through customs or immigration."

"Yes, sir, but there is a complication." O'Reilly enjoyed telling the president about complications, so he perked up now. "Canadian sovereignty is at stake, according to their ambassador, and they are being sticky. State is drafting a formal request."

The president stared at his shoes, then into the mirror at his powdered nose and forehead, which didn't shine anymore, and at his balding pate. Finally he said, "O'Reilly, you are a good chief of staff because you are a first-class son of a bitch."

He speared O'Reilly with his eyes and continued, "Still, there are a lot of sons of bitches out there, and if you want to keep this job you had better prove to me that you are the meanest and toughest of the bunch. Light a fire under that ambassador. Light a fire under ours. I don't care if you burn their balls off. *I want that saucer.* I want Adam Solo and Egg Cantrell. I want that youth serum or pill or suppository. And, by God, I want them *now!*"

THE NEW DAY CAME SLOWLY AT THE CAVE ON THE BAY. An ice fog obscured the ocean and surrounding land and filtered the daylight. It also penetrated the cave, despite the fire that kept the temperature just above freezing.

The four travelers sat huddled around the fire eating from the bag of grub Rip had packed and washing the food down with bottled water.

"It's going to be difficult to stretch our supplies for a week," Egg said, frowning at his ham sandwich. "When your ride arrives, where will they meet you?"

Solo shrugged. "Anywhere I ask them to. In orbit would probably be best."

"Another week," Rip mused. "I suppose we could stay here that long, unless someone finds us. The bay is full of fish."

Solo laughed. "I once spent a winter here. There were caribou in the forest and fish in the bay. With your rifle, we are well equipped to hunt caribou, and we can chip holes in the ice to fish."

"Heck. This little penknife is the only blade we have," Rip said sourly, holding up his. "Won't cut much fire-wood or skin many caribou with this."

"We're also a little short of coffee and soap and a way to wash clothes," Charley added.

Solo looked amused. "I would bet there are at least a half-dozen knives within ten feet of where you are sitting."

"Show me one."

Adam Solo began scraping at the loose dirt near his feet with one boot. When it seemed soft enough, he be-gan digging with his hands. In a moment he pulled up a shard of a flint blade. He laid it aside and kept dig-ging. Pieces of flint, a broken arrowhead and an intact arrowhead were revealed as the hole got wider and deeper.

After another minute he said, “Aha,” and pulled a flint blade from the dirt. It was perhaps three inches long, and both sides were edged. There was no handle.

“A knife.”

Rip inspected the blade, turned it over repeatedly in his hands and held it so the fire illuminated it. Solo rose and walked to the Viking ship. In a moment he was back with a sword. It was short, broad and covered with rust. “I can scrape this rust off, and we can sharpen this on a stone. It’ll cut wood and butcher game and, if need be, cut people.”

Adam Solo slashed the air with it. The weapon seemed to fit his hand, Charley noted with a start.

Solo gave the sword to Rip, butt first. “Now, if you will loan me your rifle?”

Rip passed it to him. “It’s loaded.”

Solo inspected it as carefully as Rip had the flint blade. “Twenty-five thirty-five. Obsolete caliber.” He flashed Rip a grin. “But adequate.” He stood and adjusted his coat. “I’ll go see what I can find.”

Adam Solo walked around the fire and headed for the opening in the rocks.

Charley Pine said, “A week in a freezing cave hideout! Robbers Roost. And they say civilization is moving right along.”

“Didn’t you ever go to Scout camp?” Rip teased.

Charley didn't look amused. She said to Egg, "How long before the U.S. government finds us?"

"Two or three days. The heat of the fire leaking from this cave will show on infrared sensors."

"Uncle Egg, we need a plan." Charley wasn't smiling. "After Solo gets rescued by his buddies and flies off into infinity, we are going to be stuck here with six billion people who think we have the formula for eternal life and won't give it to them."

"The formula is in the saucer's computer," Egg admitted, "and you are right. I *won't* give it to them."

"Six billion crazy people," Charley said. "You are going to have to give them the formula or we are going to have to get the hell off this rock while the getting is good."

"Go with Solo, you mean."

"Uncle Egg, you can't resist a tidal wave."

Egg added another dead limb to the fire. They sat staring into the fire, thinking their own thoughts.

Rip broke the silence. "Who wants to go fishing?"

"I'm saving fishing for my old age," Egg replied. "So I'll have something to look forward to."

"I caught my fish at Scout camp," Charley said dryly. "That was enough."

"No sense of adventure," Rip grumped. He put his fishing pole together, checked the reel and line and hook, then made a little ball of bread and impaled it on the hook.

He walked to the edge of the water lapping at the dirt and cast the hook and bread in.

"You can't catch a fish in here," Charley objected. "You'll have to go outside."

The words were no more out of her mouth than something big hit the hook and the line bent and started ripping off the reel. Rip laughed and played the fish.

Charley Pine was watching Rip fight the fish and didn't see Uncle Egg enter the saucer and close the hatch.

ADAM SOLO WALKED NORTH ALONG THE SHORE OF THE bay. To his right the escarpment that held the cave was gradually getting lower, becoming first a hill, then just a swell in the land, then petering out altogether.

The shoreline curved around to the east. Solo paralleled it, walking through low birches and scrub covered by several inches of snow. The air was below freezing. A light snow, almost a visible mist, was sifting down on the westerly breeze. Visibility in this gray world was no more than two hundred yards.

In just a few days, Solo knew, the bay would begin to freeze along the shore, and the ice would march out into the bay, sealing the water from the snow and wind. Winter was on its way—not the winter of the temperate zone farther south, but a subarctic winter. Fortunately the snow was not accumulating much just now. He pulled his hat down hard on his head, turned his coat collar up and buttoned the top button.

He walked deeper into the forest, looking for tracks. He kept the rifle balanced under his right armpit with the barrel down and his hands in his coat pockets. His feet would be wet within an hour or so—if he didn't find anything he would have to turn back. If he got lucky with a caribou, he could make good boots and gloves, even a hat that covered the back of his neck and kept snow from going down his coat.

All these things he had learned the hard way, once upon a time. When he was much younger.

He tried to recall how the land lay, but the memory was old and the forest no longer looked the same. Trees had grown old and died in the intervening centuries; beavers had altered the streams; meadows now existed where once creeks had flowed through gullies.

Solo was standing behind an alder, looking across an old beaver meadow, when he saw movement. Just caught it out of the corner of his eye.

Without turning his head, Adam Solo searched with his eyes and saw the flash of white moving through the brush on the other side of the meadow. He stood frozen, watching.

A bear. A white bear. With two cubs. They were heading north. When the ice froze on the bay, they could get out on it in search of their favorite prey, seals.

Solo made no move to lift the rifle. First, he didn't have a bullet heavy enough to stop a polar bear unless he made a perfect, lucky shot, and there were three of them. Killing two and wounding the third would be as fatal as missing with the first shot.

The large adult paused and sniffed the breeze. Fortunately the gentle wind was in Solo's face, not behind him.

She turned her head and visually searched downwind. She looked right at Solo and didn't see him. She wouldn't, unless he moved.

The Vikings had thought the white bears enchanted and were frightened of them. He remembered the bears and the contagious fear. With only shields, swords and battle axes, the Vikings lost many bear encounters, which meant the bears ate some of them. The bears had never met a creature they couldn't kill and eat. Standing now with an inadequate rifle and no other weapon, Adam Solo felt the fear again. He stood as still as he possibly could, trying to minimize the white cloud caused by his exhalations.

Today, thankfully, the white bear and her cubs moseyed on north along the creek until they were out of sight. Solo waited for several minutes, listening to the silence, the whisper of the wind.

He heard something, just a suggestion of a sound, then a breathing in and out. The hairs on the back of his neck and arms prickled. He turned slowly.

Turned, and there stood a bear on its hind legs, just a few feet from him, its black eyes in its expressionless white face looking down upon him.

Instinctively Solo dropped to the ground, bringing

up the rifle. As the bear lunged he was under it, with the rifle coming up, thumbing back the hammer. He jabbed the barrel toward the descending head as he pulled the trigger.

9

AFTER SOLO LEFT THE CAVE TO HUNT, EGG CANTRELL wriggled his way into the saucer and turned on the power. Then, carefully, he donned a headset and arranged it just so on his balding dome.

He knew what he wanted—Solo's memories of the Viking ship—and the computer provided it almost instantaneously. It was as if Egg remembered the event himself.

The ship was riding a heavy sea; he was wet and cold; the wind was howling and rain blew sideways. He shouted at the crew, gestured to row harder to maintain steerageway downwind, and felt the ship respond sluggishly as the oars bit into the foaming sea.

Time passed . . . the storm ended, the ship made a headland, Solo (Egg saw it as Solo had) ran the ship up on the beach, and the men leaped out to secure it to rocks and trees. Solo led a party inland, and soon they came to a village . . . a deserted village, because everyone had fled.

Solo's men ransacked the village and took all the food and drink they could carry. Several of them searched the nearby woods, and two of them dragged out a young mother. They raped her as the others searched for hidden food or valuables.

Soon the ship was at sea with the sail up, and the men were laughing and drinking mead. Egg could sense what it had tasted like. A bitter, creamy beer full of impurities.

Egg forced himself to think about America, and he saw the Viking ship approaching a beach with a cliff. It was this cliff, he sensed, and he saw the sheltered beach, now a cave, as Solo remembered it from oh, so long ago. The memories were hazy at times, the features of some faces hard to distinguish, and the timeline was scrunched and wavy. Whole weeks and months were missing.

What remained was vivid, powerful, images that Solo had never forgotten, images and sounds and smells and sensations and emotions that he *could never forget.*

Blood, murder, combat with swords, learning to use bows and arrows, sacking villages, burning, looting, raping . . .

Curiosity, hunger, anger, anxiety, revenge, longing, depression, guilt, revulsion, lust, rage . . . fear, panic . . . and joy.

There was a village, and a woman. Solo remembered her very well indeed, and—

Egg ripped off the headset. All those sensations left him drained and breathing hard. His emotions now were a tangle. He sat, trying to sort it all out.

Yes, he was sitting here in the pilot's seat of this saucer; the machinery in the compartment behind him was humming ever so faintly; through the canopy he could just make out the flickering campfire.

Egg turned off the reactor and watched the instrument panel go dark.

Several more minutes passed before he felt able to climb out of the saucer.

There stood the Viking ship, with its soaring prow and stern, resting on the sand, almost as if it were waiting for its crew to return and take it back to sea.

The emotions Egg felt now were almost overpowering. That ancient wooden ship was fear and adventure and the pure essence of life . . . a life lived to the hilt each and every minute. He forced himself to turn away from it and staggered toward the fire, trying to put the inputs from the computer into some kind of perspective.

Charley and Rip were wrestling a dead limb into the cave. Uncle Egg sat on a handy stone while they got it just so and stuck a tip of it into the fire. As the flames ate into it, Rip said to Egg, "What did you learn in the saucer?" Rip knew Egg had been in there only to wear the headband and communicate with the computer.

"Solo remembers the Viking ship," Egg managed and hugged his knees.

"And?" Charley asked. She picked up a fish and the flint knife and began cleaning it. Rip had caught six nice ones, each a meal in itself.

"That ship," Egg said, motioning with his head, as he

searched for words. "Solo remembered being at sea in it. Vividly remembered. Wild storms, wind, blowing spray, wet, cold, bad food, good companions, shouts to the gods in Valhalla . . . He remembered."

"It's so small," Charley said, examining the Viking ship with new eyes.

"They were men. No doubt of that. Crossed the Atlantic in those tiny ships. Sailed into the Med. Rowed up rivers into the heart of Europe. Sacked cities and villages. Sacked monasteries . . . Solo did all that and more. Watched his men carry away screaming women, cut down monks, kill farmers with pitchforks trying to protect what little they had. He was a pirate. They all were."

"My God."

"It was more than a thousand years ago, Charley. That was just a toss-off number. I'd say his memories on earth go back at least twelve hundred years, maybe thirteen hundred."

"He's a guilty man."

"Who isn't?" Egg demanded. "By God, who isn't?"

Charley Pine wasn't buying. "He wasn't some illiterate barbarian from a Norwegian fjord," she said acidly. "He was a space traveler, a voyager between the stars, a man from a higher civilization."

"Whatever *that* is," Egg remarked.

"You don't just leave your morals at home when you go slumming," Charley shot back. "Robbery, rape, murder?"

"Adam Solo was a saucer pilot marooned on a savage planet, amid savages, and he was going to have to become one of them or die," Egg said heavily. "There was no other way. So he became a Viking. The best one. He was adopted by Eric the Red, claimed as a son."

Rip stared. "So he was Leif, Eric's son?"

Egg nodded affirmatively. "Leif the Lucky."

"Talk about situational ethics," Charley said tartly and tossed another handful of fish guts into the dark water. "Old Mister Whatever-It-Takes."

"The ultimate survivor," Rip said softly. " 'Judge not, and ye shall not be judged.' "

"I wonder how that fine old philosophy plays with the boys from Alpha Theta Six, or wherever in the universe Solo is from," Charley said darkly. "If it ever occurred to them."

"The human memory is such a strange thing," Uncle Egg mused. "The things that happened yesterday, or in the recent past, you can recall, almost like a movie. But the things that happened long ago are lost except for specific vignettes, almost like snapshots engraved in your memory. How a certain person looked, an overwhelming emotion, an impression." Egg shrugged. "Solo has many such scenes in his memory. Most are frozen, without context, vignettes of a past that is mostly forgotten. The rest of it—*ai yi yi*—gets jumbled and sometime mixed with things that might be imagined. Or the timeline gets bent, the memories get jumbled. Sorting truth from falsehood is the computer's strength. It is man's weakness."

"Are you trying to say Solo didn't do those things?"

"No. I'm saying the only things the computer captured

are vivid memories, and they aren't linear. It isn't like a movie. That's what I'm trying to say. If you want to see for yourself, get in that flying plate and put on a headset. Just ask for Solo's memories."

Rip looked at his watch. "He's been gone almost three hours. The sun is low and it will be dark soon." He stood and jammed his hat down over his ears. "I'm going after him. Wish I had some gloves."

"If the wind rises, it will wipe out your tracks," Egg said. "Come straight back." He handed Rip the flashlight.

Charley stood and kissed him. "Be careful, Ripper." Her kiss was sensual, promising. Her eyes were warm.

He hugged her, then headed for the crack in the rock that led outside.

SOLO'S TRACKS WERE PLAIN STILL, ALTHOUGH BEGINNING to fill in with tiny snowflakes driven by the breeze.

Rip hurried along in the subarctic half-light.

A half hour from the cave, he came across the bear tracks. They were big, almost six inches across, and the claw marks were deep and vivid. They came into Solo's tracks at an angle, and Rip could see where the bear had driven his nose into the snow, smelling the tracks Solo had left. Then the bear's tracks were superimposed on Solo's.

Rip began to trot. The cold air cut his lungs.

Ten minutes later he found Adam Solo . . . and the bear. The polar bear lay across Solo's legs. Blood spattered the snow.

The bear, a male, was dead. A bullet had gone in under

his chin and come out the top of his head. Death must have been almost instantaneous. Even so, one paw had caught Solo on the top of his head and ripped his scalp open. He had bled profusely.

Rip checked to see if Solo was still alive. Well, his heart was pumping and he was breathing shallowly. His hands seemed warm enough, despite the temperatures. Amazing, that.

Solo, can you hear me?

No response.

Rip grabbed Adam Solo by the armpits and pulled mightily. The bear was a lot of dead weight; after repeated tugs, Solo's legs came free.

"Solo, can you hear me?" He said it aloud this time, and still no response.

Rip checked the rifle, opened the action, ejecting the spent cartridge, and ensured the barrel was free of snow. He closed the lever, chambering a fresh round, and lowered the hammer. He laid the rifle carefully in the snow and checked Solo again. No other visible injuries.

A pirate. Murdered monks and farmers. Carried women away to be enslaved and raped. Leif the Lucky. Ah, yes . . . *Lucky.*

There was no tension in Solo's body. He was unconscious. Whether from loss of blood, a concussion, or internal injury, Rip didn't know.

He lifted Solo, marveling at how slight he was.

Rip draped the spaceman over his shoulder. He was tempted to abandon the rifle, but afraid he might need it later. With great effort he retrieved the rifle with his free hand and started following the tracks back the way he had come.

His burden was heavy and he was soon tired. The wind began to rise, blowing against his back as he trudged on into the gathering darkness.

Rip was at least a mile from the cave when he felt Solo stir. The muscles in his body tightened.

"Solo?"

A grunt in reply.

Rip laid the man in the snow on his back. He didn't stay down but raised himself slowly to a sitting position. He looked around, looked at Rip and saw the rifle.

"You killed the bear and he darn near killed you."

Solo merely nodded, then shoved his hands into the snow and tried to stand.

"Don't do that, you idiot!" Rip ordered. "You've lost a lot of blood and probably have a concussion."

Solo ignored him and got upright. He swayed, then steadied himself. Looked around.

"I can't understand," Rip said, "why you didn't get hypothermia lying out there. Temp is damn near zero. Your hands ought to be frozen."

Solo felt his head, examining the wound with his fingers. He scraped some of the dried blood away. His hair was coated with it, but there was nothing that could be done about that. His scalp seemed to be in place and it wasn't bleeding.

"We gotta get back and see what we can do about

sewing you up," Rip said. He picked up the rifle and started walking. Solo followed. He staggered a time or two, but he remained upright with his feet going.

When they were back in the cave, Egg seated Solo by the fire and examined the wound while Rip explained about the bear. For illumination, Egg used the fire and the flashlight, which still had some juice left in its batteries.

"It's very sore," Solo said.

"It's almost healed," Egg said in amazement. "The wound is completely closed."

Charley made a noise. "Let me look." She took the flashlight and examined Solo's scalp.

"Just an angry red line," she said softly, and went around the fire to take a seat.

"Rip?" Egg queried.

"That polar bear nearly ripped off his scalp. He bled a lot and was unconscious when I found him. I carried him a mile or so, then he woke up and walked the last mile. There he sits."

"Mr. Solo?" Egg murmured.

"Mr. Cantrell. I have been shot with bullets and arrows, stabbed, slashed, and have fallen from cliffs. I survived several explosions, extraordinary low temperatures that killed several of my companions, and two airplane crashes. And now, a bear attack. My body's ability to repair itself has been enhanced."

"Enhanced?"

"Enhanced. An induced genetic mutation."

"Ye Gods," Charley Pine moaned. "If those drug moguls find out about that, they'll slice and dice you and put the pieces under a microscope."

"Let's hope they don't find out," Adam Solo said, fingering his healing scalp wound.

"Can you be killed?" Rip asked.

"Of course. If the wound is severe enough, I'll die before my body can repair the damage." Solo shrugged. "It will happen someday, a traumatic death, or my body will just wear out. I am mortal, as is every living thing. To be honest, as that white bear charged, I thought my time was over."

In the silence that followed that remark, Charley asked, "Were you scared?"

"No." He thought about that answer and added, "Relieved, perhaps."

Adam Solo eyed the fish. Before anyone could reply to his previous comment, he suggested, "One of those would be superb just now."

His companions agreed. In minutes they were roasting fish on sticks over the fire and Solo was telling them about the bear.

The conversation moved to the coming starship. "How is it powered?" Egg asked.

"Nuclear fusion," Solo replied. "The reactors in these saucers use fission, but the starships use fusion, the same reaction that goes on inside a star. Light elements, like hydrogen, are fused into heavier elements, and the energy from the reaction is used to power the ship."

"Fusion has never been achieved here on earth," Egg remarked.

"The reaction requires a force field to hold it; no material known in the universe can. Suspended in the electromagnetic field, a few grams of light elements are so compressed that nuclear fusion begins. A tiny star beings to burn."

"The computer had information about it that I couldn't understand."

"I don't," Adam Solo replied. "No man can know everything."

They discussed fusion reactors as the fire burned, more wood was added and the fish roasted.

"How is the energy used to move the ship?" Rip asked.

"The energy powers artificial gravity fields, which are used like the rings in the saucer to repel a gravity force, or to attract it, whichever is most efficient at the time. In effect, the ship hurls itself toward a star or black hole, or pushes it away."

"What is your world like?" Charley Pine asked, changing the subject rather dramatically.

"It's been a long time," Solo said. "A few years ago I was in Hollywood when the Star Wars movie projects came around. I drew up some pictures of what the cities of my youth were like, turned them in to the studio artists, who embellished them more than a little." He laughed. "When I saw the first movie, I wasn't sure exactly what I remembered."

"So how's your head?"

"Sore."

"So you survived another adventure."

"That's the definition of experience," Solo said with a trace of a smile, "which is underappreciated by those who don't have it and overvalued by those who do."

10

AFTER DINNER EVERYONE TOOK TURNS EXAMINING Solo's scalp by firelight. The wound was completely healed, leaving only an angry red scar, which would probably disappear soon.

"Amazing," Egg said.

Charley and Rip had no comment. They looked askance at each other, then wandered toward the Viking ship.

"Oh, man," Charley moaned softly. "Oh, man! If you thought eternal life got them lathered up, imagine what will happen when they hear about enhancing the body's ability to recover from wounds. The military will pull out all the stops. Gotta have it, gotta have it, gotta have it."

"No one will believe that you and I know nothing about this."

"Even if there is one chance in a million that we have the formula for antiaging, or body quick-repair, we're toast. Even if the Americans leave us alone, there are the Russians, Chinese, North Koreans and Muslim fanatics. With eternal life and a quick fix for wounds, the diaper-heads would be Allah's supermen."

"So what do we do?"

Before Charley could answer, the faint hum of a passing airplane sounded in the cave. The sound waves were muted, because they entered through the crevice to the outside world, and through the stone, which was not a good conductor.

Rip and Charley stood frozen. A minute passed, then two. As one, they broke and ran for the crevice so they could hear better.

They raced through the stone crack into the cold evening air. Twilight, a hint of breeze . . .

They heard the plane. Then they saw it, circling over the lake and starting back this way. A Beaver on floats.

"Infrared," Charley said. "They've seen the heat from the fire coming out of this cleft in the rock."

Rip said a dirty word and went running back into the cave. Charley followed.

"Pack up and saddle up," Rip shouted to Egg and Solo. "They've found us."

"WE GOT 'EM, MR. MURKOWSKY," THE PILOT SAID. "A heat plume where there shouldn't be one."

Dr. Harrison Douglas looked at the screen of the portable infrared radiation detector, which was sitting on the empty seat beside the pilot, where the copilot would sit if there were one. There was only the one hot spot on the screen, and it was a plume, indicating the gases from a fire. A small fire. "Gotta be it," he agreed.

Sitting shoulder to shoulder with him, Murkowsky grinned. He nodded at the pilot, who dialed in a frequency and started talking.

Johnny Murk spoke to the pilot. "Land as close as you can."

"Gonna be tough, Mr. Murkowsky. We can land in the water, but you'll have to swim ashore. And the water is very cold."

"The other Beaver. It's on wheels. Find a place for it to land."

Murkowsky and Douglas were so excited they could barely contain themselves. The second Beaver fifteen minutes behind them contained four gunmen as passengers. Their job, if they could be placed on the ground, was to capture Adam Solo. Well, not really. Their job was to get him dead or alive. After all, the drug moguls believed, Solo's body held valuable secrets that would improve the life of every person on earth—and, incidentally, make them filthy rich. Solo was being "unreasonable." Too bad for him.

The pilot was an old hand at bush flying. He scanned the beaches, which were reasonably flat. All he needed was a straight stretch of a thousand feet or so without rocks or trees or a creek.

He found just the place, less that a mile from the heat plume, pointed it out to his passengers and began talking to the other Beaver. Johnny Murk enthusiastically pounded Douglas on the back. Oh boy, oh boy!

"MR. PRESIDENT," THE AIDE SAID EXCITEDLY, "THE pharma people have found the saucer in Canada."

"How?" P. J. O'Reilly demanded.

"Two Beavers were searching the shore of Hudson's Bay and discovered a heat plume. One is going to land. We're picking up their radio transmissions on the satellite and have them triangulated."

The president nodded. P. J. O'Reilly swung into action. He had two C-130s sitting on the ramp at Duluth with mountain-trained paratroops aboard, ready to go with five minutes' notice. The C-130s were equipped with wheels and skis, so they could land on runways or snow or frozen lakes, if a place could be found. If not, the paratroopers could jump.

O'Reilly issued the orders, and the aide hurried off to the situation room to pass them on.

Of course, the Canadian government didn't know of the planned invasion by U.S. military forces. Sometimes it is easier to ask forgiveness than get permission, and this was one of them. Those confounded Ottawa politicians were still huffing and puffing about sovereignty.

"Murkowsky and Douglas," the president fretted aloud. Now there was a pair.

When the aide strode back into the room, he asked him, "How long until the C-130s get to Hudson's Bay?"

"Over two hours," the aide said.

"Get some fighters up there ASAP. Have them make life difficult for Murkowsky and Douglas. Set up a shuttle and keep a couple fighters on top of that location until the paratroopers get there."

"It's getting dark up there, sir, and the Canadians—"

A glare from the president shut him off. The aide charged out of the room again.

THE BEAVER ON WHEELS LANDED IN THE TWILIGHT ON the beach. The pilot was an old hand; he had his bird completely stalled just as all three wheels touched the sand. When the plane stopped, the four gunmen leaped out with their weapons and set off on a trot for the rocky promontory a mile away along the beach.

Above them in the other Beaver, Harrison Douglas and Johnny Murk monitored their progress.

"How long can we stay?" Douglas asked his pilot.

"Another hour, then we have to head back to base. "

"An hour should be enough," Johnny Murk cackled gleefully. "I'll bet Solo and the Cantrells don't even know we're coming. Tough for them, great for us."

Douglas told the pilot, "Radio the guys on the beach. It's Solo we want. Ignore anyone else they find."

The pilot nodded and keyed his lip mike.

• • •

CHARLEY PINE WAS IN THE PILOT'S SEAT OF THE saucer when the others got aboard and Rip closed the hatch. She already had the computer running, had run the built-in-tests and was ready. As everyone else strapped in, she lifted the saucer, snapped up the landing gear, and spun the saucer so that it was pointed toward the underwater cave entrance.

Carefully, using the landing light, she submerged the saucer in the lagoon as she edged it forward. The water was murky, but she had just enough visibility. She found the entrance and eased the saucer through into the open water of Hudson's Bay. Keeping the saucer as near to the bottom as possible, she slowly turned it north and proceeded at a walking pace. Too fast, she thought, and the saucer would create a wake in this shallow water.

What is your plan? That was Solo.

I'm going to give these bastards something to think about.

Killing them won't solve our problem.

That's rich, coming from you. If these guys were monks in some Irish abbey, you'd chop them up quick enough. And steal their habits, wooden plates and potatoes.

She gradually increased speed as the water appeared to get deeper. The bay was certainly no ocean, so there wasn't going to be a shelf that allowed her to drop into the depths.

She glanced over her shoulder. All three of the men were strapped into their seats. Their expressions were a study. Solo was expressionless, Egg was calm, and Rip's face mirrored his excitement.

THE GUNMEN ARRIVED AT THE ROCKY PROMONTORY eight minutes after they exited the Beaver. They were in excellent physical shape. From the Beaver overhead, Douglas and Johnny Murk described where the crack in the rock face was that the heat was pluming from. Not that the gunmen needed directions; they had found the tracks of Solo and Rip.

In they went, weapons at the ready.

Two minutes later, one of them ran back outside and radioed the Beaver overhead. "They're gone. No one there. Fire still burning. Marks from the saucer's gear pads. And you aren't going to believe this, there's an old Viking ship in this cave. Been here forever."

Douglas and Murkowsky looked at each other and both said the same dirty word simultaneously.

After ten seconds or so, Johnny Murk told the pilot, "Have them look around outside. Maybe they sent the saucer somewhere and are hiding."

The pilot was transmitting this message when the first F-16 fighter made a pass right by his plane. The wash rocked the Beaver viciously.

Another went roaring down the beach toward the bush plane sitting there idling. It cleared the bush plane by no more than ten feet.

As Johnny Murk and Harrison Douglas watched, horrified, the first fighter made a long, lazy turn, then steadied out in a shallow dive toward the Beaver on the beach. The water beside the Beaver boiled furiously.

"He's shooting, he's shooting," the pilot on the beach shouted into his radio. He didn't wait for another pass. He spun his plane 180 degrees and began his takeoff run. After an amazingly short distance he was airborne.

Another jet was inbound on a strafing run, so the bush pilot laid his Beaver over in a hard right turn and skimmed away over the forest eastward.

"THEY'VE BOOGIED," P. J. O'REILLY TOLD THE PRESIdent. The duty officer in the White House command center was giving him the blow-by-blow over a telephone. "Douglas and Murkowsky's thugs found where they had been, and the marks of the saucer, but the saucer and crew are gone."

The president indulged himself in the same dirty word the Big Pharma guys had used.

"So we're back to square one," the leader of the free world said to no one in particular. "Well, that saucer is somewhere. Tell those satellite people and air force weenies to find the thing or I'm going to start biting heads off." He grabbed his coffee cup and threw it at the wall.

THE SAUCER BROKE SURFACE ABOUT TEN MILES FROM the cave. Charley Pine lit the rockets and took it out over the surface of the bay for another ten miles, accelerating quickly, and turned while still subsonic. A nice, clean four-G turn back toward the cave and the Beavers.

"Charley!" Egg said sharply.

"When you go gallivanting to kidnap and murder people, you gotta expect to find a few potholes in the road," she replied.

The saucer was now pointing straight at the Beaver circling off the beach. It was about a thousand feet above the water and turning from right to left. Charley adjusted her course as the saucer rocketing toward the Beaver accelerated though Mach 2. The two craft came together almost too quickly for the human eye to follow; then the saucer was by.

Without turning for a look, Charley raised the nose and turned the rockets full on. The nose rose until the saucer was climbing straight up into the dark northern sky on a pillar of fire.

THE WASH OF THE SAUCER HIT THE BEAVER LIKE A punch from God. Only the craftsmanship of the de Havilland engineers who designed her—and a whole lot of luck—kept the bird from losing her wings under the hammer blow. The pilot fought to control his steed even though the instruments vibrated so badly that he couldn't read them. Just as he realized the bird was responding to his control inputs, the radial engine quit. Dead. A vast silence engulfed the pilot and Johnny Murk and Harrison Douglas.

It was broken by the muted roar of a jet engine. An F-16 was coming in slow, with the gear down, apparently to look them over.

The pilot ignored the fighter. He was pushing levers and pulling knobs and flipping switches and resetting circuit breakers, trying to get the engine to crank. It wouldn't.

The pharma moguls could hear the whisper of air passing the fuselage.

"It can't end like this," Douglas cried. "Oh, God, no!"

Johnny Murk was holding on to the back of the seat in front of him so hard that his knuckles turned white. He rested his head on his hands and closed his eyes.

Down the Beaver came, with a stationary prop. The pilot abandoned his efforts to start the engine and concentrated on finding a place to land. Open water along the beach. He turned hard, got set up, slipped to lose some excess altitude, then straightened her out and flared onto the water. The floats kissed and the bird drifted to a stop.

Another jet went over a few hundred feet above them.

"Now what?" Johnny Murk belligerently demanded of the pilot, who was in no mood to be abused.

"Well, fuck you, asshole," that craftsman said. "I guess I'll tinker with the motor while you clean out your underwear."

"I'll have your job—"

"Oh, fuck you again. And shut up. If you don't behave yourself, I'll throw you in the water and you can swim home. Maybe next spring we'll find you entombed in a big ice cube."

11

WHEN THE SAUCER WAS IN ORBIT AND THE EARTH WAS slowly spinning beneath, Adam Solo came forward and donned a headset. He said nothing aloud.

After a bit he took off the headset and said to his comrades, "I've talked to the other saucer again. It will leave orbit in about three hours and create a diversion."

"What kind of diversion?" Charley asked suspiciously. "Gonna kill a few folks to keep the rest honest?"

"Certainly not. Let not your heart be troubled. Now, let's put our heads together and see if we can come up with a plan to avoid capture until the starship arrives."

Egg was still strapped into his seat. He rubbed his face vigorously. When he finished, Solo said, "I appreciate the risks you are taking on my behalf. I could have merely zoomed off in a saucer and you could have stayed in Missouri, watching the adventure on television. It's me they want, not you."

Egg said nothing.

"Oh, I know," Solo continued, looking at Egg. "You thought about that and rejected it. Too dangerous for Rip and Charley. You didn't even think about yourself. You three are good shipmates. I hope I am your friend."

"I hope so too," Egg replied. "Okay, does anyone have any ideas?"

MEANWHILE, IN CANADA, A STICK OF PARATROOPS dropped onto the beach near the rocky promontory where four armed thugs huddled. They surrendered instantly, without a shot being fired. The pilot of the Beaver drifting off the beach set Johnny Murk and Harrison Douglas rowing. He put them on the floats and gave them paddles. After much effort, they beached the dead Beaver. They too instantly surrendered to the waiting paratroopers, who were laughing at them.

Then the assembled contingent waited for helicopters from the States to arrive to pick them up. The whole crowd went into the cave and soon had the fire blazing brightly. While the captain in charge of the soldiers inspected the Viking ship in the cave, Johnny Murk and Harrison Douglas conferred in low tones.

"We're not beat yet. That Solo thinks he got us, but you and I know that this is just one battle. We're going to win the war."

"Amen to that," Harrison Douglas said. He remembered how he felt when he thought the gunmen would capture Solo in mere minutes. Filthy rich. He and Murk would own this damn planet. And everyone on it.

They made their plans.

"A SAUCER IS COMING OUT OF ORBIT, MR. PRESIDENT." An air force colonel from the command center delivered the news to the president the next morning while he huddled with his national security team.

"Where will it come down?"

"First indications are the trajectory will bring it into the Washington area in about an hour."

"Is this the saucer that just left Hudson's Bay?"

"No, sir. It's the one that has been up there for several weeks."

The president, O'Reilly, the secretary of state, the national security adviser, and five of O'Reilly's aides stared with open mouths at the colonel.

The president recovered first. He made a shooing motion at the officer as he said, "Keep me advised."

When the door was again closed, hubbub broke loose. "Here? Washington? What could this mean?"

"Is this an attack?"

"Are aliens arriving?"

"They'll probably demand our surrender."

"Maybe they just want to negotiate for Adam Solo, establish friendly relations, get some fresh food."

"And lay some of the local dollies, perhaps? You're a moron."

"If they land on the lawn outside, will you go out and meet them?" This from O'Reilly, directed at the president.

The president's eyebrows rose dramatically as he pondered the implications.

Here. Washington. Oh, man! This might be it!

It!

The Arrival!

Aliens from another solar system. Maybe from another galaxy.

He surveyed the people around the table, all educated apparatchiks without enough common sense to pour piss out of a boot, even if the directions on the heel said, "Turn up."

"Where's Petty Officer Hennessey?" he asked the nearest aide. "Find him."

The aide obviously didn't recognize the name. "Hennessey?"

"He's in the honor guard. Go."

THE PRESIDENT AND PETTY OFFICER HENNESSEY WERE standing on the South Portico of the White House as the incoming saucer raced across the heartland. The cabinet and leaders of Congress, hastily summoned, and the top brass from the Pentagon all stood behind them. Aides scurried up to the president to keep him and Hennessey updated. It was over Iowa. Over Indiana. Over West Virginia. Well below 100,000 feet. Slowing. Trajectory seemed to be aimed right at the heart of Washington. The FAA was rerouting airliners away from Dulles and Reagan National airports. F-16s were overhead, just in case the president wanted the saucer destroyed.

"What do you think of just shooting the damn thing down?" the president asked the sailor standing beside him.

"Might work, sir, if there was only one of them," Hennessey opined. "Kinda doubt that, though. Then it's got a nuclear reactor, or so I heard. A crash might be messy."

"Yeah."

The president could see the television cameras being set up on the edge of the lawn, just in case. No doubt they would be beaming live to every television network on earth if the saucer landed here.

The president felt hot and used a hanky to wipe his brow. Some of his makeup came off, but he didn't care. The aliens wouldn't give a damn either.

Hennessey looked calm, cool and collected.

"Where you from?" the president asked the sailor.

"Oklahoma, sir. Joined the navy to see the world, and I did see a little of it, then they sent me here to Washington, which ain't what it's cracked up to be."

"No, I guess not," the president agreed and shot his cuffs.

The tension was building nicely, and the president was acutely aware that he had to pee when the saucer came into view flying over the Potomac River. It turned and came over the top of the Washington Monument aiming right at the president and Petty Officer Hennessey.

"This is it, I think," Hennessey said. Then he remembered and added, "Sir."

The president realized something was wrong when the saucer came over the White House fence and didn't continue to descend. It leveled off about a hundred feet in the air and flew toward the White House, slowing. About a hundred yards in front of the president, about where *Marine One* always landed, the saucer came to a stop. It was still a hundred feet up there. Stopped dead.

The president and everyone else on the portico and the gathered press and billions of people all over the planet watching on television held their breath.

Nothing happened. It just sat there, stationary, a black, ominous, silent flying saucer.

After a while one of the officers in the honor guard walked toward the saucer. When he hit the repulsion zone under the thing he felt it and quickly retreated. The saucer and the earth were repelling each other; anything that entered the zone of repulsion would be instantly crushed.

After a bit the people behind the president became restless. "Well, hell, what's it gonna do?"

The president conferred with Petty Officer Hennessey. "What do you think?"

"Darn, sir, I kinda think it's parked up there."

"What do you think they're doing in that thing?"

"I'm wonderin' if there's anybody in there a'tall. Maybe a helicopter could hover and take a peek through the canopy and tell us."

That, the president thought, was good advice. He acted

on it quickly, and within minutes a chopper from Homeland Security made its approach to the saucer, which didn't move an inch.

The chopper hovered, then flew all the way around the thing at a distance of about twenty feet, and the answer came back. "It's empty."

The crowd bled away. The television crews stayed longer, but eventually they made an agreement among themselves. One camera would remain aimed at the saucer and the feed would be shared by all the networks.

The saucer was still there, steady as the Rock of Gibraltar, when the sun set, so lights were rigged.

In the White House all the options were considered, and one by one rejected. The hatch was in the bottom of the ship, so with the antigravity system on, entry there was impossible.

A helicopter could deposit a crew with blowtorches on the top and they could try to cut their way inside. If they got in, then what?

Shooting down the saucer was considered. The idea was a nonstarter, for the very reason that Hennessey had articulated. If it were shot down it would fall close by, perhaps hit the White House, and the thing was nuclear powered. If the reactor were breached all of Washington would have to be evacuated. The cleanup could cost billions. If the mess could be cleaned up. If not, Washington might become a wasteland for thousands of years. Tens of thousands.

Hmmm.

The president conferred one last time with Petty Officer Hennessey before he went to bed. As he looked out his bedroom window at the saucer parked in the sky, he asked the Oklahoma sailor, "What do you think?"

"Somebody put it up there, sir. I reckon it's gonna stay there until somebody takes it down or flies it away. Probably that Solo fella, I figure."

The president nodded. "You going to be on duty tomorrow, Hennessey?"

"Actually, sir, tomorrow's my day off."

"Liberty is canceled until further notice. See you in the morning."

"Yes, sir." Hennessey snapped to attention, did an about-face and marched out.

IT WAS TWILIGHT IN WESTERN AUSTRALIA WHEN THE saucer's crew saw the little crossroads village. Two dirt roads crossing in the desert made a giant X. Around the crossroads Rip counted seven buildings. A telephone line ran east-west through the village.

They landed a mile away, along the deserted road. Rip dropped out and went over to examine the nearest telephone pole. He paused behind the saucer to relieve himself, then climbed back inside.

"I think it's just telephone. Push the pole over and I might be able to cut that wire." From his gear he extracted a souvenir Viking sword.

He climbed out and waited.

Solo maneuvered the saucer against the pole and pushed gently. As the line came in reach, Rip gave it a mighty whack. Hmm. Two more mighty whacks, and the line broke.

He climbed back inside. "Better go around the town and do it over there too."

Solo avoided the village by at least a mile, staying about a hundred feet above the ground. Rip got the wire with two whacks this time.

They parked the saucer on the edge of the village, got out and closed the hatch. It was almost dark, but two medium-sized boys were standing in front of the nearest building, a house perhaps, and gawking. A dog must have been tied out back, because they could hear him baying at the top of lungs.

"Say, lads," Rip called, "is your mom or dad home?"

They turned and fled. A moment later, a woman in pants came out on the porch with a flashlight, which she put in their eyes. "And who might you be?" Her voice quavered a little. The dog kept on barking.

Egg made a sign to Rip and stepped forward, towing Charley along. "Ma'am, my name is Egg Cantrell, and this is Miss Charlotte Pine. We dropped in to see if we could get something to eat and drink. Be glad to pay you, of course, in American dollars."

"Oh, my Lor . . . You're that saucer crowd that's all over the telly that everyone's looking for. Why on earth are you *here*?"

"Well," Charley said patiently, "we are hungry and thirsty and tired, and our ship isn't designed for many creature comforts. I hope we didn't frighten you."

"Well, bless me, you surely did. The cats are inside climbing the walls, and the boys are scared half senseless. If my man was here he'd have fired some shots."

"I see. We were indeed fortunate to arrive when we did. Now back to our request—"

"You just stay away from this house or I'll turn the dog loose. I have Jim's rifle and know how to shoot it. I don't want my boys kidnapped and flying off God knows where." She retreated inside and slammed the door.

Egg took a deep breath and scratched his head.

"Obviously our vibes are not good enough," Charley remarked. "Despite the fact that we are nice, wholesome American spacemen with our little round flying saucer." She paused, then added, "Along with one thousand-year-old Viking alien with a very checkered past."

Rip set off for the center of town, such as it was, with Solo trailing along. Egg shrugged at Charley, and she and he followed side by side.

There was a bar, or pub, and it was open. Rip led the way inside. Two men were huddled over pints at a table in the corner. Rip bellied up to the bar. The barman was a skinny, rangy redhead with only one eye. He squinted at them and asked, "What'll it be, mate?"

"Four pints. Do you have anything to eat?"

"Steaks."

"Four steaks."

"I didn't hear you drive in."

"We didn't drive."

Before the barman could assimilate that comment, a youngster ran in, shouting, "Harry, there's a *flying saucer* parked out there!"

Dead silence for several seconds, broken when Rip said, "That's our ride."

The men at the table stood and whooped. Harry, the bartender, slapped the counter and howled, "You're *that* bunch? The ones they're after?"

Assured that was indeed the case, the patrons of this fine establishment pounded the four fugitive travelers on the back, and the barman served overflowing pints of beer. Everyone asked questions at once as more people magically appeared in the room. Over a dozen. Someone turned on the telly, which was hooked up to a satellite dish, and they all shouted and cheered at the video of the saucer hovering on the White House lawn.

"Drinks are on the house, mate. Glad you dropped in."

Charley Pine watched Solo's eyes and facial expressions. His eyes flicked from person to person, sizing them up, and he kept a friendly grin plastered in place. Nevertheless, he maneuvered himself into a corner so he could see anyone coming in or going out of the room. When his steak came, he ate it standing at the bar.

Adam Solo, Charley decided, was a careful man.

• • •

THE SAUCER PARKED ABOVE THE LAWN ON THE WHITE House captured the imagination of the planet's population. They looked at it on television—a saucer-shaped black presence, menacing, threatening, yet inert—listened to the hot babes and political types pontificate on what it might mean and talked among themselves.

The saucer didn't move. It simply sat in one place, repelling the earth with power supplied by its nuclear reactor, waiting for a signal it recognized to tell it to do something else. The signal didn't come. The machine waited with infinite patience. It had enough plutonium in the reactor to sit here for a hundred thousand years. Time meant nothing to the machine.

In Vegas the people partied on with occasional glances at the television picture of the stationary saucer. In churches across America and around the world, people prayed. Teenagers kept screwing, with occasional glances at the hovering saucer's image on their cell phones. In bars all over America patrons stared at the immobile saucer on the televisions that usually showed sports while they imbibed record amounts of liquor. Bartenders noted that the regulars who normally drank beer and wine were on the hard stuff now.

Meanwhile, a starship approaching earth was decelerating so it could orbit this medium-sized blue planet. Although the sleeping president and the people of earth suspected aliens, voyagers from the stars, were coming, they didn't really know. They would soon find out.

• • •

DURING THE NIGHT CROWDS BEGAN TO GATHER ON the sidewalks and in the streets surrounding the White House. Due to the position of the saucer, most of the people could see it parked in the sky. From all over the metropolitan area, people took the metro into town, or drove and parked their cars willy-nilly wherever they could find space, and walked closer. In New York and Connecticut and Boston, people packed trains to Washington. When the agents announced the trains were full, they jumped turnstiles and crammed aboard anyway.

By dawn over a hundred thousand people filled every square foot of space for blocks around the White House. The nervous Secret Service officer in charge asked the army for troops to control the crowd, which didn't need controlling. The people were orderly and quiet. They stood or sat whispering to each other and looking at the saucer and snapping photos with their cell phones or cameras. Thousands of pictures of the saucer were uploaded to Facebook and YouTube. A crowd control specialist with the district government quickly ordered hundreds of porta-potties and asked that they be delivered immediately. Sidewalk vendors, indomitable capitalists, set up shop to irrigate and feed the assembled multitude and sell them souvenirs. The crowd continued to grow. Thanks to the aroma of pot smoke wafting over everyone and to beer and liquor people had brought from home, the crowd was pretty mellow.

Surveying the saucer, which hadn't moved, and the gathering sea of humanity, P. J. O'Reilly got plenty worried.

If the crowd panicked, this mess had the makings of a real disaster. On the other hand, if the army and police tried to move them away, there might be a riot.

O'Reilly went down to the command post and found the White House telephone switchboard was out of service. Too many incoming calls. O'Reilly pulled out his cell phone and tried to log on. No service. No doubt the cell towers were overwhelmed too. He was busy talking to the Secret Service and government cops about crowd control when an aide interrupted to tell him that the saucer that left Hudson's Bay was no longer in orbit. O'Reilly had more important things on his mind just then.

The chief of staff decided to awaken the president and brief him on the situation in the streets of Washington. He enjoyed telling the Head Dog bad news, so he trotted off to the presidential bedroom with a spring in his step.

DR. JIM BOB SPICER, THE FAMOUS EVANGELIST, WAS ON top of his game. He knew an opportunity when he saw one. He managed to rent a construction hydraulic lift and got a permit to park it on a sidewalk from a crooked bureaucrat in the D.C. government. Armed with his piece of paper, he and the rent-a-lift people spent two hours maneuvering it through the packed streets to the head of Pennsylvania Avenue, where he had the crew put it on a sidewalk and elevate it with him and his cameraman as high as the thing would go. It was just high enough to give the camera a good view through the treetops of the stationary saucer and the floodlit White House.

With the camera rolling and the saucer as background, Spicer launched into a fevered prayer for the human race—indeed, for all of the world's species large and small, from germs and worms and beetles right on up. The camera sent the digital feed to a satellite. From there it was rebroadcast to the studio where Spicer recorded his cable religious shows.

With his prayer finished, Spicer looked straight at the camera and started in. The morning sun illuminated the saucer over his right shoulder.

"Judgment Day is here," he roared into his handheld mike. "In fulfillment of biblical prophecy, the Anti-Christ is almost here. There"—he gestured grandly at the saucer behind him—"is his chariot! Do you doubt the word of God? Do you doubt the evidence of your own eyes? Repent, you sinners, and be saved. Repent, I say, and God will save us from the Anti-Christ and evildoers who accompany him . . ." His harangue went on and on while his producer told him via an earphone that he had the largest audience in the history of his ministry. The news gave him new strength.

With the saucer looming ominously behind him, Spicer wrestled with the Lord over the fate of the earth's sinners, which was everybody, of course.

Ten minutes into his oration, Spicer had a larger audience than Fox, MSNBC and CBS combined. Given the news over his earphone, Spicer had to suppress his glee and keep a somber look on his sour old puss while he ranted on.

Government cops decided to run Spicer off and started making noise; the rapt crowd nearby shouted ugly things, so they backed off.

AFTER LISTENING A WHILE TO O'REILLY'S SUMMARY OF the coming Götterdämmerung, the president got out of bed, pulled the curtains aside and peeked out the window. Yep, that damn black plate was still there. For all he knew, it might remain there until Judgment Day. Hell, the next election was only a year away; then the next president could worry about it.

"The D.C. chief of police estimates the crowd at a quarter million and growing," P. J. O'Reilly said ominously.

"Tell them to shut down access to the city," the president said. "Stop the trains. Put up roadblocks. Don't let anyone else in."

A look of surprise crossed O'Reilly's face. Why hadn't he thought of that? He rushed away to issue the order.

The president turned on his television and flipped through the channels with his remote. One of the news shows was now broadcasting Spicer, so the leader of the free world watched almost a minute of the divine's tortured anguish, then surfed on. The hot women were worried, the experts in a dither, and a dingbat congresswoman from California was demanding action, although of what kind, she didn't say.

A news ribbon streaming across the bottom of the screen on one network quoted the Russian president as saying the saucer should have come to Red Square in

Moscow. Nothing the Americans agreed to with aliens would bind Russia. Paris echoed that sentiment.

Muslim clerics in the Middle East denounced the saucer news as Hollywood fakery designed to tarnish the holy image of the Prophet. Large riots were promised. Just in case it wasn't fakery, one cleric issued a fatwa for the saucer people.

Frowning, the president flipped off the television. He wondered where Rip, Charley, Egg and Adam Solo were. Wondered what they were up to. In the depths of his devious soul, the president knew those four were somehow responsible for the saucer parked outside the building. *His* building. He was getting almighty peeved at those people.

He cussed a while, put on his slippers and stomped off to the bathroom.

12

JOHNNY MURK AND HARRISON DOUGLAS GOT BACK TO Connecticut eventually. The military dropped them in Duluth, and they rode Johnny Murk's private jet to Connecticut. They were in a foul mood when they arrived. Solo and the Cantrells had made monkeys of them, not to mention nearly killing them with a near-miss flyby of the saucer.

"The government is after those bastards, and with all their assets, we'll always get there late," Johnny Murk said.

The FBO bar was closed and locked, so Johnny had brought a bottle of Scotch from his plane. The two were sitting alone in the lounge drinking it neat from paper cups. Heidi the masseuse was sacked out on one of the couches, dead to the world, with her magnificent breasts pointed straight at heaven. The pink sunrise through the windows was gorgeous. Neither Murk nor Douglas paid any attention to any of these attractions.

"There is just no way we can get to Solo before the

Army, Navy, Air Force, Marine Corps, Coast Guard and Boy Scouts."

Murkowsky's cell phone buzzed. He pulled it from his pocket, checked to see who the caller was and immediately answered. "Yes."

He listened for a while, asked no questions and ended the conversation with a curt, "Keep me informed."

He stood to pocket the phone and looked around as if seeing his surroundings for the first time.

"Well?" Douglas asked.

"My Space Command spy. The saucer is in Western Australia. No doubt about it. The White House has been informed, but nothing is happening in Washington that he knows about."

"Oh, hell, the prez probably called the Aussie PM and the diggers are on their way right now to bag 'em and tag 'em."

Johnny Murk turned on the television in the corner of the room, and the two men stood in front of it. Of course, the picture was of the saucer suspended over the White House lawn. Then the video switched to the quarter million or more people gathered in the streets. A sea of people. After three minutes of listening to the delicious female anchor—she never mentioned the Cantrells' saucer—talk about the rising excitement, the fact that the police had sealed off the city and the media's demand that the president appear before their cameras to tell the world what was happening, the network began to air man-in-the-street interviews. Everyone interviewed was absolutely certain that aliens would soon arrive. They wanted to be there for this historic occasion. The excitement and anticipation were palpable.

The two pharma moguls looked at each other.

They turned back to the television, which now aired a moment of Jim Bob Spicer praying for salvation for all the earth's people.

"It's like they're waiting for the Second Coming," Johnny Murk murmured.

"It's a ten-ring circus," Douglas proclaimed.

"Bet you that no one in the White House has bothered to tell State to call the Aussies."

They looked at each other again. Simultaneously they both said, "What are we waiting for?"

Galvanized into action, each man grabbed his cell phone. Douglas called his friends in Philadelphia and promised big money; Murk chartered a Boeing 747-400 to fly a crowd across the Pacific. The plane was huge, carried a zillion gallons of fuel, and with a light load could fly the world's biggest pond nonstop. The moguls even called their homes and told the maids to pack suitcases with clean underwear and a change of clothes and have the chauffeurs bring them to the airport. Both men's wives were asleep. Neither man left a message for his spouse.

Heidi the masseuse continued to sleep, her magnificent trophy chest rising and falling in a gentle rhythm.

THE WHITE HOUSE WAS IN FULL CRISIS MODE. AIDES ran hither and yon, telephones rang continuously, e-mails flooded the computers, and teletypes spewed out important messages from prime ministers and ambassadors and foreign heads of state. Politicians of every stripe, in offices large and small and out of offices large and small, demanded to be heard. Meanwhile, huddled behind locked doors, the president's hard-core advisers weighed how the crisis would affect the president's polls and his ability to get his agenda, such as it was, through Congress.

P. J. O'Reilly was in his element. He loved the hubbub. He made decisions, stroked the people he thought important, ignored everyone else, and generally behaved like the petty tyrant he was. More importantly, he refused everyone access to the president. He had the press secretary tell the press that the president was working on the saucer crisis. Discussing the situation with experts. Meditating. Preparing himself in case he would soon have to meet and negotiate with "aliens from outer space" as ambassador for all the world's people. All six billion of them, including the French.

The president, however, was actually in his study in the family living quarters watching a John Wayne Western on television. He liked the fact that the Duke didn't suffer fools or take any sass, unlike the president, who was surrounded by fools and listened to copious amounts of bullshit day in and day out.

He also liked the way that John Wayne kicked ass. Very satisfying.

When the movie ended he turned off the idiot box and sat thinking about all the asses he would like to kick. That line of reasoning took him to Egg Cantrell, Rip and Charley, and that toad Adam Solo. Boy, would he like to take them out behind the woodshed. Especially Egg, with his smashed computer trick. That was low-down mean! The Duke would have drilled him.

Finally the president began to turn the situation over in his mind. He wondered where the Cantrells and Pine and Solo might just happen to be. Were they still in orbit? He picked up the phone and was soon speaking to O'Reilly.

"Where's Cantrell's saucer?"

"Haven't heard a thing, Mr. President. Space Command will keep us advised. D.C. police say they don't have enough officers to control the crowd in the streets, which is still growing. Nearly a half million, they think. Right now we're talking to the army, bringing in troops. We're also bringing in every federal cop we can find, stripping the office buildings and museums bare. We're afraid if the aliens land the crowd will surge right through the fences onto the White House grounds. It'll be an out-of-control mob; people might get trampled. The aliens might react violently in self-defense."

"That would certainly be exciting. But do you really think sane people would want to get close to an alien?"

"There aren't any sane people out there in the streets." O'Reilly's credentials as a pessimist were impeccable.

"Doesn't anybody ever watch *War of the Worlds* these days?" the president muttered.

The chief of staff ignored that comment. "Before the

aliens arrive, Fox and CNN would like exclusive interviews with you."

"About what?"

"Your diplomatic strategy. How will you communicate with the aliens if they don't speak English? Will you ask for the superdrugs that extend life? Will you—"

"No interviews. Tell the press secretary to schmooze the bastards. He gets paid for that."

"Sir, the political staffers seem to think—"

"That's an illusion. They haven't had a thought in years. They are good at pretending."

"And then there is the matter of protocol. The alien ambassador—"

"For God's sake, O'Reilly!"

The president hung up. Ate two more Rolaids, turned the TV back on and flipped over to the Western Channel to see what was airing there. Aha! An episode of *Gunsmoke.* The president liked Matt Dillon too.

JOHNNY MURKOWSKY AND HARRISON DOUGLAS WERE leading an army. A small army, it is true, but an army nonetheless. Eight men, armed to the teeth. They looked like extras in an action movie: lean, mean and ready to kill somebody, with lots of tattoos and mustaches and bulging muscles. All wore pistols and knives. Submachine guns and bags of spare magazines were tucked under their seats. The warriors lay sprawled across the center aisle seats of the big Boeing, reading comic books and playing computer games on their iPads.

They looked like Attila's Huns, and Johnny Murk liked that. Yet he felt a nagging sense of unease. Something wasn't right. It took him fifteen minutes to figure out what it was. He had forgotten Heidi. He had left her sleeping on a couch at the airport.

He had a bad moment. Johnny Murk needed sex three times a day, regardless, and he paid Heidi well to provide it. What was he going to do? His white count would build . . . and build and build . . . Could he go on?

"Get some rest," Douglas told him, pulling at his sleeve. "We're going to need every ounce of smarts we have to outthink that alien creep Solo and those Cantrells."

"Hmm," Johnny Murk said distractedly.

Douglas had known since takeoff that Heidi was missing. Now, through Sherlockian logic, he concluded her absence was bothering Murkowsky.

"Get some sleep," Douglas advised his fellow pharma pirate. "Some rest for your poor little pecker will do it good."

Their big Boeing was high over the Pacific, in and out of clouds. In the cockpit the crew watched the GPS and computers and talked of inconsequential things as the plane bored into the opaque night. The moguls made themselves comfortable in First Class and were soon snoring loudly, Johnny Murk dreaming of the pleasures of the flesh, Harrison Douglas dreaming of money. Back aft, some of their Huns drifted off to the land of Nod dreaming of violence and blood and personal catharsis.

• • •

AS BOTH THE NIGHT AND THE DRUG MOGULS' CHARtered Boeing 747 raced across the Pacific toward Australia, the four saucer adventurers ate dinner at the outback saloon and began thinking about sleep even though the jackaroos were buying the drinks and the sheilas were all agog. Egg slipped off to bed down in the saucer.

Charley and Rip sat trying to drink as little as possible amid a crowd of Aussies pouring the beer down. At the bar Adam Solo entertained a dozen men and women by singing. He sang the old Irish songs and he sang Italian opera. He had a superb baritone voice; soon everyone in the room was silent and listening. More beer was put in front of him. At the end of a song Solo paused and drained the mug. Then he went on, now singing classic Spanish love songs.

"He really loves life," Charley whispered to Rip, squeezing his hand.

"Yes," Rip muttered, slightly surprised. "The amazing thing is how he absorbs the best of what is around him and appreciates it."

"Why is that amazing?"

Rip glanced at Charley. "A rapist and killer connoisseur."

Charley rolled her eyes. "Let's get out of here," she said, "while he has the crowd."

They sneaked off. The sun had set and the stars were out. Only a whisper of wind stirred the air.

As they walked toward the saucer holding hands, Rip said, "What will happen when the mother ship arrives?"

"Well, Solo will go winging out of our lives, and they'll zoom off to another planet to check the DNA library."

"We're going to have to get rid of both saucers," Rip said with conviction in his voice. "Give them back to the aliens. If their computers are gone, maybe you and I and Egg can keep living on this rock."

"What kind of people will the aliens be?"

Rip hadn't thought much about it. "Like Solo, I guess."

"Meeting them will be the biggest adventure of our lives," Charley Pine said, throwing her head back to take in the stars. It seemed as if Rip's discovery of the saucer in the Sahara Desert just a little over a year ago had somehow been leading to such a meeting. Travelers between the stars. People from another star system, perhaps even another galaxy. People out there . . . coming here!

"We're like the Indians on the beach who first saw the sails of Columbus' ships on the horizon, coming closer," Rip mused. "All the speculation, all the dreaming, all the wonder . . ."

When he fell silent Charley squeezed his hand and said, "I wouldn't repeat that Columbus-and-the-Indians analogy if I were you," she said lightly. "A lot of people think the Indians would have been better off if Columbus had stayed home."

"You know what I mean."

She put her head on his shoulder and he held her as they both gazed at the stars.

The saucer's hatch was closed, no doubt to keep out

the curious, and presumably Egg was asleep. Rip opened the hatch and stuck his head inside. He could hear Egg snoring. He slithered in, got his and Charley's sleeping bags and passed them out to her. Then he climbed down, closed the hatch and latched it.

"Where . . . ?"

"Over here by the landing gear. That's good enough."

They zipped both bags together, shed their clothes and crawled in. Thirty minutes later they slipped into exhausted sleep.

ADAM SOLO STAYED IN THE BAR UNTIL HE WAS THE last man left standing. The women had wandered out hours earlier. He had drunk more beer than any of the Aussies but was apparently unaffected. Four men were passed out on the floor when he drained his mug for the last time. Solo nodded at the bartender and stepped over a drunk on his way to the door.

Outside he paused and looked around to see who was watching in this last hour before dawn. Solo suspected there was a satellite telephone or shortwave radio somewhere nearby, and if so it was absolutely inevitable that news of the saucer's arrival had gone forth. He wondered just how much time they had before the Australian army or Harrison Douglas and Johnny Murkowsky came charging over the hill.

He heard a voice in his head, speaking breathlessly and quickly. **They are here. The saucer is here!**

Solo walked the half mile to the saucer and stood looking around. He saw no one except Rip and Charley sound asleep, wrapped together like otters. Solo opened the saucer's hatch and climbed in.

Egg was stretched out on the back bench seats snoring gently.

Solo pulled the power knob out to the first detent; he heard the gentle hum from the machinery spaces behind him as the computer screens exploded into life. He donned the headset lying on the console in front of him.

Perhaps it was the gentle, barely audible hum from the panel behind him that woke Egg. He realized he was awake and opened his eyes to see Solo's back partially blocking one of the computer screens. The other two were filled with symbols flashing and dancing, actually three-dimensional holographic displays, constantly changing.

Egg arose and stood. He moved so he could see all three screens. The light reflected from Solo's face, which was almost in profile. Egg could see his serious expression, concentrating.

His eyes went to the screen. It was as if he were watching a motion picture on fast forward. Some of the images registered on Egg's retinas: ships, combat, castles, Indian villages, Vikings in helmets, tall sailing ships, World War I combat, factories, perhaps a university . . .

Solo was transmitting his memories, his report, to the starship. More than a thousand years of life, everything he had learned. On one screen Egg saw formulas dance, squiggling and squirming in constant mutation. On the third were plants, trees, animals, snakes, bugs, beetles, mosquitoes, insects of all types . . .

After five minutes or so the screens became composed. Two of them faded to dots, then went dark. Only the center screen continued to change, but more sedately. Finally it too went into a rest state.

Solo took off the headset and, for the first time, looked at Egg.

"When are they coming?" Egg asked.

Soon.

The fact that Solo didn't speak, yet Egg heard his voice, unnerved him. "How soon?" he asked aloud.

Solo seemed to sense Egg's discomfort and spoke aloud. "They are inside the moon's orbit, decelerating. These things take time."

"So do we stay here?"

"Someone has called the Australian government on a shortwave radio. A man. He may be believed, he may not. They may come today, they may not."

For the first time, Egg realized that Solo didn't look as he had since he had known him. He looked older. His face was lined; his shoulders sagged.

"How much did you have to drink?" he asked accusingly.

A grin flickered across Solo's face. "Too much," he said. "It used to be that alcohol didn't affect me much. If at all. But tonight . . ." He sighed and rubbed his face with his hands. "I'm a bit intoxicated. I can feel it."

Solo looked at his hands in the glow of the cockpit

lights. Even Egg could see that they looked older, looked like the hands of a man in his sixties or seventies. Lean, gnarled, scarred, mottled.

Solo drew his hands away hastily.

Time is marching on.

Yes, it is, Egg thought. **It does that for all of us.**

What a life I've had. I want to go home, but that's ridiculous. My family has been gone for a thousand years. I know none of these people who are coming. None of them know me. They thought I was dead, dead for a thousand years. I am a living fossil, a fossil with too many memories, too many things to regret. Too many dreams that ended in ashes.

"How long can we stay here in Australia?" Egg asked. He hadn't gotten used to communicating without talking.

Solo threw up his hands. "I don't know." He paused. "Rip and Charley need their sleep, and so do I." He punched in the power knob, turning off the saucer's machinery. Slowly, carefully, Solo eased himself out of the pilot's seat. He took several steps over to the bench seats and spread his sleeping bag.

As he crawled into it, Egg asked, "How do you feel about reporting to your people?"

"I don't know." He paused. "Mixed emotions. A load off, I guess."

Egg went to the hatch and looked down. He heard Solo's voice in his head. **They say it's the journey, not the destination, that is important. But sooner or later, eventually, you get there. Then the journey is over.**

Egg lowered himself through the hatch. He sat with his back against one of the saucer's legs as the stars faded and dawn slowly crept up the sky. He was still there, watching, when the sun finally peeped over the earth's rim.

13

"DO WE REALLY NEED ADAM SOLO OR A SAUCER computer?" Johnny Murkowsky asked Harrison Douglas. They were sitting in two First Class seats just behind the cockpit of the Boeing 747 taking them to Australia. Their private army was still sprawled out in the cheap seats aft snoring loudly. "We're only three or four years from having drugs that alter the human genome; after all, that is all that Solo could tell us. We're almost there without him."

"Are you sure?" Dr. Harrison Douglas grumped. "Heck, how do your scientists even know they are on the right track?"

"They are! They are. We're getting results."

"On *mice*! Get real, Johnny. With the secrets from a saucer we could jump a couple of generations of research, leapfrog forty, fifty, maybe even a hundred years into the future. Skip the errors and blind alleys that lead nowhere. What would that be worth?"

When Murkowsky didn't immediately answer, Douglas pressed. "In billions?"

SPACE COMMAND SAW THE STARSHIP FIRST. IT WAS merely a blip on a radar used for keeping track of satellites. At first there was some confusion, since the blip didn't coincide with any known satellite position, and when it quickly became apparent that the blip wasn't in orbit, alarms sounded. Could it be an ICBM inbound from North Korea or Iran? No.

The duty officer called his superior, a general, who called his boss. The civilian spy in Space Command put in a satellite call to Johnny Murkowsky and got him at 36,000 feet over the coast of Australia.

"A starship, they think. Inbound. Maybe two days out at its present distance and velocity."

Johnny Murkowsky's eyebrows went up toward his receding hairline. Holy jumping cats!

"Keep me advised," he told his spy.

"I am thinking of retiring next month," the man said. "I'll need a job that pays a couple hundred thousand a year. Maybe work half a day, three days a week."

"You son of a . . . Keep me advised. You're storing up acorns for the winter. You got a lot in the hollow tree already. Keep putting them in there and be happy with that."

Murkowsky rang off, turned to Douglas and gave him the news.

• • •

TEN MINUTES AFTER JOHNNY MURKOWSKY HEARD THE news, the White House received a call from the four-star air force general in charge of Space Command. The call was patched through to P. J. O'Reilly, who was in a way relieved. That saucer hovering over the lawn had gotten billions of people all over the world in a real uproar, and now the suspense was about over.

They were coming!

He hurried off to tell the president.

The president took it well, O'Reilly thought. Then he changed his mind. The color drained from the president's face. He began perspiring profusely. This wasn't merely the Roswell saucer parked over the White House lawn, a sculpture with no visible means of support that couldn't hurt anybody. This was *it*!

Aliens were coming to earth!

O'Reilly managed to suppress a smile at the president's discomfiture.

"Should we do a press release?" O'Reilly asked, digging the needle in a little deeper.

The president made a gesture that could mean anything, O'Reilly knew. When His Royal Arrogance didn't want to deal with something, he often waved vaguely at O'Reilly, a signal for him to handle it.

P. J. O'Reilly decided to take the gesture as an assignment. He was up to the tasks he saw before him. The Secret Service and Homeland Security were in crisis mode over the crowds. If they were told the aliens were two days away, perhaps the crowds would go home to eat, sleep and do an alcohol refill. *Maybe we can get a breathing space,* O'Reilly thought. He turned and trotted out of the room.

The president melted down into a panic attack. His gut tried to tie itself into a knot. He grabbed the Rolaids bottle and dumped some into his hand, how many he didn't know, stuffed them into his mouth. Chewed them up and swallowed them, then chased them with some good bourbon whiskey from the bottom drawer of his desk.

This was *it*! He was going to have to *meet* the aliens! Stand straight and tall as the first human sacrifice on the altar of intergalactic peace. Maybe the aliens were green froglike creatures that speared their victims with long, sticky tongues and gobbled them down; or small blobs of odiferous bacterial slime that oozed along consuming everything in their path; or giant dung-eating beetles with mandibles that had won the evolutionary battles on some postatomic-war world . . .

The president felt his heart galloping. The leader of the free world had another drink and tried to light a cigarette; he had to forgo the cancer stick because his hand was shaking too badly to work the lighter. He wiped his forehead with a coat sleeve and sent for Petty Officer Hennessey.

JIM BOB SPICER, THE FAMOUS EVANGELIST, WAS RUNning down. He didn't have any more juice left in him, he thought, until an aide handed him the White House press release. The aliens were two days out. In two days—Oh, my God!

Two days!

Galvanized, Jim Bob straightened his tie, ran his fingers through his mop of gray hair and stepped in front of the cameras to preach.

"And behold, I looked and saw a Lamb standing before the elders, and on the Lamb were the wounds that had caused his death . . . As I watched, the Lamb broke the first seal and began to unroll the scroll . . . When the fourth seal was broken I beheld a pale horse, and its rider's name was Death . . ."

In Lafayette Park a television network had set up a table with the White House behind it as a backdrop. Here the pretty people were interviewing scientists, politicians and dingbats, in whatever order they could be corralled. Life was the topic, not Death.

"With the medical knowledge we will gain from the aliens," Senator Blohardt promised, "the people of earth will enter a new era, one remarkably free of the diseases that have plagued our species since the dawn of time. The aliens are crossing the vast reaches of interstellar space using technology we can only dream about. They couldn't do it without good health. The secrets of long, healthy life will be their greatest gift to us."

Several other politicians echoed that sentiment. They were talking to the White House, advising the president. They would make sure any necessary legislation sailed through the Congress. They wanted good health for their constituents, and they wanted the political credit for getting it for them.

After they got rid of the politicians for a while, the talking heads interviewed a scientist, a thoughtful one. "When you cross a scientific tipping point," the scientist said, "a great many new technologies flow from that, almost automatically. Think about how the understanding and harnessing of electrical energy has revolutionized the lives of everyone on this planet. Even people living in mud huts in Africa have cell phones. The arrival of aliens will be an even bigger event."

The arrival. *The Arrival.* Bigger.

Bigger than the World Series. *Bigger* than the Super Bowl. *Bigger* than the inauguration of a new president. *Bigger* than the end of a world war. *Bigger than everything.*

"It'll be as big as the Second Coming," one congresswoman from California said, quite seriously, to the tens of millions of people in the television audience, even though she was known for her oft-stated opinion that all religion was drivel. No one remarked on that incongruity.

The president, in his private family room in the White House, nibbled Rolaids while he waited for Petty Officer Hennessey, who was apparently stuck in the crowd outside. He flipped the channel back to Jim Bob Spicer. The famous evangelist was still going over the gory details of the Arrival with his audience. According to Spicer, it was going to be a real mess.

The president listened a bit longer, then turned off Spicer and poured himself another rather large tot of bourbon. He felt self-pity flooding through him again.

Why me? Of all the billions of people on this round rock, *why me?*

ADAM SOLO DROPPED THROUGH THE SAUCER'S HATCH and walked over to Egg Cantrell. The sun was well up, the day was streaming on, and Rip and Charley were trying to get their clothes on before they got out of their sleeping bag.

The crack of a rifle split the morning, flat and loud. Solo spun and hit the ground.

Egg turned him over. Solo had been shot through the body. He was coughing blood. The entry hole was in his chest—apparently the bullet had missed his heart—and he had a large exit hole in his back. The back of his shirt was being quickly soaked with blood.

"Rip!"

The young man came running, just as a young Australian man, perhaps twenty years of age, came charging up with a rifle. An old Winchester Model 94, Rip noticed.

"I got him! Damn, I got him. A million dollars dead or alive, the Internet said. And I got him!"

The Aussie had his eyes on Solo, had his rifle pointed at him, ready to shoot him again. Rip let go with a roundhouse right to the chin that lifted the man off his feet and dropped him in the dirt, out cold. Rip grabbed the rifle and began pounding it against the nearest landing-gear leg. The stock splintered; Rip kept swinging, again and again; the barrel and magazine tube separated. He threw the rifle away and kicked the supine Aussie.

"Solo's hit bad and bleeding," Egg said. "Let's get him in the saucer and get the hell out of here."

Stuff a rag in the bullet hole to slow the bleeding.

Rip and Charley helped Egg lift Solo up through the saucer's hatch.

An infuriated Rip kicked the unconscious Aussie again, then dragged him away from the saucer so he wouldn't be crushed by the antigravity field. He left him lying about twenty-five feet away on his stomach. Just for good measure, he kicked him in the ribs as hard as he could, one more time.

Rip climbed aboard and closed the hatch. Charley Pine was in the pilot's seat wearing the headband. Solo was lying on the seats at the rear of the compartment with Egg sitting beside him. Nothing could be done to help Solo while the saucer was under the G forces of acceleration, so Rip grabbed the back of the pilot's seat with a death grip.

Charley lifted the saucer off the ground, snapped up the gear and lit the rocket engines. The roar from the rocket engines woke up everyone within twenty miles, even the drunks. The young man who had shot Solo had his eardrums shattered.

Inside the saucer Charley Pine asked the computers for full power. Gs pushed against them like the hand of God. As the saucer's airspeed passed Mach 1, she pulled the nose of the ship up into the morning, away from the earth, toward the invisible stars.

WHEN THE SAUCER WAS IN ORBIT AND WEIGHTLESS, Rip, Charley and Uncle Egg gathered around Solo, trying to bandage his wound and assess how badly he was injured. Solo was conscious.

He was bleeding a bit from his mouth. "Lung, I think," he whispered.

"You've been injured a lot worse than this plenty of times before," Rip said, more to Charley and Egg than to Adam Solo. "Hang tough and fix yourself up."

Solo closed his eyes. His face was lined, spare, his eyes deep within their sockets. The scar the polar bear had given him just a few days ago was a solid white line that led into his hair.

"This man needs a doctor," Egg said flatly. "He's bleeding internally."

"He can fix himself," Rip said confidently.

"Just how are we going to get him to a doctor?" Charley asked.

Solo opened his eyes again.

"I know a place," he whispered, "in the Grand Canyon." He coughed blood.

It's been seven, perhaps eight hundred years since I was there, but there was usually water and it's almost impregnable. No one can approach by land. Take the saucer to Lake Powell and refuel it. We will go to the place I know. Then you must send the saucer into

orbit. Tell the computer to calculate an orbit that will allow the saucer to return to us with the minimum amount of maneuvering. That will probably be a polar orbit.

Rip glanced at Charley and Uncle Egg.

"Let's do it," Rip said. He motioned with his head, and Charley Pine climbed into the pilot's seat.

THE PRESIDENT WAS RELIEVED TO SEE PETTY OFFICER Hennessey, who looked natty in his blue uniform with the bell-bottom trousers and a splash of color on his left sleeve. He even had a couple of ribbons on his jumper, decorations, but the president didn't know one from another. Hennessey had his round, white sailor hat in his hands since he was indoors. Without his hat he couldn't salute; it was a navy thing. Hennessey stood at attention, though. The president pointed to a chair and Hennessey dropped into it. He put his hat on his lap.

"These aliens," the president began. "Space Command says a starship is approaching earth. Be here in two days."

Hennessey's expression didn't change.

"What do you think?" the president prompted.

"I think it's gonna be fun, Mr. President. Don't sweat the program. After all, if these guys are smart enough to get here from there, they gotta have something on the ball. They'll really appreciate a drink and a decent meal. Probably would like to get laid too, but I don't think you oughta get into that."

The president nodded. Damn good advice, he thought.

"Long voyages are pretty much all alike," the sailor observed.

Why, yes, the president thought. *I can see that.*

"They'll be just as curious about us as we are about them," Hennessey continued. "If we use a little common sense everything will come out okay. These guys didn't come all this way just to see how mad they can make us. When you go visit the cannibals you try not to end up in the stew pot."

They talked a while longer. When Hennessey left, the president felt better. Yeah. A little common sense. Of course, the problem with common sense is that it is so uncommon. Hennessey was a rare repository of the stuff, the president thought.

THE DRUG MOGULS' BOEING WAS DESCENDING INTO Sydney when the call came from Johnny Murkowsky's Space Command spy. The saucer had left Australia and was in orbit.

Douglas and Johnny Murk cussed vividly.

"We can't just go chasing them around the world until the aliens arrive and they hop in some starship and go tootling off," Douglas protested.

"Our strategy is wrong," Johnny Murk mused. "Well, let's land and refuel and head back for the States."

"Man, I could use a bath, a decent meal and a good night's sleep," Douglas said, yawning.

"Enough already," Johnny Murk shot back. "I would

also desperately like to get laid. All right? Are we going to tough this out and get filthy rich, or are we going to watch television in some Aussie hotel as the aliens ascend into heaven to sit on the right hand of God?"

Douglas yawned again. "We haven't been doing so well so far. Frankly, we'd have been better off staying at home. If you have a better strategy, I'd like to hear it."

The plane's wheels squeaked on the concrete. As it taxied Douglas and Murkowsky analyzed the situation yet again and plotted their course.

WHEN THE PRESIDENT WAS TOLD ABOUT THE SAUCER coming out of orbit—headed once again for the United States—his heart fluttered. The *western* United States, the aide said.

Well, at least it isn't coming here, the president thought.

He recalled his conversation last night with his wife. She and a few friends were vacationing in the south of France. She told him in no uncertain terms that she wasn't coming home until this whole mess was over and things returned to *normal.* She had bought several cases of wine that she was shipping home. She was thinking about getting a face-lift. The French plastic surgeons were excellent, she had heard, and very private; the press wouldn't get wind of it. By the way, she needed some more money.

Normal? What was that?

He marched down to the situation room with Petty Officer Hennessey in tow to find out if the crowds on the streets were going to storm the White House. P. J. O'Reilly was very much in charge. He informed the president that after his announcement that the starship was days away, the crowd was dissipating, a few actually going to work, some going home, the rest filling up restaurants and bars eating or getting drunk, or both. Everyone looked at the monitors that showed video of the crowds on the streets.

"Fifteen senators and twelve congressmen and -women want to meet with you. They want a statement they can pass along to the press and their constituents."

"Have someone write out something. But I want to read it first."

"Yes, sir. A delegation of preachers also wants a few minutes of your time, Mr. President. They want some reassurance they can take back to their congregations."

"Tell them to read their Bibles. Who am I to compete with Jesus and the prophets?"

"An excellent point," O'Reilly said with just a detectable hint of sarcasm. "And a delegation of foreign ambassadors, about a dozen at last count, wants to meet with you, today if possible. As bad as things are here, they are beginning to spin out of control in foreign capitals."

The president scowled. "If we can keep the people in the Washington area and out in Peoria calmed down, that will be a feat. What on earth could I possibly say that will oil the waters in Paris and Rome and Beijing?"

Petty Officer Hennessey cleared his throat. The president looked at him with raised eyebrows.

"Perhaps, sir, you could say that you are actually *looking forward* to the aliens' visit. That you plan to bring your granddaughter along. I'll bet she'd get a real charge out of meeting the alien captain."

The president's first reaction was that *his* daughter would never, ever let *her* daughter within ten miles of an alien. Then again, maybe she could be finagled. His daughter was a nervous Nellie, but his granddaughter, Amanda, who just had her tenth birthday, certainly wasn't. Heck, she had even ridden with him in a saucer flown by Charley Pine six weeks or so ago, when Charley and Rip were preparing to zip off to the moon to fight it out with the Frenchies and save the world. He would ask Amanda and let her handle her mother. Yeah.

"That," he told Petty Officer Hennessey, "is a darn good idea. When we get back upstairs, I'll call Amanda to see if she is up for the adventure." He skewered O'Reilly with his eyes. "Wish we had some other folks around here doing some serious thinking."

That comment merely bounced off O'Reilly. He had spent too many years with the president to let the old fart's jibes bother him. "About the saucer just now reentering the atmosphere after launching from Australia . . . perhaps an announcement by the press secretary? He's feeling a bit left out of the excitement."

"No announcement. Tell that moron if he opens his mouth I'll throttle him. Tell Space Command to keep the lid on too."

People nowadays get too much information, the president

told himself, *and they don't know what to do with it.* He often found himself in precisely that situation.

Just for the heck of it, he flipped a television to CNBC, the business channel. Another rough day on Wall Street. Would the impending alien visit be good or bad for business? Apparently the day traders, speculators, mutual fund managers and mom-and-pop investors couldn't decide, so the market was going up and down like a pump handle. The richest old crock in America, multibillionaire publicity hound Warren Buffett, gave a two-minute interview. He was buying on the dips, he said. "The world is not coming to an end. People will still need food, clothes, housing and wheels. Plus cell phones, liquor, diapers, pills and all the rest of it."

The president glanced at Hennessey, who met his gaze and nodded. Yep, more common sense.

Reassured, the president began to feel better. His stomach stopped aching, at least for a moment.

"Mr. President," P. J. O'Reilly said, in his take-charge persona, "I want to have the photographer take some shots of you at your desk in the Oval Office looking pensive and serious. Somber, but in charge. Thinking deep, complex thoughts, conscious of your moral responsibility for the fate of the world, which you are holding in your two mortal hands. Maybe we could get a couple of shots of you actually looking at your hands. I'll release the photos immediately. The world will see that you are on the job, managing the alien crisis, like JFK during the Cuban Missile Crisis."

The president's eyes rolled back into his head. He fought to refocus on his chief of staff, who looked particularly loathsome today. Perhaps he could offer him to the aliens as a protein snack.

"Okay. Hennessey, come with me. O'Reilly, have someone bring us dinner."

14

AFTER THEY REFUELED FROM LAKE POWELL, CHARLEY Pine flew the saucer south through the deepening canyon of the Colorado River. It was a night full of stars, with the moon still down, so she hoped that no one along the canyon would see the black saucer ghosting along at about a hundred knots low above the river. She could see on the computer screen the canyon walls rising vertically on both sides above her vision, so she felt as if she were a little girl tiptoeing along a hallway.

She was perhaps thirty miles below the Glen Canyon Dam when she hit some power lines stretched across the river. She had about a second's warning—they appeared as thin filaments across her screen—then she hit them. The saucer slipped between them effortlessly, forcing one line over the top and one underneath. A power surge shot through the saucer, and the instrument panel went black.

Charley Pine felt the adrenaline surge through her veins. *The Roswell saucer crashed during a lightning storm.* Then the computer screens came back to life and all again appeared normal. To her infinite relief, she saw that she was still in the center of the canyon, still level, still in control . . . *Am I in control?*

She flicked the stick automatically. The saucer responded, like an obedient dog. Five degrees left wing down, now five right, now level again.

"That was exciting," Rip said. He was standing beside her.

"That was a lummer," she told him nervously. "A shot of cold urine to the heart."

"You live for those."

"Right. How is Solo?"

I am okay, Charley. Now I need to explain what to do. There is a beach on the north side of the river, perhaps a hundred miles ahead. It is not sand, but erosional debris that washed down a canyon and accumulated for perhaps ten million years. The river won't move it for a long time. We will land there, get out of the saucer, and get on top of it.

"On top?"

On top.

On they flew, deeper and deeper into the Grand Canyon, with Charley keeping the saucer about a hundred feet above the ribbon of water that stretched like a crooked road on the computer screen before her.

About an hour later she found the ledge. It slanted toward the river but looked okay. She gingerly lowered the legs of the saucer and set it down.

We will need all our supplies. We can remain here until they come.

They.

Until *they* come.

Charley Pine felt a shiver run down her spine.

Rip opened the hatch and began shoving sleeping bags and sacks through the opening. Egg helped Adam Solo walk over to the hole, sit on the edge and ease himself through; then Rip assisted him out from under the saucer.

"Next time, tell them to put the hatch on top," Rip told Solo.

"The belly was the cheapest spot."

When he had Solo out of earshot of Egg and Charley, he asked, "So how are you really doing?"

"I'm dying, I think. Bleeding internally. My body isn't repairing itself quickly enough."

Rip took that comment in silence.

"Don't tell the others," Solo said. "They have enough to worry about."

"And I don't? But I think they already know."

"Perhaps," Solo admitted. "When we have our gear unloaded and the hatch closed, have Charley lift the saucer and raise the gear, then lower the ship onto its belly so that we can climb on top. The place we want is a cliff dwelling in the side of a cliff about five hundred feet below the South Rim, about two miles west of here."

"And when we're there?"

"Program the saucer to go into a polar orbit that will bring it back over us on every pass."

There were many things Rip wanted to ask Solo, who was the most unique human he had ever met. Twelve hundred, thirteen hundred years on earth, a youth from a planet in another star system, crossing the interstellar vastness . . . and yet Rip didn't want to ask. Perhaps, as Solo remarked once in passing, he had lived too long, experienced too much, left too many loved ones behind.

As Rip watched the saucer descend onto its belly, held level by Charley, he helped Solo climb onto its dry, slick surface. He thought about the past, not about the immediate future.

Charley, on the other hand, was thinking hard about the task before her. Flying the saucer with its antigravity rings up the cliffs, finding the place Solo wanted in the starlight, keeping everyone from falling off the rounded top of the ship. My God, if they fell off . . .

Solo sensed her concern. **If we fall, we fall.**

She heard his voice in her head and sensed the wisdom, even if she didn't like the message. Keeping this flying plate level was going to take all the flying skills she possessed. Sure, the computer would help, but she had to tell the computer what to do. If she screwed this up . . .

well, the fall wouldn't take so long. Then she and Rip and Egg and Solo would begin the next adventure, whatever that would be.

That's right.

Your mind reading is very tiresome, she thought.

There was no reply.

EGG CANTRELL WAS THE MOST FRIGHTENED. HE GLUED himself to the saucer—he had Solo sprawled flat right on the crest—and held on for dear life. His rounded middle seemed to push him away from the saucer, making him feel like a basketball that was balanced just so and could at the slightest nudge begin to roll.

Charley sensed his fear. She was in front of him, sitting up, where she could see. "We'll be okay, Uncle Egg. Hang on to Solo."

"I can't hang on to anybody," Egg informed her, trying to keep his voice calm. Even as he said the words, he felt the saucer lift off. Something like an elevator, yet smooth and effortless. He closed his eyes and tried to get a grip with his hands and feet, even though there was nothing but the glass-smooth surface of the saucer to hold on to.

"If it was raining, we'd be in big trouble," Rip remarked. He was the eternal optimist, Egg thought, with the confidence of youth. Yeah, things could always be worse. That's one of life's profound lessons.

Egg could feel the cold air flowing over him. Charley

was moving the saucer forward, but climbing. He could feel the saucer pressing against his body, lifting, rising, higher and higher. He risked a look around. The cliffs were visible in the starlight, which made the snow on the canyon rims glow. He couldn't see much detail. He could see that the saucer was moving, however, and the aspect of the cliffs was changing. He squeezed his eyes shut and tried to fight the cold.

The flight seemed to take hours. Charley kept the speed under control. Once the saucer flew over a ledge of a cliff—the sides of the canyon rose like a giant's stairsteps—and the thing began to tilt. Egg felt the panic rising in his throat. He clung to the ship, which somehow came back level.

Well done, Charley. It was that damn Solo. The guy had steel balls. Egg pressed a cheek against the saucer's skin and kept his eyes shut.

After a while Solo gave Charley directions. **Left some. Higher. Along that ledge.**

"Use your flashlight, Rip," Charley ordered.

"Maybe the saucer's landing light would be better."

"Too bright. No use advertising. Just the flashlight."

Finally Egg felt the saucer stop. A total lack of motion. Or so it seemed. He opened his eyes and looked in the direction his head was pointing. He was looking along the upper edge of the Grand Canyon. A sliver of moon was up now, and the entire sweep of the great tear in the earth was spread before him. Yet the saucer was stationary, solid as one of the canyon's cliffs. He raised his head.

Ahead of the saucer was a ledge below the rim of a mesa. Upon it he could just make out what appeared to be a stone wall, built by human hands. With windows. Charley was standing, and so was Rip. They picked up Solo, one on each arm, and led him down toward the front of the machine. Then they stepped across the narrow gap onto the ledge.

Rip hopped back onto the saucer and began off-loading gear. He passed items to Charley, one by one, and she tossed them back away from the edge. A bag of food, sleeping bags, a few other odds and ends.

This took several minutes, with Rip skipping around fearlessly while Egg held tight to the ship.

"Come on, Uncle," he said at last, standing on the apex of the saucer with his hand out. "It's time to get off."

Egg was frozen with fear. His muscles refused to work. Yet Rip's outstretched hand was irresistible. He forced his cold muscles to obey. He tried to rise, stretched out his hand and slipped.

He felt himself sliding down the slope of the saucer toward the edge. He grabbed with both hands and kept sliding.

As Egg slid along, Rip ran after him. Egg went over the edge and Rip was right behind him, launching himself at his uncle.

Fly the saucer, Charley.

Falling into the dark abyss, Egg Cantrell felt his

nephew Rip grab his hands. In a way, it was comforting. He knew then that they would die together.

Standing on the edge of the ledge, Charley Pine told the saucer what to do. Her commands reversed the anti-gravity field. Instead of repelling the earth, now it attracted it. It didn't fall; it accelerated downward faster than the falling men. Three hundred feet below them, it arrested its fall at Charley's command and slid under them, still going downward.

Egg and Rip landed on the top. Rip had both of Egg's hands in his. The impact knocked the wind from both of them. The saucer slowed and stopped. The Gs mashed the two men into the surface of the ship, imprisoning them like bugs against a windshield. Then the saucer began to rise.

"Hold on, Uncle!"

"Holy pickles, Rip. I—my God, I thought we were dead!"

The saucer lifted them back to the ledge. Charley ran across and helped Rip drag Egg to the ledge and push him across.

Egg fell heavily to the ledge and held the rock with both hands. He was spent.

Nicely done, Ms. Pine.

Rip gathered Charley into his arms and kissed her.

JOHNNY MURKOWSKY WAS TRYING TO SEDUCE THE flight attendant, a tall, leggy brunette with come-hither eyes and a nice figure, when he got the call from his Space

Command spy on his satellite phone. The Boeing 747 was somewhere over the vast Pacific eastbound.

"The saucer came down and went into Lake Powell," Johnny Murk's spy reported. "The FAA's radars reported that it then crossed over Glen Canyon Dam and headed down the Colorado River, apparently. Best guess is it's somewhere in the Grand Canyon."

"Has the White House been notified?" Johnny Murk queried.

"Sure. But there is a starship coming in from deep space. It'll be here in a couple of days, and the head dogs are all worked up about that. They don't give a hoot about the saucer."

"Keep me advised."

"Listen, Mr. Murkowsky. Just telling you all this could cost me my job. I want a job after I retire, and I want your promise."

"You got it. If I get to that saucer before the damned Army, Navy, Air Force and Marines. If I don't . . ."

"Did anybody ever tell you you're an asshole?"

"Three or four people a day. And they are right. But, asshole or not, I pay my debts. Now if you want that job, keep telling me what is going down. I want to know where that saucer is every damn minute. Got it?"

"Yeah."

The connection broke.

Johnny Murk and Harrison Douglas put their heads together; then Murk went forward and told the chief pilot to land at Grand Canyon Airport, on the South Rim. The captain protested. He had enough fuel to get there, just, if the winds held, but there were customs and immigration laws and all that. Johnny Murk made some large monetary promises. Those didn't impress the pilots, who had licenses to worry about.

Johnny Murk whipped out his checkbook and wrote checks for a million dollars each for every person in the crew, all five. The pilots examined their checks, looked at each other, folded the checks and pocketed them, then reprogrammed their flight computers and pushed the appropriate buttons. Grand Canyon Airport, here we come!

Johnny Murk went back to the flight attendant. He was desperate, and she *loved* her million-dollar check. Lust and money had cemented many a romance since the earth began to spin. She poured two glasses of champagne, opened a can of caviar and got out some gourmet crackers. She and Johnny snuggled up on a couch in the First Class lounge.

THE PRESIDENT'S GRANDDAUGHTER, AMANDA, answered the telephone when the president called. "Oh, Grandpa," she burbled, "is it true? Aliens are coming to the White House?"

"Appears so, kiddo. I was wondering if you'd like to be here, go out with me to meet them? Kinda say hi and inspect their spaceship and see what's what and stuff?"

"Holy Bananas! Of course! I was about to call you. Mom is being *such* a drag, but I know you can persuade her. Is Charley Pine going to be there? When I grow up, I'm going to be just like her. She is *so* wonderful, *so* true blue, *so* real. *So everything!*"

"Well, I don't know about Charley Pine. Haven't heard from her in a while." The president fervently wished he had his hands around Charley's throat right then, but he had the tact not to say that to Amanda. "Never can tell," he added.

"Will they have their kids with them?"

"Well, heck, I don't know. We'll have to meet them and see."

"Oh, golly, you are the world's *greatest* grandpa. I'll put Mom on."

So he had to talk to his daughter after all. She had informed him after the last election that she voted for the other guy. Every politician should have a daughter like this, he thought gloomily.

"Do you think it's safe?" she asked. "Aliens?"

"*Of course* it's safe! I wouldn't be inviting Amanda if there were the *slightest* iota of danger. After all, Amanda flew with me in a saucer just last month."

"Well . . ." One thing about his daughter, she was easily persuaded. Which was probably why she voted for that other bastard.

"I'm going to be right there holding her hand. She'll love it! It'll be historic as hell. She'll be in every history book written for the next thousand years. People will name their kids after her."

"Well . . ."

He could hear Amanda, demanding to go. She was wailing, "Oooh, Mommmm . . ."

His daughter caved.

"I'll send a helicopter. Have her pack her nightie and toothbrush."

He hung up, then called O'Reilly and told him to send a helo after Amanda. And to have the press mouthpiece announce that the president and First Granddaughter Amanda would greet the aliens when they arrived.

When he completed that conversation and had the telephone back on its cradle, he smiled benignly at Petty Officer Third Class Hennessey. Truly, the darn sailor was a genius.

"Want another drink?" he asked Hennessey.

"This is mighty fine bourbon, Mr. President," the sailor from Oklahoma said, nodding. They taught you how to drink in the navy.

"Let's hope the aliens don't eat us all," he said to Hennessey, raising his glass.

"Amen to that," the sailor replied.

THE FOUR TRAVELERS STOOD ON THE LEDGE WATCHing as the saucer ghosted away across the canyon. Black as it was, it soon disappeared into the gloom. Charley had programmed it to fly several hundred miles north into Utah on the antigravity rings before using the rockets to climb into orbit.

When the saucer disappeared, the cold seemed to seep ever deeper into their clothes. Adam Solo sagged. Egg and Charley helped him into the cliff house.

The first thing we need, Rip thought, *is a fire.* Searching the old Anasazi ruin, he found three pack-rat nests, which would make nice kindling. He still needed wood to burn. Part of the ancient cliff dwelling had collapsed, and the round poles that had held up floors were still there.

He dragged two inside and arranged them so the ends would catch in the fire, which was soon burning fairly well and giving off warmth. The room they were in had obviously been used for fires in times long past; the ceiling was blackened. A hole high in the wall acted as a chimney.

Rip found four cans of soup in the food bag, cut the tops open with his knife and put them beside the fire to heat up.

They arranged Solo on a sleeping bag by the fire. Egg used a spoon to feed him soup. With it down, he went to sleep.

The others ate their soup, sharing the spoon, and crawled into sleeping bags around the fire. All were asleep within minutes, except for Egg, who lay there in the firelight listening to the others' deep-sleep breathing, thinking about falling toward certain death with Rip holding his hand. He was still coming down from the adrenaline high.

He had never before been so close to death. The fear washed over him again and again . . . and yet, thinking about it now, he had been ready.

I've had a good life, he told himself. *To have a nephew like Rip, to have shared the saucer adventure, to have met all these extraordinary people, well, I'm truly blessed.*

With that thought in his mind, he dropped off to sleep.

AN EXPLORATION OF THE LEDGE IN THE EARLY DAWN the next morning showed how isolated the old cliff dwelling was. The Grand Canyon was spread out before them. The ledge they were on was perhaps fifty feet long and twenty feet deep at the widest point. Soot from ancient fires blackened the sloping stone over their heads and the walls of the stone house.

Rip found a water source, a place where water trickled from a soft formation. This morning the little stream was frozen due to the overnight temperatures, but later this morning it should flow again. So they had water. A dab of food to eat, water to drink and wood to burn. They could last a few days here. Until Solo's people arrived, anyway. No doubt the National Park Service would get peeved if they ever figured out he had burned these old logs from the Anasazi ruin, but that was a problem for another day.

Looking to the right and left along the ledge, it was obvious there was no easy way to access the cliff dwelling. Rip estimated they were perhaps fifty feet below the top of this mesa, which Solo said was an island, separated from the South Rim by a thousand-foot-deep chasm. No doubt there were handholds in the cliff that would allow you access to the top, if you knew where they were and had absolutely no fear of heights.

The ancients had climbed here from below, along a trail now completely overgrown except for the last forty feet or so. Rip looked it over in the early morning light and thought he could descend it if he had to. Had to real bad. He figured Charley could too, but not Uncle Egg. Nor Solo in the condition he was in. So they had to stay put.

He rebuilt the fire with another pack rat's nest and shoved the old logs deeper into the blaze. Soon the warmth filled the main room.

They would be safe enough here, for a little while, Rip reassured himself. However, Adam Solo had taken a turn for the worse.

He looked physically older, and his color wasn't good. The bullet holes were still leaking. His wound would have killed any normal man; of course, Solo wasn't normal. Still, this one might have been one too many. His pulse was steady yet weak. His breathing was okay, between fits of coughing, which brought up blood.

"You've been here before?" Egg asked after taking Solo's pulse.

"In the thirteen hundreds. A family still lived here. I was starving. They took me in."

"Starving?"

"War between the tribes. Apaches were tough, fierce warriors."

Solo fell silent, his eyes examining the stone room they had laid him in.

"I thought your body could repair itself," Rip whispered.

"Nothing lasts forever, Rip." After a bit, the voyager between the stars added, "Pretty proud of you last night, son. I've seen a great many men in serious straits; you are right up there with the best. I'm proud to have known you."

Rip was embarrassed. "Is there anything we can do for you?"

"Leave me alone with my memories."

So they did. Rip, Charley and Uncle Egg sat on the ledge and watched the sun rise.

"I was pretty scared when I fell off the saucer," Egg admitted to Rip and Charley.

"Me too," Rip said.

"But you jumped after me."

"I figured Charley would save us. And she did."

"What if she couldn't have?"

"Unc," Rip said with a big grin, "you and I would now be going over our accounts with St. Peter. Gonna have to do that sooner or later anyway."

Just thinking about the fall made Egg's heart thud

powerfully. Another dose of adrenaline. He had looked death in the face, yet lived to tell the tale. This morning that seemed a good thing. There was more life to be lived.

The three of them watched the sunlight chase the shadows from the great canyon, watched the colors change, watched the extraordinary eternal panorama as the earth spun on its axis, just as it had done since the dawn of time. Snow on the rims . . . an early winter morning in the greatest canyon on earth.

Meanwhile, inside the stone room by the fire, Adam Solo had a conversation with the captain of the starship. He told him who he was, when he was marooned on this planet, who he was with; he informed the captain of his many adventures as fast as he thought them and told him the starship exploration landing team should go to Washington, the White House. **Washington is the capital of the United States, the largest, most advanced economy on the planet, and a democracy. That is the best place for diplomacy with the people of this planet, who live in over one hundred eighty nations in every stage of economic and moral development.**

Solo also informed the captain that Egg Cantrell, Rip and Charley had a saucer and access to another, which was now parked above the lawn of the White House.

I may not be alive when you arrive, Solo added. **Rip**

and Egg Cantrell and Charley Pine are people you need to talk to. They are brave, wise and compassionate. In my thirteen centuries on this planet, I have met few who are their equals.

15

ADAM SOLO LAY INSIDE THE ANCIENT CLIFF DWELLING watching the sunlit sky through the window, which was just a hole in the stone wall. His wound pained him greatly, yet he was thinking about the people he had known here. It was so long ago . . . and they were of course long dead. Dead for almost seven hundred years.

There had been a man and his wife, and kids, and the wife's mother, and several young men from the tribe who had yet to find wives. In this place they had planned their lives, their future, their children's future. They were safe here from the nomads who would have killed and robbed them. Safe. On this tiny ledge facing this great canyon.

There was food if they worked hard to get it, water was accessible. Survival was the challenge. What more did men need?

Indeed. What does anyone need but people to love and cherish, food, water, clothes and shelter?

The Indians had lived their lives, loved, raised children, passed on what they knew and surrendered to their own mortality eventually, when enough years had passed, leaving another generation to carry on . . . and a generation after that, and so on.

Solo knew that was the way of life. The way of life wherever it was found in the universe.

So he lay on a sleeping bag trying to ignore the pain, thinking of these things and of those people who had lived here whom he had known. Remembering.

Ah, I have too many memories, he thought. *Too many people who have gone on before me, leaving me here to struggle and try to survive. And in the end, I was shot by a fool who saw the glimmer of a big reward.* Those Indians who lived here, the Vikings, the Iroquois, the white settlers who tried to wrestle a living from the land and so often failed, what would they have thought of the Internet? Of flying saucers? Of starships?

Most of those people had been happy, like the Indians who had lived in this house overlooking the Grand Canyon. Happy! They had been contented with their lives in a way he had never been.

He had always been searching for a way home. For a way back to the life he had once known. Oh, he had tried. Tried to be as content as the people around him. Tried to be content with a good hunt, a good crop, or with rain when the fields needed it. Tried, but it was never enough.

Now as he lay in pain, trying to ignore it, he thought about being content. Somehow that great gift had escaped him. He had never been content. Never accepted life on its own terms. Always he wanted to escape from this savage planet. Wanted a starship to rescue him.

What a fool he had been! A fool!

He had everything life had to offer for hundreds of years, over a thousand, over half a hundred earth generations, and hadn't appreciated it.

He could hear Egg and Charley and Rip talking outside. They were worried about *him*!

Adam Solo began weeping.

Soon he drifted off to sleep.

He awoke when Charley Pine tried to gently roll him over to check the wound below his right shoulder blade.

"Sorry," she muttered and rolled him over anyway. She took the sodden bandage off, left the bit of rag in the exit wound and used one of Rip's old tee shirts as a body bandage.

When she rolled him back onto his back, her face was drawn, pale. "You're still bleeding," she said. "No doubt internally too. You really need a doctor that can pump you full of platelets."

"Too big a risk," he muttered.

"Don't be such a cynic."

You know as well as I do what might happen if a DNA

sample from me fell into the wrong hands. The people of this planet aren't ready for knowledge like that. They aren't politically, ethically or morally ready. When they are, they'll get there by themselves.

"You're dying. You know that, of course." It was a flat statement, not a question.

I should have died a hundred times already. I'm ready for what comes next. If anything.

"Christ, you *are* a cynic!"

I've seen many people die. It's as natural as going to sleep. I don't fear it.

"So what was your closest escape from the grim reaper?"

Adam Solo thought about that, sorting through the memories. Finally he told her, **It was a cattle drive, bringing a herd up from Texas. Crossing the Canadian my horse got into quicksand. I threw a rope at something on the bank—I forget what—and missed. The horse struggled and sank and I tried to get off and got trapped. If I had gone down with the horse I would have died. I knew it. My body's ability to repair itself would have counted for nothing. Then a friend of mine rode up and threw me a rope. He dragged me out. His name was Billy Vance, and he was nineteen, a young nineteen, full of himself.**

"So you made it."

Yeah. Lived to die another day.

"So what happened to Billy Vance?" Her face was serious, pensive, as she tried to understand.

We made it to Dodge; the owner sold the herd and paid us off. I talked Billy into going with me to Colorado to hunt for gold, and he agreed. But on our last night in Dodge he caught a gambler cheating at cards and called him on it. The gambler got a bullet into Billy and two into me. Billy died and I didn't. A month later, when I recovered, I went to Colorado by myself.

"You've buried a lot of friends."

More than I care to remember.

"What happened to the gambler?" she asked.

He didn't make it. Billy and I each got a slug into him. Took him a long week to die. They buried him with his marked deck.

"We need to bring the saucer back and get you to a doctor."

No.

She crawled through the low door and went back out onto the ledge above the kiva. A good woman, he reflected. He hoped Rip realized just how good. Maybe he did. That Rip . . . he was a lot like Billy Vance. Billy with the wicked smile and crooked teeth and terrific thirst for life. Billy Vance, dead of a gunshot wound to the gut at the age of nineteen, but game all the way.

Solo lay thinking about those days long ago, about the American West and the Indians he loved and longhorns and thunderstorms, blistering hot endless days on horseback, nights of exhausted sleep and the cow towns at the end of the trail. Thinking of the men. Companions for the trail of life. If only he could do it all again, see all those men and women he had known and loved through the centuries one more time, hear their laughter and voices . . .

He had been so blessed. Adam Solo knew that. That fool who stole the saucer long ago and marooned Solo on this savage planet had done him a great favor. The thought gave him peace.

"WE NEED A PANEL OF EXPERTS," P. J. O'REILLY HAD told the president. "A panel of experts will give the public the assurance that you are talking to the right people, getting yourself fully informed."

"Experts in what?" the president had asked skeptically.

"Oh, you know, whatever. Experts are experts, people with degrees from out of town. It's a PR thing. Keep the Joe Six-Packs calmed down."

The president groaned inwardly. He was certainly a master of listening to bullshit and making appropriate noises, but he doubted if he would get any light at all from any group O'Reilly could assemble. Another waste of time. Yet he was politician enough to appreciate that O'Reilly had a point. The art of politics is to appear to be leading, even when groping in the dark. Petty Officer Third Class Hennessey from Oklahoma had nodded sagely, so the president had reluctantly agreed to an audience with some "experts."

Now, as he faced the hastily summoned group, he was tempted to make some excuse to dismiss them, but refrained. The White House photographer was snapping pictures, and the mouthpiece, the press secretary, was standing against the wall, ready to spin the event for the media in the White House Press Room.

O'Reilly introduced the delegation. There was a philosophy professor from Harvard, an astrogeophysicist from the University of Houston, a scientist from NASA and two women from the National Science Foundation who had been looking for intelligent life in the universe for some years now, at government expense, with no results to show for their efforts. The president was tempted to ask if the women had checked in Washington but held his tongue. There was also some guy who wrote best-seller science fiction, none of which the president had ever read. He was famous, though. Even the guy from Harvard smiled warmly at him. All were duly introduced, and all had something to say.

The president listened carefully.

The experts agreed, more or less. The aliens would be more technically advanced than we are and would have high moral and ethical principals. Very high. They would not be eaters of flesh. Would not be here to conquer and enslave. Would be very "progressive," according to the Harvard philosopher. Since that was a loaded political term here on this little round rock, in this day and age, the presidential eyebrows rose a fraction of a millimeter. The chief executive glanced at Hennessey, whose face was deadpan.

"What about weapons?" the national security adviser asked. O'Reilly had let him attend this soiree, the president thought sourly.

Well, of course the aliens had weapons. The Sahara saucer and the Roswell saucer both had antimatter weapons; technological progress being what it is, no doubt the coming alien delegation had death rays of some sort to protect themselves from monsters and predators and dragons on whatever planet they happened to visit.

"Dragons?" said the national security adviser.

The president glanced at Petty Officer Hennessey, who had one eyebrow raised. The president had always admired people who could do that. He had tried for years but couldn't.

"Who knows what forms of life other planets in the universe might contain?" the science-fiction writer asked rhetorically, warming to his subject. "They must be prepared. We must assume they are; ergo, superior weaponry."

The universal nods of affirmation from all the experts silenced the national security adviser.

Ergo, indeed!

When O'Reilly finally ushered the experts out, the president asked the petty officer what he thought.

"These aliens are just sailors. Kind of like Christopher

Columbus' guys. They fly starships because it pays fairly well, but the brains are back on the home planet, wherever that is. These guys didn't design and build the starship or figure out how to fly it. They will be just a bunch of average Joes. You'll see."

The president felt reassured. With Amanda there at the great event, he didn't want anything to go wrong. His wife and daughter would never forgive him. Of course, there was the future of the human species to consider too: Aliens, First Contact, and all that.

The experts had agreed unanimously: The future of the humanity, indeed, the future of the whole planet and every species on it, hinged on how he, the president, handled this first meeting with the representatives of an advanced civilization with unknown but extraordinary capabilities. After all, voyaging between the stars . . . "Not to put any pressure on you, Mr. President, but facts are facts."

Back in his office the president remarked to Hennessey, "Damn, this will be historic," and glanced at the television, which was still showing that saucer sitting over the South Lawn with no visible means of support.

"Yes, sir," the navy said.

Just a bunch of sailors driving a starship. Yeah. *Hey, how are you? Did you have a nice trip?*

Amanda wouldn't be here for a few hours, so the president asked Petty Officer Third Class Hennessey, "Want another drink?"

"One more wouldn't hurt," the sailor admitted and held out his glass.

P. J. O'REILLY WAS SHOOK AFTER THE EXPERTS LEFT. He went to his office and had a snort from a Scotch bottle he kept in his desk. This time His Arrogance wasn't up to the challenges that lay before him, O'Reilly thought. He looked kinda pasty and had that sailor with him all the time now. O'Reilly had caught those glances at Hennessey when some expert had said something rather startling, something almost profound but not quite.

None of them had anything profound to say, O'Reilly thought. Rather humdrum, actually. No doubt the experts were pontificating on the networks just now—telling the boobs watching worldwide what they had told the president—and this weekend, if the aliens hadn't destroyed Washington and the planet, they would have oped pieces in all the big newspapers. An expert's reputation must be constantly polished.

O'Reilly put his face in his hands and sat that way for a long moment. If this went bad, he was going to be dead sooner rather than later. The aliens might decide that all humans were equivalent to stink bugs and just step on them. Or they might want some humans to take aboard their ship as protein. Protein must be hard to come by on a starship. How many cows or hogs or chickens could one of those things carry, anyway?

Hollywood movies from the past sprang to mind. He remembered the one in which a gruesome alien sprang from someone's stomach. It had taken a really sick mind to think of that! And the aliens as zombies! Then there was the Arnold Schwarzenegger movie *Predator:* invisible ten-foot-tall sport hunters who crossed interstellar space to kill for the thrill of it.

Oh, baby . . .

He put the bottle away and tried to arrange his thoughts.

What if some horror along those lines was really what First Contact was going to be like? The president and that kid sailor didn't seem worried, but the old man always did lack imagination. The kid from Oklahoma . . . well, who knew? Two dimwits had found each other.

P. J. O'Reilly looked again at the TV in the corner with its permanent display of the hovering saucer just outside the building. What to make of that? What kind of twisted intelligence would park a saucer *there,* of all places?

The phone on his desk buzzed. His executive assistant. O'Reilly picked it up and grunted.

"That saucer that came in from orbit went back up, or so say the FAA and air force. They aren't absolutely certain, but they think it's probably the same saucer. Thing's now in a polar orbit."

"Has the press got this?"

"Not to my knowledge. We're keeping a solid lid on information about saucer and starship movements. Should I inform the president?"

O'Reilly thought His Greatness had enough on his plate just now. "No, and don't let this leak." After all, even if hundreds of saucers were scattered from pole to pole in every pond, lake and fishing hole, what could the U.S. government do about it?

O'Reilly was meditating on what might happen if the aliens weren't the space-cruising diplomats the president seemed to think they would be when the press secretary popped in without knocking. He handed O'Reilly a list of the points he intended to make with the press.

"The First Granddaughter will arrive in an hour," the mouthpiece said brightly as the chief of staff scanned the list. He kept his job, the chief of staff knew, because he was a consummate actor who could make the most outrageous lies sound plausible.

"We've got television crews from every network on the planet out there," he continued smugly, "to film Amanda coming down the stairs of the helicopter and the president waiting to welcome her. I called her mom to ensure Amanda is bringing her teddy bear. Having Amanda here for the alien arrival has really calmed down the crowds and pols. That teddy bear will be the icing on the cake. Her arrival will make her the most popular female on the planet. Great television, great politics."

"Let's hope the aliens don't eat her first as an hors d'oeuvre," O'Reilly snarled.

The press secretary's smile disappeared. "Yeah," he said slowly, his face growing pale. "I hadn't thought of that."

"Did anyone ever tell you that you're a moron?"

"My ex-wife. She said that's why I landed this gig."

"Get out of here," P. J. O'Reilly snapped, pointing toward the door. "And knock next time, dammit!"

"So the list is okay?"

"This administration has the situation well in hand—that's the company line. If you panic the peasants, I'll have your empty little head bronzed and use it as a paperweight."

"What about the Russian government? The Russian president says they have known for dozens of years that aliens are here, sneaking around, planning to take over."

"Aliens could probably do a better job of running Russia than those idiots in the Kremlin."

"And what about the French government? They say—"

"The aliens can land in Paris if they want the French government's considered, enlightened, progressive opinion. Or if they want to gobble garlic-flavored snail-eaters. By God, I wish they would make a French port call!"

After the door closed behind the press dude, he got out the Scotch bottle and had another swig. "Screw the French," O'Reilly muttered.

With bottle in hand he sat staring at the saucer on the television screen. After two more snorts he swiveled his chair and looked out the window at the real thing.

THERE WAS A DELEGATION OF PHILADELPHIA THUGS waiting on the tarmac at Grand Canyon Airport when the Boeing 747-400 deposited Harrison Douglas, Johnny Murkowsky and their mercenaries, whose ranks were swelled by six men waiting for them. Nearby were parked two National Guard attack helicopters.

The two pharma moguls conferred with their troops.

"We know where they are," one Philly soldier told Douglas. "Got them pinpointed with infrared. Used one of the choppers."

Johnny Murk looked the choppers over. They had sensors and machine guns sprouting all over and looked rather fierce. "Where in hell did you guys get those things?"

"You can get anything on this planet if you are willing to pay for it. Douglas said you were."

"Damn right. We want Adam Solo, dead or alive, and hang the cost."

The Philadelphia contingent smiled benignly. It looked as if they had struck the mother lode. This was almost as good as having access to the U.S. Mint.

"What are we waiting for?" Harrison Douglas shouted, loud enough to be heard by all the troops. "Let's man up and go get those bastards before the sun sets."

Johnny Murk put a hand on Douglas' arm. "Let's you and me stay out of the choppers. I've got this feeling . . ."

"Bad vibes?"

"Those choppers look tough, but a saucer would make short work of them. Let's let these guys earn their pay, and you and I will take a guy with a sniper rifle out as close as we can get to the edge. Now wouldn't be a good time to wind up dead."

Most days aren't, Douglas reflected soberly. They climbed into a van with a shooter with a rifle—his name was Vinnie, he said—and away they went. They were through the gate in the airport fence when the helicopters went over their heads, heading for the rim . . . and Adam Solo.

THE HELICOPTER CARRYING THE FIRST GRANDDAUGHTER landed on the White House lawn just a hundred feet from the stationary saucer. When the door opened Amanda emerged with her teddy bear clutched in her arms. The president was there to meet her. It was the most-photographed arrival at the White House in the history of television. Every network on the globe carried Amanda's arrival live. The queen of England and Vladimir Putin didn't get a reception like this, nor did the president of China.

A band played lustily. Amanda waved to the cameras and federal employee gawkers as she walked across the red carpet through a double line of saluting soldiers, sailors and airmen standing at attention, the honor guard, to her grandfather, the president. She gave him a hug, kept a firm grip on the bear with her free arm and took his hand to walk into the White House. Halfway there they paused to examine the hovering saucer. Amanda pointed at some feature, the president nodded knowingly, and they resumed their stroll toward the Executive Mansion.

Reporters shouted questions, which the president and First Granddaughter ignored, yet Amanda let go of her grandfather's hand to wave. Then she again grasped the presidential appendage and they disappeared into the presidential mausoleum together.

The talking heads on television instantly began analyzing the Little Arrival. She had done it well, they agreed unanimously. The president looked relaxed, and everything seemed well in hand. Experts speculated about what saucer feature Amanda found interesting in light of the fact there were no obvious knobs or appendages protruding from that dark, perfect, ovoid shape.

Obviously the White House wasn't sweating First Contact with the aliens, the Big Arrival, and the rest of humanity shouldn't either. After all, they knew things at the White House that the rest of us didn't. Or so the commentators said.

Perhaps, one curmudgeon suggested on Fox, the Russians had shared what they knew about the aliens with the United States government. This comment led another iconoclast to wonder why the Russians knew more about the aliens than the good guys in the white hats. Away they went on this tangent. One network segued away to various politicians for their thoughts. A competitor network sent its crew across the street from the White House to Lafayette Park for man-in-the-street interviews, carefully ensuring that they got a diverse sample of ages, races, genders and airheads.

Another producer, more enterprising, aired a live interview with a group of old farts forted up in Idaho. The aliens were already here, their spokesman said, and were probably running the White House and Congress. That was the only logical explanation for the last ten years of political theater in Washington. The militia in Idaho shook their rifles at the cameras and flipped the world the bird.

In his office, P. J. O'Reilly nodded in silent agreement at the comments of the forted-up crazies in Idaho, then used his television remote to surf on to yet another network.

Jim Bob Spicer's face appeared on the screen, and his booming voice filled the room. "Washington is at the root of this *evil.* The wickedness of the sinners who inhabit this Sodom on the Potomac has dragged us to the edge of the pit. We must *repent* to earn salvation!" Spicer had more to say, a lot more.

There, P. J. O'Reilly thought, *is a truly poisonous man.* He had another snort from his Scotch bottle.

• • •

THE SOUND OF THE HELICOPTERS, FAINT AT FIRST BUT getting louder, alerted Charley, Rip and Uncle Egg. The sound began echoing from the cliffs of the great canyon and sounded somewhat like a percussion band gone mad.

Rip darted into the first room of the ancient cliff house and grabbed his old Winchester and the rest of his box of shells. He climbed to the top level of the house—it was only two stories—and knelt to look out a window. The first helicopter, an evil-looking Apache, circled some distance away.

Then he went back downstairs to join Charley and Egg. "What now, Ripper?"

"Better get that saucer here, Charley, if you can. We're going to need it."

"Take a while," Egg suggested.

"Better late than never."

Adam Solo dragged himself toward them. The bandage on his back, under his shirt, was leaking again, staining his shirt with blood.

"Just sit here," Charley said, helping him seat himself against a wall. "You should have stayed where you were."

"They want me," Solo said. "Or my body. If they kill me, throw my body into the canyon, then use the saucer to shoot them down."

Rip said nothing, merely checked that the Model 94

had a shell in the chamber and set the hammer on half-cock. He didn't take his eyes off the helicopter. It flew out of view to the right.

"They'll put people on the top of this little mesa," Charley told him. "They'll rappel down. When they're on the ropes, shoot 'em."

"Better to just scare them off until the saucer arrives," Egg advised. He was worried. Who knew how many thugs the Big Pharma guys had out there? How, he wondered, had the bad guys found them in this aerie? If the thugs were here, were the U.S. government's legions close by, coming fast?

Almost on cue, Rip said, "Those are Army or National Guard helicopters."

"Maybe these are the good guys," Egg said hopefully, his voice rising in pitch.

The Apache appeared again, this time from their right. Now a loudhailer could be heard. Amid the *whop-whop* echoes and exhaust noises, the words were hard to distinguish. ". . . Throw down your weapons and come out with your hands up . . . two minutes . . . we only want Solo . . . let you go."

"I didn't get all of that," Rip muttered.

"They just threatened to kill us all if we don't surrender," Charley Pine said acidly.

"Saucer on its way?"

"Oh yes."

Now they heard a chopper on the mesa directly behind them, just out of sight from the Anasazi ruin where they were.

"They're rappelling down," Charley shouted, because the engine and rotor noises were now very loud.

"Get your heads down," Rip roared and settled in with his rifle on the sill of the window. Almost as if he had planned it, the chopper turned so that he had a good look at the right engine nacelle. About a hundred yards, he figured.

He cocked the rifle, aimed and fired. The report was almost lost amid the noise. He worked the lever, chambering another round, and fired at the engine nacelle again. Then a third time.

The chopper accelerated away to their right with its tail up and nose down.

Rip and Charley saw it at the same time: a wisp of smoke trailing behind the machine, which climbed straight ahead for the rim of the canyon, perhaps three hundred yards away and several hundred yards above them.

Charley Pine pounded Rip on his back.

Her second slap missed. Rip rushed through the low door that led outside. He kept close to the adobe wall of the Anasazi house and worked his way to the corner of the ledge. It sounded as if one of the choppers were right over his head.

What, he wondered, if Uncle Egg was right? Could these be army dudes? What if he shot some soldier? How would he live with that?

Rip scanned the ledge above as the sound of the helicopter changed pitch. It sounded as if it were moving away . . .

He leaned out slightly to see if he could see it above the mesa . . . and a bullet smacked into the rock just inches from his head, spattering him with rock chips.

Holy . . . !

Rip launched himself flat on his stomach as another bullet smashed into the wall—right where his head had been.

He got behind a pile of old stones that had crumbled from an Anasazi tower and looked through a small gap in the stones with one eye, examining the edge of the rim. Two men were standing . . . one with binoculars, it looked like.

Then he saw the prone man, obviously behind a rifle.

A bullet struck the rock just in front of him and threw rock dust in his eyes. He curled up in a fetal position and rubbed his eyes, trying to clear his vision.

That took maybe twenty seconds. The helo above the mesa was gone now. Soon someone was going to come down the ropes, trying to get onto this ledge.

His eyes were blurry . . . He blinked mightily and rubbed them some more. Eased up to look through the gap in the stones.

The two guys were still standing there like a couple of tourists from Iowa seeing the big ditch for the first time.

Rip eased the rifle through the gap. Cocked it. Rested it right on the stone. He put the front bead on the man with the binoculars and lowered the rear of the rifle so the bead was sticking up a little in the notch.

Then he squeezed that old Model 94 off ever so gently. He knew the muzzle flash would give him away, so he ducked down and was pulling the rifle toward him when another bullet smashed into the rock right above him and whined away.

"I'M HIT! *I'M HIT! THE BASTARD SHOT ME!*" HARRISON Douglas fell to the snow clutching his right arm with his left hand. He looked down. Blood oozed between his fingers.

The prone shooter didn't look up. He had his cheek weld and was trying to reacquire the kid on the ledge. Lucky. The kid was lucky. He was bobbing and weaving and staying down, showing himself too briefly for the rifleman to get a shot.

As Douglas moaned, Johnny Murkowsky pounded on the rifleman's leg. "They told me you were good. Prove it! Get that kid! Get him, I say!"

"You wanta do the shootin', old man?"

Johnny Murk whacked him again. "That's your job, you Philadelphia moron. But if you keep missing, I might as well. Couldn't do any worse."

The sniper kicked Johnny Murk. As the mogul recoiled away, he settled back into position and looked again through his scope. Actually, his target—he never thought of people he was shooting at as people—had found a good position, by luck or happenstance or . . .

skill? The kid had made an excellent shot, 312 yards. Wounded his target but didn't kill; still, a fine shot for open sights.

Harrison Douglas lay writhing in the snow, which was three or four inches deep. His wound, bleeding from both the front and back of his arm, was beginning to hurt terribly. Maybe the bone was broken. He tried to move his hand and couldn't. He moaned softly. Johnny Murk and the rifleman ignored him.

AS HE LAY BEHIND THE PILE OF STONES, RIP CANTRELL reloaded his rifle. He filled up the tubular magazine and made sure he had a live round in the chamber. He left the rifle cocked.

He was safe here behind this rock pile, he thought. Safe enough, anyway. That sniper couldn't see him.

With the rifle reloaded and ready, he lay waiting, watching the ledge above him. They would have to come over that, he thought. Rappel over the edge and try to get onto this Anasazi ledge. There was only the narrowest of ledges leading away from the cliff dwelling behind him, a path so narrow that only a suicidal fool would try it. The far end of the ledge ended in a sheer wall; a great slab of the old rock had slipped away sometime in the ancient past, carrying the old Indian trail, if there had been one, with it into the great canyon.

"Come on," he whispered. "Come and get it."

A bullet slapped into the rock above him. Then, fifteen

seconds later, another. They were trying to make him keep his head down. The bad guys were coming . . .

Above him, a rope came snaking out into space, then fell to hang vertically. Then a second one, a bit closer to the sniper. Then a third.

16

ADAM SOLO WAS OVERWHELMED BY THE MOMENT. ALL his long life had led to this: He was dying, and these three earth people were risking their lives for him anyway. The flat crack of Rip's .25-35 Winchester had died away, as had the booming reports of whoever was shooting at him. The sound of the bullets smacking into the rock was quite audible here in this sanctuary.

"I'm dying," he whispered to Egg Cantrell, who was checking his bandages.

"We all are," Egg shot back. "Sooner or later."

"I'm a sooner."

"Charley," Egg said. The female test pilot rose from her position at the window and came over to where Egg was tending to Solo. "How much longer until the saucer gets here?"

"Perhaps ten minutes. I don't know exactly, Uncle Egg. It's on its way, I think."

"What are you going to do with it when it arrives?"

"I'm going to use the antimatter weapon on these poor, misguided fools. Introduce them to the wages of sin."

"You are going to kill them," Egg said flatly.

Charley's head bobbed affirmatively. "They are going to find out rather quickly if there is life after death."

"Charley, Charley, Charley . . ." Adam Solo whispered. "I've killed a lot of men. All were trying to kill me. But I've had to carry it for all these years. Sometimes at night I can see their faces, see their death agonies, hear their screams. After all these years."

"I'm not going to live as long as you have," Charley said, frowning. "What do you want us to do? Let them kill us? Take your body away and dissect it so those fools can get filthy rich making eternal-life pills? *I don't think so.*"

Solo swallowed three or four times. His mouth seemed unnaturally dry. "I hope Rip understands the quality of his lady."

"By God," she said fiercely, "he'd better."

AFTER THE THREE ROPES CAME OVER THE OVERHANG, Rip waited expectantly. His hands were sweaty despite the cool temperature of the day. The sun shone brightly on the ropes, a nice contrast to the shadow under the overhanging cliff. Rip didn't notice. Nor did he pay much attention to the spectacular view, the vastness of the canyon, the shadows and sunlight on the rocks, or the narrow gorge far away and below where the river ran hidden from sight. He waited for the ropes to twitch, to show that someone was hooking up to them.

They hung lifeless, stirred only by the gentle breeze.

A sound behind him—he turned and pointed the rifle all in one motion. A man was there on that narrow ledge, and Rip was just a split second faster. He merely pointed the rifle and pulled the trigger.

The impact of the bullet made a whacking sound as it hit the man chest-high. The man teetered for a second, trying to regain his balance as Rip worked the lever. He didn't need another shot. The gunman toppled over the edge and fell, his submachine gun hammering. He was twenty or thirty feet down when Rip realized that the man must have been wearing a bulletproof vest. Still, the impact of the .25 caliber bullet had pushed him off the ledge to his death.

Rip didn't watch the man hit hundreds of feet below. He was already concentrating on the ropes.

The far one. A pair of feet came into view. Rip aimed at a foot, snugged that front bead down into the notch and squeezed the trigger. A scream. Now the man's crotch and torso fell into view. He was slipping on the rope, which apparently went through a carabiner ring. Didn't have the strength to hold on. Down he came, his submachine gun dangling uselessly.

The man on the rope fought to regain control. Another bulletproof vest. No, he couldn't hold on to the rope, which ran through the ring until the man hit the end of the rope and kept on going.

A bullet tagged Rip on his neck. He whirled and fell on his back. It stung like hell, and he couldn't move his head.

He reached and felt—couldn't help himself. His hand came back bloody. Well, if the slug severed a vein he was going to pass out in seconds and bleed to death.

He didn't. Gritted his teeth and said a few dirty words he knew while watching the ropes.

That damn sniper!

Maybe he thought he killed me. Or disabled me. I went down pretty quick.

Here they came, two more men down the ropes. He didn't wait but shot them when their legs came into view. One man lost his grip and went zipping down the rope into space. The other hung on for dear life. When he got stabilized, he tried to get his submachine gun into action. Rip hesitated—if he wasn't careful he was going to run out of bullets—and was rewarded with a shower of slugs that he miraculously avoided by rolling behind a rock.

The fool used his entire magazine, spraying slugs without a target. Rip risked a peek. The guy was dangling there and trying to change magazines with one hand. He was only perhaps fifty feet from Rip now.

"You have a choice," Rip called. "You can tell them to haul you up or I'll shoot you again. Which will it be?"

The guy dropped the submachine gun and it dangled on a strap. His leg was turning red. Maybe an artery severed. He spoke into a mike arranged on some sort of helmet, and the people on top began hauling up the rope.

If the guy doesn't pass out before they pull him up, maybe he'll live, Rip thought. He did pass out, though. Lots of blood on the injured leg. He lost his grip and began sliding down the rope, faster and faster. He was in free fall when he ran out of rope.

He hit about two hundred feet below on the scree fan and began rolling. Rip closed his eyes and felt his neck. *Ai yi yi.*

JOHNNY MURK'S SATELLITE TELEPHONE RANG. HE looked at the number. The Space Command spy.

"Yeah."

"Mr. Murkowsky, that saucer is coming back. It's reentering the atmosphere, and from its trajectory, it looks like it's headed right for the Grand Canyon."

"When?"

"Eight minutes or so."

Murkowsky broke the connection without saying another word. He kicked the sniper. "Their saucer is eight minutes away and coming fast. Better start shooting or we're all going to end up poor."

The sniper opened fire, sending a fusillade toward the old Anasazi ruin even though he had no targets.

"THIS IS PETTY OFFICER HENNESSEY," THE PRESIDENT said, introducing the sailor, who was in his blue uniform with his red chevron on his left sleeve.

"Are you a Boy Scout?" Amanda asked.

"No," Hennessey replied with a smile. "I'm in the navy."

"Oh," she said.

"I used to be in the Boy Scouts, though."

Amanda, the First Granddaughter, was comfortably ensconced in the Oval Office with a plate containing a half-dozen Fig Newtons, her favorite cookies, and a glass of milk.

She turned her attention to her grandfather. "I am so excited. This is so cool! People from outer space. Coming here. When will they arrive?"

"In a day or two," the president replied evasively. The truth was, he had no idea. The starship was in orbit, NASA said, but if the intergalactic voyagers were trying to communicate, no one had told him about it. Nor had he any idea what they were doing up there circling the earth, or indeed, what their plans were. Maybe they would go to Paris to eat snails after all.

"I'll bet they get here tomorrow in time for lunch," Amanda said and picked up another Fig Newton. She dipped it in her milk and began nibbling. "Is that their saucer parked out there?"

"I don't know that either," the president admitted. He thought it probable the aliens were saucer people, but who knew? Maybe there were dozens of civilizations all over the universe sending starships out to explore willy-nilly.

The president certainly hoped they were saucer people. When he and Amanda took their saucer ride with Charley Pine last month, she told him the computer interface was designed for human brains. Or humanlike brains.

The archaeologist, Professor Hans Soldi, became famous when Rip Cantrell discovered his saucer in the Sahara by arguing with force that the saucer people might well be ancestors of the people here on earth today. That had caused a sensation, of course, and to date, as far as the president knew, no one had successfully refuted Soldi's idea. Still, although plausible, Soldi's theory remained just that, a theory.

Nevertheless, in the presidential mind Soldi's theory and the fact that Rip and Charley and even Egg Cantrell had all successfully flown not only Rip's saucer but the one recovered in Roswell, New Mexico, and secretly stored in Area 51, seemed to make it probable, indeed, likely, that the saucer pilots were people, more or less like us.

More or less. Ye Gods . . .

"Can I go aboard the spaceship when it comes and see what's what?" Amanda asked. "Oh, I do hope they bring kids about my age. It'll be such fun showing them around."

The president looked beseechingly at Petty Officer Hennessey. *Do something,* his look said. Hennessey obliged. He began asking Amanda about her school and her friends.

Hennessey was still at it when P. J. O'Reilly rushed in with some eight-by-ten photos in his hands. "Mr. President, here are some photos of that starship in orbit that were taken with very-long-lens cameras."

Everyone gathered around the president's desk to look. The starship resembled a giant doughnut. It had a central core and spokes that led out to the ring. Six spokes.

Above the central core some sort of thing was attached that looked a bit like a blimp.

"Hmm," said the president. "How big is it?"

P. J. O'Reilly rubbed his hands. "The thing is over a mile in diameter, Mr. President. According to the people at NASA. It should be visible as a bright star right after dark and before dawn."

"A mile?" the president muttered skeptically.

"It's big, bigger than any transportation vehicle ever designed or built on this planet. NASA thinks it could hold something like ten thousand people."

"Wow!" Amanda said. "We are gonna have a party!"

"Of course," O'Reilly continued, enjoying the look of distress on the president's face, "it could be full of troops. They may have come here to conquer the world."

"By God," the president said heavily, "if they can balance the federal budget they can have this piece of it."

Petty Officer Hennessey snorted. "More than likely," he said, "that thing is full of scientists and college professors dying to find something super to spin theories about."

The president eyed Hennessey and smiled his gratitude.

"Should we release copies of these photos to the press?" O'Reilly asked.

The president hesitated, eying Hennessey, who nodded.

"Go ahead," the president said, "and get the staff on the phones. We need some scientists of our own to welcome these folks. Or things. Or whatever. Get Professor Soldi and ask him for recommendations. Biologists, anthropologists, linguists, astronomers, a delegation of NASA engineers, anyone you can think of."

"Some congressmen and senators want to attend," O'Reilly pointed out.

"No damn politicians," the president said and smacked the table.

"How about some teachers?" Amanda piped up. She wasn't the least bit frightened of her grandfather.

"Certainly, teachers. O'Reilly, invite a bunch from around Washington and the suburbs. Elementary, middle school and high school." The Grand Poobah made a gesture, and O'Reilly shot out of the room. He left the photos.

"Boy, oh boy, oh," Amanda enthused as she examined each picture. "The kids in my class are going to be sooo jealous."

Hennessey looked at the president and the president looked at him. They nodded.

Hennessey left the room to find someone who would make the calls to invite Amanda's entire fourth-grade class to Washington.

RIP CANTRELL HEARD THE MUTED ROAR OF THE rocket engines before he saw the saucer. It was high, perhaps ten degrees above the far canyon rim, coming quickly, now without power. Silent and coasting. It looked as if it were headed straight for the cliff house. In fact, he wondered if it might not be able to stop before crashing into it, but indeed it did stop. Maybe a hundred feet away.

He heard Charley calling his name.

"Yeah." The word came out hoarse. His throat hurt fiercely.

"Look at the sniper's location. Just look at it, think about it."

Rip rolled over and crawled to the slit in the rock pile that he had used to shoot at the sniper's group. No one standing there erect now, of course.

The sniper had to be there, though. Or close by. Rip stared. *There,* he thought. *There.*

His peripheral vision caught the saucer turning and moving, going right for the spot where he was looking. A beam much like a child's sparkler, only straight and fierce, illuminated the place. That was the saucer's antimatter weapon, which spewed forth antimatter particles that obliterated atoms of normal matter when they encountered them. Yet for every one that self-destructed, a million continued on . . . Rip saw sparks—little flashes that looked like sparks—around the area where he thought the sniper was concealed.

He took that opportunity to haul himself erect. Bracing himself on the wall of the old stone house, moving carefully toward the door, he tried to keep his eyes on the sniper's position. He gave up when he reached the door. He fell through the opening, landing right at Charley's feet. She didn't look at him. She was staring through the door at an oblique angle at the impact point of the antimatter weapon.

THE ANTIMATTER PARTICLES THAT SMASHED INTO the area around the cliff's edge penetrated everything until they hit a regular particle and exploded in a small burst of pure energy. $E = MC^2$. They buzz-sawed through trees and rocks and dirt; bits of wood and rock and dirt flew everywhere. They also went through the sniper—an antimatter particle met its opposite number in his brain. The explosion killed him instantly.

Dr. Harrison Douglas was lying behind a rock trying to tie a piece of his shirt around his wounded arm. The antimatter particles penetrated the rock, and he died after explosions in his lungs, kidneys and heart.

Johnny Murkowsky avoided being wounded by the shower of antimatter particles. Dozens went through him without obliterating themselves. It was just the sheer dumb luck that sometimes protects fools and morons.

He gripped his submachine gun tightly and waited for the assault to stop. It did, finally, and he eased his head out from behind a stone where he was cowering in time to observe the saucer turning and climbing, heading for the top of the mesa where the Philly boys were hunkered down and shooting assault rifles at the saucer.

Oh, too bad, too bad! They were so close.

Damn that Charley Pine. Damn Rip Cantrell. And damn Adam Solo. Just a lock of hair was all we needed. Just a lock of hair.

• • •

AS UNCLE EGG SLAPPED A RAG ON RIP'S NECK AND EXamined the bullet wound, Rip heard some kind of rocket exhaust amid the staccato hammering of assault rifles firing bursts.

Charley Pine saw something strike the saucer and explode. It had no visible effect on the ship. She also saw sparks all over it—no doubt bullets from the top-of-the-mesa crowd.

She ordered the ship to turn and use the antimatter beam on the people and machines on top of the mesa. Climbing and turning, the saucer soared back toward the mesa above the ledge where the cliff house stood. Now she saw the flashes along the leading edge where the antimatter was pouring from the weapon, then saw the beam of smoke and flashes reach toward the top of the mesa. The particles traveled at the speed of light, so the river of them resembled a searchlight. On, then off, then on again. Finally off.

Charley heard an explosion that sounded as if it came from atop the mesa. A helicopter blowing up, perhaps? Or one of its weapons detonating?

"Charley, did you get the sniper?" Rip asked.

For the first time Charley glanced down and saw that Rip was bleeding on the right side of his neck. Egg's rag was becoming sodden with blood.

"What—?"

"Bullet grazed him," Egg said. "Not hurt badly, I think.

But boy, Ripper, when we get the bleeding stopped, your neck is going to be stiff and sore."

Egg tore up the last T-shirt and used it as a bandage.

"Did you get the sniper?" Rip asked again.

"I don't know."

Finished with Rip, Egg checked on Adam Solo's condition. He looked haggard, and his face had lines. The entry and exit bullet wounds were still leaking.

"Solo needs a doctor, and he needs one now," Egg stated. "Let's get aboard the saucer and go find one."

"Okay," Charley said, turning back to the window.

"How are we going to do this?"

"Same way we got here. We're going to ride on top. Let's get ready. I'm bringing it around."

Rip hoisted himself erect and gripped his rifle fiercely. He paused and ensured he had a live shell in the chamber and shoved two more shells into the magazine. He only had a few cartridges left in his pocket.

Egg helped Solo, who could scarcely stand. Rip draped the other arm over his shoulder, and the two men moved Solo to the door.

Thank you. Egg, Rip and Charley heard the unspoken words in their head.

Charley brought the saucer close to the edge of the cliff, turned it around and backed it up until the rocket nozzles were resting right against the stone.

They charged out, Charley in the lead. She climbed onto the saucer's back and helped Uncle Egg and Rip get Solo aboard. "Don't look down, people," she warned.

Once again, Egg was struck with how precarious their position was on top of the mounded-up saucer shape, with nothing to hang on to except the now-dry, smooth, warm, dark surface of the spaceship. In other words, nothing at all. As they lay down and spread themselves, the saucer began to move, gently, almost imperceptibly.

As they moved away from the cliff, Egg scrunched his eyes tightly shut.

He opened them again when he heard the thumps of bullets hitting the ship and the zings of bullets flying off. Then the reports. Someone was shooting an automatic weapon at the saucer.

"Assault rifle," Rip shouted and raised his head to see where the fire was coming from. *Whump, whump, whump,* and howling whines as the bullets ricocheted away. "Climb, Charley! Show them the belly."

"I can't. We can't climb any higher without the rockets. We'll fall off."

Rip scanned the top of the mesa. Saw no one. Then he looked toward the place the sniper had been on the rim. Saw a man standing there . . . muzzle flashes.

The guy was no marksman. He squirted another magazine full of bullets at the saucer, and maybe half of them struck.

When the guy emptied his weapon, Rip got to his knees and cut loose with the Winchester as fast as he could work the lever.

"Go at him, Charley," he shouted. "Fast as you can."

Adam Solo writhed uncontrollably.

A feeling of intense pain shot through Rip, Charley and Uncle Egg. Horrible pain. Egg almost lost his grip on the saucer as he groaned.

Adam Solo began to slip. Slowly he went down the side of the saucer toward the edge. The pain paralyzed Rip. He could do nothing but watch helplessly as Solo slid to the edge and went over without even trying to arrest his descent.

Someday I'll see you on the other side.

Then the pain stopped.

Shaken, without thinking, Rip pulled two more shells from his pocket, stuffed them into the rifle, worked the lever and took careful aim as the saucer closed the distance to the rim of the canyon. A hundred yards now, then seventy, then fifty. The guy showed himself and Rip fired. Knocked him off his feet.

Charley had the saucer moving at perhaps twenty knots. The cold wind was in their faces.

The saucer crossed the rim and bore down on the shooter, who was struggling to scuttle away.

Rip recognized the man. Johnny Murkowsky.

Johnny Murk screamed as the saucer approached. He disappeared under the nose and the scream stopped abruptly.

Now Charley brought the saucer to a stop and lowered the landing pads.

It sank to the ground. "Come on, Uncle Egg," she said. "Let's get inside. Rip, watch for anyone who wants another shot at us."

They scrambled down, and Charley went under the saucer to open the hatch.

Rip saw what was left of Johnny Murkowsky, squashed like a road-killed squirrel. As he scanned about, he saw Harrison Douglas' corpse and the body of a man in a camo outfit lying in blood-spattered snow. A bolt-action rifle with a scope lay beside him. That was probably the sniper. They were obviously dead, no doubt victims of the antimatter weapon. He saw no one else.

Rip was the last to crawl through the hatch. He pulled it shut and latched it.

Charley adjusted the headband in the pilot's seat.

"They killed Solo," Rip said. "Why did he have to die like that?"

"He was dying anyway, and he knew it," Egg said flatly. "I think he intentionally let go up there. Did you feel that pain?"

"Yes," Rip said, trying to hold back his tears.

Charley sat for a long moment with her head in her hands.

After a bit she felt Rip's hands on her shoulder. She looked up and saw that he had tears streaking his face.

"We can't leave his body in that canyon," Egg said.

Charley Pine nodded and the saucer lifted off.

They swung around over the mesa and examined the carnage. Indeed, one helicopter had blown up. Bodies lay scattered about in the thin snow. Charley eased the saucer over every body she saw, squashing them in the saucer's antigravity field, just in case someone was playing possum. She was feeling rather vengeful just then.

In the first shelf, a thousand feet below the rim, they found Adam Solo's body. Charley had to proceed for several hundred yards before she found a flat place to park the saucer. All three of them hiked back to the body. Solo's head was smashed, and shards of bone protruded from his clothing. He had obviously hit the scree fan and rolled for hundreds of yards.

The cliff above them seemed to rise into infinity. Behind them was the mesa with the small shelf that contained the old Anasazi cliff house. They could just see the front of it from here. The canyon was silent except for the whisper of the wind. The rock faces and flats were broken by stark sunlight and shadows; sunlight glistened on the snow on the rims. Above them in the cerulean blue two hawks soared.

Without a word, the three of them picked up Adam Solo and carried him in stages to the saucer. They shoved the body up through the hatch as gently as possible, then climbed aboard themselves.

"Do you want to give his body to the aliens?" Charley asked the two men.

"No," Rip said. "A volcano, I think."

"That's right," Egg muttered. "This planet was his adopted home. We'll keep him here."

They fueled the saucer in Lake Mead. An hour after the battle in the canyon, the saucer rose on a column of white-hot fire and the roar of the rocket engines washed over Las Vegas and the revelers who packed it. The exhaust plume gradually faded to a burning speck in the sky, then to a star, then winked out altogether. The echo of its engines also faded, more slowly, until finally the murmur was also gone.

In Las Vegas, the party resumed.

17

THE FLIGHT BACK FROM THE VOLCANO ON THE ISLAND of Hawaii gave Charley Pine plenty of time to think. She again tapped into Solo's memories that were embedded in the saucer's computer. She saw Solo as an Indian, killing enemy wounded and the wounded of his own tribe who were too grievously hurt to travel. Too grievously hurt to survive. She saw him gun German airplanes in World War I, saw them fall in flames, and felt his emotions. She forgave him. Forgave him everything.

It was after midnight when she landed the saucer in front of Egg's hangar in Missouri and Rip dropped through the hatch to open the hangar door. Inside, she set the saucer down and secured the power. She and Egg eased themselves through the hatch.

Rip closed the door, and the trio climbed the hill to Egg's house. Turned on lights. Egg busied himself in the kitchen making a meal. Rip went upstairs, found another box of cartridges, filled the Winchester's magazine and his pockets, grabbed an empty grocery bag and trekked off to Egg's mailbox by the front gate. It was full. In the darkness of a Missouri night, listening to the night sounds, alert for anything, Rip emptied the mailbox into the sack and walked along the road through the woods back to the house.

In addition to all the usual mail, there were dozens of letters from children addressed to Adam Solo, in care of Arthur Cantrell. Rip and Charley read a few of them, then had to quit. Their emotions were too raw.

After a quiet, subdued meal, the three of them went to bed. Charley found she wanted and needed Rip badly. With his rifle propped against the dresser, they made love and fell asleep in each other's arms.

P. J. O'REILLY BRIEFED THE PRESIDENT ABOUT THE saucer going into orbit from Lake Mead. The National Guard in Phoenix had had two helicopters stolen the day before, and they were seen on the ramp of the Grand Canyon Airport when a chartered 747 dropped the pharmaceutical titans. The president told him to have the National Park Service look around the canyon when the sun came up.

Just before he went to bed, the president was told about the saucer arriving in Hawaii and soon departing. An aide woke him up later to inform him the saucer was back in Missouri at Egg Cantrell's farm.

The president lay in the darkness thinking about things. He suspected the pharma moguls had been outmaneuvered and perhaps outfought by Rip Cantrell and Charley Pine. Now there was a pair to draw to. It seemed logical to the president that those two thought Douglas and Murkowsky were no longer threats or they wouldn't be hiding in plain sight at the Cantrell farm. Along with Adam Solo. The self-proclaimed alien. The guy who stole the Roswell saucer after it was raised from the Atlantic, stole it right from under Harrison Douglas' nose.

He reviewed the few moments he had spent with Adam Solo . . . what, ten days ago? It seemed like ten years. Yet he remembered that humorless face, the eyes that bored right into you, almost as if the guy were reading your thoughts. Solo . . . the guy who got the whole world fired up.

A pox on him!

Ah me.

When are these damned aliens going to arrive? The spring is getting wound tighter and tighter. That starship is circling the earth, almost every whacko, nutcase, screwball and nincompoop who doesn't live near Washington is on his way here, the politicians are over the edge of sanity promising their constituents a Fountain of Youth pill . . . and the people most responsible for this state of affairs are probably in bed in Missouri sleeping like babies.

As it happened, he was right about the sleeping.

LATE THE NEXT MORNING UNCLE EGG, RIP AND CHARLEY awoke to the sound of rain on the windows. They snuggled a while in bed, then finally dressed and went downstairs. The smell of coffee and bacon frying assaulted them as they descended the stairs. Uncle Egg was busy, busy, busy, wearing an apron and wielding a spatula.

Rip leaned his rifle in a corner; then he and Charley dived into fried eggs and potatoes, bacon and sausage. There was no bread. Egg apologized. The bread had gone moldy and he had thrown it out for the squirrels and birds.

The television in the corner blared away. The White House had announced that the people in the starship had talked to them and were going to land tomorrow, the announcer said. The president, the first granddaughter, and all the members of her fourth-grade class, plus a delegation of scientists, would meet the intergalactic voyagers. Tomorrow, the announcer assured his audience, would be the most historic day in the history of the planet. Tomorrow.

Rip finished his breakfast and went over to the coffeepot for a refill.

"Too bad Adam Solo won't be around to see it," Rip said sadly.

Uncle Egg paused in his kitchen duties and watched the raindrops smear the kitchen window. After a moment, he shook his head and went back to scrubbing a frying pan. From where she sat at the counter Charley Pine could see that he was weeping.

"Hey, you two," she said. "Adam Solo lived a long life, a life filled with living and love and adventure. Stop the moping: He would tell you that. He told you that someday he would see us on the other side. Let's rejoice. All of us will come to our end eventually, and after that . . . well, he had faith. We should too."

Egg swabbed at his eyes. Rip put his coffee cup on the counter and hugged Charley. "Yeah," he said. "Yeah."

Egg dried his hands on a towel and said, "I'm thinking of going to town. Going to visit the local television station and tell them what happened in the Grand Canyon. Tell the world that Solo is dead."

Rip nodded his concurrence. "Someone is going to find that shot-up chopper and those bodies on the mesa before long," he mused. "Might be better getting our version out there before the FBI swoops down and arrests us."

"Charley?" Egg asked. "What do you think?"

"Better put on a tie and jacket, Uncle Egg. We'll hold the fort and watch you on the tube."

So Egg suited up, got into his pickup and drove away.

Charley poured herself another cup of coffee and began opening random letters to Solo. After reading two or three, she passed them to Rip with the comment, "Someone should answer these."

"Let's each pick one to answer," Rip suggested. "Then I need to refuel the saucer and clean it out, just in case we have to boogie again."

Charley took back a letter from a girl who said she was twelve years old. She wanted to know how Solo liked living on earth, and if he was looking forward to going home.

With paper and a pen, Charley sat for a moment composing her thoughts, then wrote:

Dear Sophie,

I am writing to you in answer to your letter to Adam Solo, who died yesterday. I got to know him well in the few days we spent together, so I think I know how he might have answered you.

He was marooned here on earth many centuries ago. I think he not only came to appreciate the people of earth and their accomplishments, I think he grew to love them. He was naturally optimistic. Life, he thought, was a grand adventure, and he certainly lived it that way. I hope you will too.

Sincerely,
Charlotte Pine

CHARLEY WAS STILL ANSWERING LETTERS AN HOUR later when Rip scampered into the kitchen and turned on Egg's counter television and flipped the channel to the one he wanted.

There was Uncle Egg. The caption below his visage read ARTHUR CANTRELL.

The local host was wise enough to stay out of the picture and merely let Egg tell it, which he did. About Adam Solo coming to the farm, about the president and the Big Pharma moguls, about Canada and Australia and the Grand Canyon.

Uncle Egg described the battle of the canyon in detail.

He gave Charley and Rip all the credit. He explained about burying Adam Solo, who fell to his death after being shot again by Johnny Murkowsky, in a cauldron of molten lava in the Kilauea volcano on the island of Hawaii.

When Egg ran out of things to say—the interview took forty-five minutes—the off-camera questioner prodded him on his thoughts about the aliens' visit tomorrow to Washington. Egg begged off. "I am not the one to comment on that," he said. "The event will speak for itself."

That was about it.

Rip flipped channels and found that the networks had shared the feed from the Missouri small-town station. Fox was running the entire interview a second time.

Rip turned the television off and sat staring at his toes.

"What are you thinking, Ripper?"

"I think the comfortable little world you and I grew up in is gone forever," he said slowly. "I am not sure whether that's good or bad. I'm going to miss it, though."

"Don't be such a pessimist," Charley shot back.

The doorbell rang. Rip glanced out the kitchen window. "It's a television crew." He snatched up the Winchester, checked that there was a round in the chamber and went to open the front door.

"Mr. Cantrell," the female reporter said as a male with a camera on his shoulder stood so he could get them both in the picture, "we're with WXYZ-TV. I wonder if you would be so good as to show us your saucer?"

Rip glanced over his shoulder at Charley, who was

standing behind him in the kitchen doorway. She shrugged.

"Sure," he said without enthusiasm. "It's in the hangar. Follow me." He led them down the hill on the path he had trod since he was a boy.

THE PRESIDENT WAS HASTILY SUMMONED FROM A CABinet meeting by P. J. O'Reilly to watch the Arthur Cantrell interview on television. The president motioned Petty Officer Third Class Hennessey to sit beside him, and together they watched Uncle Egg.

"So Solo's dead," the president murmured.

"And Johnny Murkowsky and Harrison Douglas," O'Reilly said. He passed the president a message from the Department of the Interior. One stolen National Guard helicopter had been found damaged and abandoned at the Grand Canyon Airport. The totally destroyed carcass of the other was on top of a mesa in the canyon. There were six bodies on the ground near the shattered chopper, four more in the canyon and three on a nearby rim. Many of the bodies were flattened "like road-killed possums." Lots of weapons lying around. Preliminary indications were most of the men were thugs from a Philadelphia Mafia family. Murkowsky had been flattened, and Douglas was dead of apparent massive internal injuries.

The president handed the message back and concentrated on Egg Cantrell's image. Listened. Watched his face. Wondered what he was leaving out.

When the interview was over, this network went back to a graphic feed from NASA that showed the current location of the starship in orbit. It was currently leaving the Indian peninsula, ninety-six miles above the surface of the planet. The president sat watching the blinking symbol as it moved, almost as if he were mesmerized. Finally O'Reilly turned off the television with the remote.

"These aliens might be a bit unhappy tomorrow if they think they are going to rescue their castaway, Solo, from the cannibals," O'Reilly said pointedly.

"Bad news rides a fast horse," Hennessey observed. "Bet they know as much as we do right now. They'll have until tomorrow to digest it. I doubt if it will be a problem. The United States government didn't kill Solo—criminals did."

The nation's chief magistrate shook his head, as if he were clearing his thoughts. "So how are we coming on the welcoming ceremony tomorrow?" he asked O'Reilly.

"We're doing an honor guard walk-though. The kids and teachers and scientists won't be here until later this evening. The television networks are setting up cameras and lights. Beyoncé has volunteered to sing the national anthem . . . for free."

The president made a noise. "She'd probably be underdressed for this," he said sourly. "This isn't the Super Bowl. No singers."

"Do you want the honor guard to have loaded weapons, just in case?"

"Holy catfish, O'Reilly! Are you nuts? These people

just crossed interstellar space, for God's sake. They didn't come all this way to gun down people on the White House lawn in front of every camera on earth!"

"You hope they are people."

"You're damn right I hope. I don't care if they turn out to be giant green beetles, we're going to do it my way! *I'm* the president!"

"Yes, Your Magnificence."

"What?" asked the surprised Hennessey.

"Forget it," the president said and shooed O'Reilly away. When the door closed behind the chief of staff, the president explained to Hennessey. "He thinks he should be president and I should be running an Ace Hardware selling nuts and bolts."

"Oh."

"My dad was in hardware. Wish I'd taken his advice and helped him with the store instead of getting into politics. Oh, well, all that's water under the bridge now."

"I see . . ."

"Have any suggestions?" the president asked the Oklahoma sailor.

"Maybe you should ask the Cantrells and Charley Pine to fly their saucer here in the morning. Seems like a good opportunity to return these saucers to their rightful owners. Get rid of them once and for all."

The president thought that the best advice he had heard in years.

He snagged the telephone on the desk and spoke to

the White House operator. "Get me Arthur Cantrell's residence, Toad Summit, Missouri." The telephone operators in the White House were justly famous for getting anybody anywhere on the line when the president wanted to chat.

The president hung up and waited for the operators to work their magic. Thought about getting rid of all these saucers. Of life getting back to political backstabbing, scurrilous lies and shady deals. Of nothing more on the morning plate than Islamic jihadists and the euro crisis, Chinese ambitions and nuclear weapons in North Korea and Iran. Normal. The president longed for normal.

"Want a drink?" he asked Hennessey.

"One surely wouldn't hurt," Hennessey said with a smile.

The president got his bourbon bottle from his desk drawer and poured into two glasses. He didn't have any ice. Hennessey didn't seem to care.

When the phone rang, the operator told him she had Charlotte Pine on the line.

"Ms. Pine, this is the president. How are you?"

"Fine, sir."

"Mr. Egg around?"

"No. He went to town for a television interview and hasn't yet returned."

"Yes, I watched that interview. Too bad about Dr. Douglas and Johnny Murkowsky."

"And Adam Solo."

"Indeed. A tragedy."

"Those cretins attacked us and we defended ourselves. Are we going to get any flak about that?"

"Not from the federal government, Ms. Pine. I can't speak for the Arizona authorities, but I imagine they have better things to do than hassle you folks about dead pill pushers and Mafia soldiers."

"Let's hope," she said coolly.

"The reason I called," the president said smoothly, for he was a smooth man, "is to invite you, Rip and Arthur Cantrell to fly your saucer to Washington tomorrow. You can land it right here on the lawn. It would be terrific if you could get here about eleven so we can have time to chat before the aliens arrive. They said they'd show up about noon, in time for lunch."

"How did you hear from them?"

"Well, it's sort of weird. Actually, very weird. I just heard this voice in my head. I said 'Hello' out loud and we talked. So either I'm going crazy, which my wife and the pundits have predicted for years, or that was a real communication."

"It was real communication, all right. They read your thoughts. Did you say lunch? Uncle Egg would like that. We've been on a very low-cal diet this past week."

"Indeed. Lunch it is," the president said. "See you tomorrow."

When the president hung up, Hennessey flashed him a thumbs-up.

The president also jabbed a thumb at the sky.

Yeah! Gonna get rid of all these saucers. Yeah!

As the president sat in the Oval Office with his drink, he tried to digest Charley Pine's statement that the aliens read thoughts. His thoughts. Holy smokes! If he looked at an alien female with lust in his heart, like Jimmy Carter, she would know it. The polite lie would go the way of the Model T. How would politicians function? Lawyers? Marriage counselors? Priests? Lovers? Adulterers?

The people of earth, he decided, probably weren't ready for that method of communication, which would bankrupt Apple and all the other cell phone manufacturers, plus the telephone companies and the spavined postal service, already on its last legs. The postal and communications workers unions would go nuts.

The future was arriving way too fast.

"Here's to mendacity," he said to Petty Officer Hennessey, then raised his glass and drank.

"SO DO WE SALLY FORTH TO WASHINGTON IN THE morning?" Uncle Egg asked Rip and Charley. He had stopped at the supermarket in town for a load of fresh groceries and was now grilling three steaks. They were sizzling nicely, which reminding him of the fresh fish they and Adam Solo had roasted on sticks in the old Viking hideaway beside Hudson's Bay. Of course, Charley had complimented him on his television interview and told him and Rip about her telephone conversation with the president and his invitation.

Rip was drinking a beer. "Why not?" he asked. "Gotta

confess, I'm curious about Solo's people. Would be fun to meet them up close and personal. Just to say we did."

"My concern is," said Charley Pine, "what are we going to do afterward?" She was having a glass of white wine.

"Do you mean immediately, or in the larger sense?" Rip asked, scrutinizing her face.

"Good question, Charley," Egg said, and turned over the steaks as he talked. "After you've had the world's greatest adventure, indeed, where do you go from here?"

"Precisely," Charley agreed.

Rip shook his head as he eyed his lady. "Did you see the size of those royalty checks that came in the mail from the computer people? We can ski down an Alp, canoe down the Amazon, camp out under a bridge in Paris, stalk man-eating lions in darkest Africa, or sail the Pacific in our own yacht. Or all of the above."

Charley Pine gave Rip the Look. "Maybe I'll just go get a real flying job," she said and strode away toward the kitchen to refill her glass.

"Guess we do have a problem, Uncle," Rip said thoughtfully.

"Looks like it."

"One we aren't going to be able to solve today. So tomorrow morning let's pack clean underwear and toothbrushes and saucer off to Washington to watch our representative democratic government in action. The day after tomorrow is going to have to take care of itself."

"If you still like your steaks medium rare, yours is ready," Egg said.

"I still do," Rip replied. "I'll get a plate." He rushed off for the kitchen.

Egg Cantrell shook his head. Well, Rip and Charley had their own lives to lead—and they were going to have to figure out how to do it. Just like the rest of us.

Rip came back with his plate and a telephone, which he offered to his uncle. "It's your girlfriend," he said with a smile. "Professor Deehring. She saw your interview. Poor woman thought you looked handsome."

18

THE FOLLOWING MORNING, THE MOST HISTORIC DAY in the history of the world according to a talking head on a network morning show, Charley Pine busied herself filing a flight plan for the saucer while Uncle Egg fixed pancakes and sausage. She hadn't been filing flight plans for saucer flights and had found a nasty letter in the mail from the FAA threatening to revoke her pilot's license. In her reply last night she had pointed out that flying saucers were not aircraft, which might stump the bureaucrats. For a little while, anyway.

Just to be on the safe side, this morning she called Flight Service and filed an instrument flight plan. Missouri direct to the White House. By presidential invitation. They could check.

Flight Service gave her some radio frequencies so she could talk to Air Traffic Control. Charley told the Flight Service dude when she was leaving and roughly how high she would fly: well above controlled airspace. The guy got rather hostile over the fact her craft didn't have a radar transponder. She replied haughtily that transponders were not required equipment in flying saucers, then hung up before the conversation could deteriorate further.

After breakfast the trio took their small overnight bags, locked the house and trooped down the long hill to the hangar. Rip opened the door. The rising sun spotlighted the saucer, which didn't look as ominous as it usually did. Rather benign in appearance, Egg thought.

Rip produced his little camera from his pocket—the one he had forgotten to take when they skedaddled with Solo—and snapped a shot of Egg and Charley in front of the thing. Egg snapped one of Rip and Charley. They were smiling, and Rip had his arms around her shoulders. Egg scrutinized the photo on the little screen, turned off the camera and pocketed it. Rip didn't seem to notice.

Then, with nothing else to do, Egg and Charley got aboard, fired up the reactor and inched the saucer out of the hangar. Rip closed the hangar door, took one look around, then climbed aboard and closed the hatch. Charley was in the pilot's seat, looking very comfortable.

She needed flying, Rip acknowledged to himself. Flying was who she was, all she had ever wanted to be. "On to Washington, Ms. Pine," he said imperiously.

She flashed him a grin, lifted the saucer and snapped up the gear as she started the ship moving. Turned to align it with Egg's grass runway, got it accelerating with the antigravity rings and lit the rockets. The acceleration came on with a heavy push. The nose came up, and up and up. In about forty seconds nothing could be seen through the heavy canopy except high, thin cirrus clouds and patches of blue sky. A minute later they left the cirrus behind, and the sky began to darken as the atmosphere thinned.

Hello, Ms. Pine. The voice in Charley's head startled her. For a second she thought it was Solo, but of course it couldn't be.

"Hello, yourself," she replied.

I am the communications officer of the starship over your planet. I wonder if I might access your computer to learn if there are any biological threats that we should take precautions for.

She tried to pick up an accent, a gender indication, something, but it wasn't there. The message was more a thought than a voice. "We have more bacteria and viruses than you can imagine," Charley said. "We don't even have names for all of them."

Precisely. No doubt Adam Solo left a great deal of information on the computer of your saucer that would be of interest to us.

"Access away," Charley said.

Thank you.

When the voice didn't say anything else, she gave Rip and Uncle Egg the gist of the conversation.

"Let's hope they all don't drop dead of something, like the Martians did in *War of the Worlds,*" Egg remarked.

"Well, Solo didn't, and he was probably exposed to

every bug and virus on the planet in his thirteen hundred years here."

Egg and Rip stood on each side of the pilot's seat and stared out the canopy at the earth and clouds below and the stars in the dark sky above.

"A SAUCER HAS GOTTEN AIRBORNE FROM MISSOURI, Mr. President," the aide said. "The FAA says Charlotte Pine is the pilot. She filed a flight plan with the White House as her destination."

"A flight plan?"

"Yes, sir. The FAA demanded a flight plan, they said."

"God bless the FAA."

The aide thought that reply sarcastic and took her leave. Petty Officer Third Class Hennessey watched her go. She was kinda cute, he thought, not for the first time. He had hit her up for a date last week and had been refused. He had gotten the impression that enlisted men were beneath her notice. Oh, well.

First Granddaughter Amanda and three of her school chums came running into the room. The Secret Service had always let her roam at will when she visited, a freedom she took full advantage of now that she had a dozen of her school friends here to share the arrival of the starship delegation.

The secretary of state eyed the kids without affection. This meeting with the aliens was going to be diplomacy of the first order of magnitude, and he suspected kids arcing around would only complicate things. He worried about protocol, about crowd control, about communications with the aliens . . .

"Just how did the aliens communicate with us?" he asked the president.

"Comm won't be a problem," the elected one said evasively, to P. J. O'Reilly's disgust. The president had merely given him a handwritten memo about a message he had received from the aliens, told him to pass it to the press and refused to answer questions about it. The Great One was playing his cards close to his vest, as usual.

Except for the kids, everyone was nervous—you could see it in their faces and body language. Well, everyone but the sailor, O'Reilly noted. He looked as if he were patiently waiting for an order to weigh the anchor—just another great navy day.

O'Reilly wandered into the hallway, which was packed with cabinet secretaries, undersecretaries, deputy secretaries, assistant secretaries and agency hoohahs high and low from all over the government. More officials stood around the conference room swilling Kool-Aid, nibbling stale cookies, nervously chewing their fingernails and watching two televisions.

The air was electric with anticipation and excitement both inside the White House and out in the streets, which one announcer said contained over a half-million people within ten blocks of the Executive Mansion in all directions. The National Guard was helping D.C. and federal police with crowd control. People with heart conditions had been warned to stay home because getting emergency vehicles through the crowds would be problematic, at best. Loudspeakers had been set up so the crowd in the streets and parks could hear the words of the diplomats as they were spoken on the White House lawn.

The kids swooped in and raided the cookie plates. They each took a handful, then scampered off, giggling and whispering and laughing outrageously. They almost knocked down the assistant secretary of defense for roll-on-roll-off (RORO). A Supreme Court associate justice spilled his Kool-Aid down a D.C. schoolteacher's dress when a kid body-blocked him.

Suddenly a whisper shot through the crowd. Rip Cantrell's Sahara saucer was just five minutes away. The crowd began to surge toward the doors. The kids cleaned the last of the cookies off the plates and, using their elbows, wormed their way through the adults.

O'Reilly was back at the Oval Office by then. He heard the secretary of defense say to the president, "All the brains in the executive and judicial branches are here. If the aliens plan to decapitate the government, it won't take much of a bang."

"If that's their goal," the president shot back, "they can do it by merely giving O'Reilly three martinis. Everyone else is just window dressing."

The Oval Office crowd swarmed out and swept the chief of staff along with them.

The weather was perfect for early November: temperature in the sixties, sunlight diffused by high cirrus, and just enough of a breeze to stir the flags, of which there were many.

Charley Pine brought the saucer down the Potomac at the published speed of planes approaching Reagan National Airport, and at the Washington Monument told the approach controller she had the White House in sight. She banked the saucer and let the computer fly the approach. The saucer hovering over the lawn was immediately visible. She decided to land beside it.

The crowd began to roar as the saucer came into sight. From hundreds of thousands of throats, an inarticulate babbling noise rose so loud that the dignitaries and kids and teachers and television crews on the White House lawn behind their crowd control ropes had trouble hearing each other speak. Still, they all shouted at each other and pointed, adding their voices to the hubbub.

The saucer came on with only a tiny growl from the rockets, which fell silent crossing Constitution Avenue. Now it rushed toward the mansion silently, swiftly, growing larger and larger. It seemed to be traveling much too fast, but the more acute observers noticed that the angle of attack was high, so the speed bled off quickly. The saucer came to a dead stop beside the Roswell saucer, one hundred feet in the air. The landing gear came down; then the saucer with Charley Pine at the controls settled slowly until it was completely at rest.

The hatch in the belly opened; Rip Cantrell dropped

out. He turned to give Charley Pine his hand, which she seized and held on to as they made their way out from under the ship. They did it gracefully, even though they had to stoop. Egg Cantrell dropped down, closed the hatch and waddled out ungracefully.

The crowd went nuts, clapping and shouting. The president and Amanda came walking over. As the president shook Rip's and Uncle Egg's hands in turn, Charley swept Amanda off the ground in a bear hug. She still was hugging Amanda when she shook the presidential appendage.

Petty Officer Hennessey led the group back into the White House and straight down the hallway to the Oval Office. This time it was just the president, Amanda, Hennessey and the Missouri trio.

"Thank you for coming," the president said. "I hope you had a good flight."

"Great," Charley said. She still had one of Amanda's hands in hers as they sat side by side on a couch.

"The shuttle from the starship left orbit twenty minutes ago." The president looked at his watch. "They think it will be here in forty-nine minutes."

Everyone nodded.

"I have a request," Amanda's grandfather continued. "Could one of you folks lower that big saucer to the ground?"

Uncle Egg said, "Sure. I can do that. I want to be close enough to watch it, though."

"If you would, please. Hennessey, would you escort him out and back?"

"Yes, sir. This way, Mr. Cantrell."

After they were gone, the president asked Rip and Charley, "Did you folks put that damn thing up there?"

"No," Rip replied. "Adam Solo did. He thought it would be a nice diversion. Give everyone something to think about besides us."

The president sighed and leaned back in his chair. "He was certainly right about that. Sorry he's no longer with us."

"He was ready to go, I think," Charley said softly, and smiled at Amanda, who grinned right back. Charley Pine had been a rock star with Amanda ever since she gave her a saucer ride.

"What I'd like," the child whispered to Charley, "is to fly up to see the starship. Can you help with that?"

"I don't know," Charley said. "Let's wait and see what happens. If things go okay, I'll ask for both of us."

"Totally cool." Amanda beamed at her grandfather and Rip. No two ways about it: She felt *fine*.

The president, however, was getting fidgety. He asked Rip, "So what do you think? Is this starship in orbit an Imperial Battle Cruiser? Are we going to be entertaining a bunch of Klingons here in a bit?"

Rip grinned. "I doubt if these people are Klingons. Adam Solo was an acute observer, a natural leader, a warrior and a survivor if ever there was one. If this starship crew is anything like him, they are basically good people."

"People like us?"

"Forget good, which is a value judgment," Rip said. "The fact is those saucers' computers recognize our thoughts. The computers were built by people with brains like ours or that feat would be impossible. These folks communicate by telepathy, which also would be impossible if their brains were significantly different. They are probably as far in the technological future from us as we are from Julius Caesar. Still, I don't think you'll find them hard to deal with. Be reasonable, and when you must, take no for an answer. After all, this isn't their first visit. Nor, probably, their tenth."

"What was Solo doing here on this planet anyway?"

"Food," Rip said flatly. "Finding ways to genetically engineer new food sources is the only real payoff for the tremendous costs involved in space exploration. They certainly weren't going to take tons of ore or rare metals into orbit and transport them to another star system. That would be impractical.

"No, Solo was undoubtedly here to collect DNA samples from every living plant and animal he could find. Learning how living creatures that had evolved elsewhere solved the basic functions of life was the goal. Heck, scientists on earth are genetically engineering crops, which are the key to mankind's future. But Solo was also a librarian. These guys use the living creatures of earth as a giant DNA library."

The president was horrified. "You mean they put their DNA in us?"

A thoughtful look crossed Rip's face. "I doubt if it's their genome. Our researchers are already storing digital data on DNA, then reading the code with lasers and reconverting it to digital computer code. Think about it: If you have a tremendous amount of critical scientific data acquired at great cost or historical data that you don't want to lose, where would you store it?"

The president look skeptical.

"A star can explode," Rip continued, "a planet can be destroyed by an asteroid impact, nuclear war could break out . . . so you convert the records you want to preserve into DNA and insert it into living species on a variety of planets in different solar systems. The creatures that carry it will be unaffected, and they will pass the coded DNA on to their descendants. The data would deteriorate at a very slow, known rate, which is basically the speed that DNA evolves under radiation.

"One of Solo's tasks was to check on the species carrying code and perhaps insert new code or read old code."

The president remained silent for almost a minute. Then he said, "Why was Solo stranded?"

"One of his shipmates went nuts and stole their saucer. It had been a hard, difficult voyage. Think of the ancient Polynesians sailing across the Pacific looking for islands. We'll never know how many set out and died at sea." Rip shrugged. "I think the other castaways with Solo died or were killed soon afterward. Solo was alone, marooned like Robinson Crusoe, on this planet. This 'savage planet,' he called it.'

"Is Earth still their DNA sample lab and library?"

"Of course. As for storing data, perhaps they didn't store it in the people of earth. Or perhaps not only in people. Other mammals and birds and reptiles could be carriers. One suspects the DNA is in a large number of species to ensure valuable records and data will survive if individual species become extinct. That is the most cost-effective approach, of course, the one with the highest probability of success."

That was a lot for the president to digest. He glanced at Charley Pine, whose face showed no emotion, then scrutinized Rip's innocent visage.

After a moment he said, "I'm going to ask the aliens to take both these saucers with them."

Rip's and Charley's eyes met. "We sorta figured that," Rip said. "They've caused a lot of trouble, and yet mankind is better off because we had them for a little while."

The president didn't want to argue. In his opinion the verdict wasn't in on the saucers. Yes, the technology was revitalizing industry, stimulating research, innovation and investment that was leading to millions of new jobs and a new prosperity here and around the globe, but this Fountain of Youth medical stuff had him worried. For the past ten days he'd felt as if he were sitting on a volcano of public and political pressure that threatened to destroy all that had been gained. Now there was the secret DNA library. If the public got wind of that there would be hell to pay.

A loud round of applause sounded outside. The president's television depicted the Roswell saucer slowly descending with its landing gear out.

"Come on," Charley said to Amanda. "Let's give your friends a saucer tour."

When they were alone, the president said to Rip, "You're a pretty bright young man."

"I get by," Rip acknowledged without a trace of modesty.

That didn't bother the president, who also had a high opinion of his own abilities. He asked, "What are you going to do with your life, after this?"

Rip sighed. "Darn if I know."

WHEN THE ROSWELL SAUCER WAS ON THE GROUND, Uncle Egg said to Petty Officer Hennessey, "Want to climb inside with me? I want to check out the condition of the ship."

"Sure," Hennessey said brightly. *Man, this navy gig is looking up. A flying saucer, no less.*

They climbed inside, and Egg sat in the pilot's seat and donned the headband. Soon he had the computer probing the health of every system. Yes, as Solo said, the communications equipment was kaput, as was one of the computers. The other two seemed to be functioning normally, however, and the engineering checks seemed fine.

Satisfied, he took off the headband, verbally sketched out the workings of the saucer for the sailor and answered a few questions.

Egg secured the reactor and closed the hatch when they both were once again on the ground.

As he stood up, he heard a voice call, "Arthur Cantrell! Arthur Cantrell!"

He spotted her in the front row of the scientists' area. Professor Deborah Deehring, the archaeologist. She was smiling and waving. Uncle Egg felt his pulse soar.

He veered and strode toward her. Some Secret Service type with a badge and earpiece, talking into his lapel, gestured to Egg to stay back, but Hennessey took a hand. He had the badge of a presidential aide, so he was a big shot. He raised the rope for Deborah.

She gave Egg a hug, in front of the whole crowd and the television cameras, a hug seen round the globe.

"I was worried about you, Arthur," she said.

"I was in good hands. Rip and Charley's."

They chatted as they strolled toward the Sahara saucer, where Charley Pine stood with a delegation of children around her as she touched the fuselage, pointed at the rocket engines and landing gear, and gave a grade-school explanation of saucer flight.

They stood back until she finished. Charley gave Deborah a little wave, then went under the saucer and opened the hatch, and the kids swarmed in. Egg and Deborah followed them.

Inside, Egg and Professor Deehring stood back while the kids romped and listened to Charley's explanations. After about five minutes, Charley shooed the kids out and followed them, leaving the two adults alone. Egg seated Deborah in the pilot's seat, put a headband on her and turned on the power.

She sat mesmerized as she once again explored the memories of the computers and the displays on the panel tracked her progress. Finally, almost reluctantly, she took off the headband.

"Oh, Arthur."

Egg laughed. "Life holds its surprises."

"No wonder you were so enthralled. There is so much information, it would take ten lifetimes to even sort through it, much less analyze it. Are you going to—?"

"No," he said firmly. "Charley and Rip thought our flight here this morning was our last saucer flight, and I think they are right. The saucer gives too much. Just too much. Mankind isn't ready yet."

Egg glanced at his watch. "The shuttle from the starship should be here within minutes. Let's get out and watch it land. See how the president handles it."

"And the First Granddaughter," Deborah added. "Amanda."

"She'll do fine," Egg replied. "It's the grandfather I'm worried about. All this talk about Fountain of Youth pills, eternal life by prescription . . . It would be madness, but the public and politicians are screaming for it."

"That information is in these computers, isn't it?"

"Yes. If the aliens don't want these ships back, Rip, Charley and I agreed to launch them into the sun."

19

THE SHUTTLE FROM THE STARSHIP CAME OUT OF THE south, so it was first visible as a black speck in the sky to the audience gathered on the White House lawn and the hundreds of thousands of people standing in the streets. Amazingly, a giant hush fell upon the crowd.

The shuttle wasn't using rocket engines. Rip noted that fact and whispered the observation to Charley Pine, who just nodded. They were standing with Uncle Egg, the president and Amanda, out front beside the two saucers. Everyone else was behind crowd control ropes strategically placed in a giant horseshoe. Television cameras were on mobile platforms behind the people, and several cameramen and sound technicians wearing badges were roaming near the presidential party ready to record the aliens' and the president's first remarks.

All over the globe people were gathered around their television sets. Outside of Washington, in every city, town, hamlet and village all over the world, streets and public places were deserted as people gathered to watch the Big Arrival. Network executives were orgasmic: Ad revenues, based as always on the size of the audience, were going to go through the roof. Never before in the history of the medium had this many humans watched the same event.

The shuttle was not a saucer. It was arrow-shaped, with stubby winglets and two short, wide, vertical stabilizers. The entire ship was a lifting body. As it crossed Constitution Avenue, stubby struts appeared on the wingtips and one from the belly, near the nose.

The shuttle slowed, drifted downward and landed facing the president. It was black, a glistening black; no doubt the entire skin was a solar panel to recharge the batteries, Rip decided, just like the saucers, and hard and tough enough to be unaffected by the near-absolute-zero of space or heat of entry into atmospheres.

Not a whisper could be heard. Seconds passed; then a hatch opened in the side of the ship, opened inward. A tiny stair came out. Then a person. It was obviously a woman, middle-aged, of medium stature, with short-cropped hair and brown skin, as if she were well tanned. She stepped out and looked around at the crowd, at the sky, at the buildings and trees and grass, taking it all in. She stood watching as other people emerged from the shuttle one by one and lined up behind her. Soon a dozen people were standing there. They wore khaki one-piece jumpsuits and some kind of footwear. No hats.

Amanda broke the spell. She had been holding the

presidential hand, but now she bolted. She ran toward the starship crew fearlessly, her face alight, her hair flying, her legs and arms flashing in the early winter sun.

To the amazement of the onlookers, the woman who was the first person out of the saucer plopped down into a cross-legged sitting position on the grass and stared at the approaching child. She ran her fingers through the grass as Amanda ran up to her.

Amanda's courage failed her then. She stopped several feet away and gazed hard at the woman. Their eyes were almost on a level. "I'm Amanda."

I am the captain.

Several of the other space travelers also sat. Standing or sitting, they fixed their unwavering attention on the girl.

Then Amanda took a few quick steps and hugged the woman, who hugged her back. As the woman ran her fingers through the child's hair and scrutinized her features, the crowd exploded in applause and cheering.

The applause and shouting didn't stop. Now some of the shuttle crew began looking around, trying to take it all in. People were waving madly; tentatively, one crewman raised his hand and waved back. That stimulated the crowd, which got even noisier. Some of the others waved as well.

Finally the president walked over. He held out his hand to the seated woman.

"Welcome to earth," he said.

Thank you. The woman got to her feet, glanced at the

outstretched hand and took it. The president sensed that shaking hands was not a custom, so he pumped her hand once and released it.

"Did you bring any kids along?" Amanda demanded.

No. Unfortunately. She addressed the president. **I am the captain.**

The president introduced himself and his granddaughter.

The other spacemen and -women, for there were three more females, gently gathered around Amanda. They looked at her straw-colored hair, felt it, touched her . . . and two of them kissed her on the cheek.

Amanda set out to hug each and every one of them. It took a while. The applause continued unabated. Finally the president pointed at the White House and the group began to move. Amanda was the center of the group, so he took her hand and she followed. Maybe she was getting a bit nervous at all the attention. One of the space people lingered to close the hatch, then caught up with them.

"Is this your shuttle crew, Captain?"

This is my starship crew. All of them.

"Oh."

They walked between the saluting soldiers, sailors, airmen and marines of the honor guard toward the open doors of the White House. All the space people were waving now. The crowd roared its approval as Petty Officer Hennessey, Rip, Charley, Uncle Egg and Professor Deehring followed the starship crew.

"Are you a mother?" Amanda asked the captain.

No.

"But you like kids?"

Yes.

"Would you like to meet my friends?"

Of course.

Before the president could stop her, Amanda scampered between two of the honor guard and ran for the area where her classmates waited. They saw her coming and slipped under the rope. They evaded the Secret Service agents like fleeing cats and ran toward Amanda, who reversed her course. In seconds the children were packed tightly around the captain, who tried to touch and hug them all.

Before the president, his party and the children disappeared into the Executive Mansion, a marine captain led a company out from behind a barricade and marched toward the saucers and starship shuttle. The marines were in combat dress with helmets and carried loaded assault rifles. When given the duty of guarding the ships, the captain on his own responsibility had ordered his marines to load their weapons. Now they circled the ships facing outward. The sergeants moved a few of them one way or another and, satisfied, went over to confer with the captain, who returned their salutes. After a short conference, the captain wandered off to talk to the Secret Service agent in charge.

The cameras caught that scene, of course. One of the network talking heads remarked over the air, "This is appropriate. After all, the streets of heaven are guarded by United States Marines."

"ARE YOU FOLKS HUNGRY?" THE PRESIDENT ASKED THE captain. "We have a lunch prepared if you wish to sample our food."

A sample of your food would be welcome indeed. With water that hasn't been recycled a hundred times.

The president motioned to two aides to take Amanda and the children away. "Get them some lunch," he said.

Then he led the adults to the State Dining Room. Uniformed waiters stood at attention. The aliens stood transfixed, staring. It took several seconds for Uncle Egg to realize they were staring at the riot of flower arrangements on the dining table. One of the starship crewmen took a tentative step toward them, smelled them. The others joined him. They drank in the aromas; then one man plucked a petal and tasted it.

The aliens broke into laughter and moved from arrangement to arrangement sniffing and tasting.

That broke the ice. The waiters held chairs, and after much shuffling, everyone was seated.

The president had conferred with NASA experts, who were of the opinion that vegetables, protein and starches would be excellent menu choices. This White House had by decree stopped serving French cuisine at state dinners years ago. The menu today was American food: all the usual vegetables and a variety of breads, roast beef, lamb, pork chops and fried chicken, plus dishes that reflected the diversity of the American population. Chinese dishes, Polynesian, Cuban, Mexican, Indian, Italian, German and a couple of French dishes with appropriate sauces that the chef had sandwiched in there anyway. Great Britain was represented by toad-in-the-hole.

Even as the president's guests were being seated, the White House mouthpiece was handing out copies of the menu to reporters, who packed the press room. P. J. O'Reilly had the situation well in hand.

The aliens were seated between members of the president's party. The president sat beside the captain. The secretary of state sat on her right. A member of the crew was next, then Egg and Professor Deehring, another crew member, Rip, another crew member, Charley, and so on. Petty Officer Hennessey had a space person on his right and left.

The secretary of defense found himself seated at the foot of the table between a Supreme Court associate justice, an old woman who talked in a whisper, and the head of NASA. A crone and a windbag. He glared at Hennessey up the table seated between two aliens from God-knows-where and chattering away. An enlisted man, no less!

There were bottles of wine on the table, California reds and whites. The secretary of defense would have deeply appreciated a couple of vodka martinis, which the waiter whispered weren't available, so he poured himself a brimming glass of red wine and drank it like milk.

Rip turned to the man on his left and introduced himself. "Rip Cantrell."

I am the first officer.

"What do they call you?"

An unintelligible noise flashed through Rip's head. He laughed.

Pick a name you like and call me that.

"Sam. I'll call you Sam."

Sam. I like that. Tell me about the saucer pilot who is marooned here. Is he here with us today?

He is dead, Rip said silently.

The first officer glanced at the captain, seated beside the president, and she looked at him and Rip.

Tell me about that, the first officer said.

So Rip did. Silently, directing his thoughts at Sam, the first officer. *Adam Solo was the chosen name of the saucer pilot marooned on earth for thirteen hundred years. He had other names at various times, such as Hiawatha and Leif Ericson, or Leif the Lucky.*

Rip was well into his explanation of the pharma moguls and their quest for drugs that would extend human life when he realized that all the starship crew had stopped talking and were staring at him. They were listening to every word. So he told of the chase and final battle in the Grand Canyon and Solo's death. Told it in the silence, with every one of the starship crew staring at him.

When he finished, he heard words that he knew were from the captain of the starship.

Thank you, Rip.

Then the first officer. **Thank you.**

"Let's have some wine," Charley Pine said aloud. She too had heard the first officer's and captain's thoughts and now broke the silence. Conversation resumed. The earth people spoke aloud, and the aliens replied silently. It was weird, yet it wasn't. In a few minutes it seemed absolutely normal to all the people seated at the table.

The waiters carried the dishes around, and the aliens always took a spoonful to try. Only a spoonful. Meat in slivers.

The first officer stared at the eating utensils and settled on a spoon. The knife he knew, presumably, because he hefted it and tested the point and sharpness of the blade, then held it ready in his left hand. He found about half the dishes palatable. If he liked it, he ate the dollop on his plate. If he didn't, he ignored the rest of it. The meat he sliced into tiny bites, which he placed one by one on his tongue using the spoon.

He delivered his verdict to Rip and Charley, who were on each side of him. **Good. Fair. Very good. Not so good. Bad. Good again.**

He liked the red wine best, Charley noted. The white he sampled, then ignored. Every now and then he picked up the water glass and drank as if the glass contained the nectar of the gods. The waiter behind him refilled it promptly.

The president was feeling mellow. The Arrival was going well, so far anyway. His wife had been giving him grief about the size of his tummy, which wasn't sexy, she said, and he had been watching his diet. He decided to splurge. He loaded his plate with fried chicken, mashed potatoes and gravy, and two enchiladas covered with cheese.

The starship captain watched him with an air of disbelief but tried a tiny amount of each. She watched her host use his knife and fork and tried to emulate him.

Charley Pine got the first officer talking about his home planet, what it was like. Compared to Adam Solo, the first officer was positively garrulous. Blah, blah, blah. He blabbed on and on. He was homesick, thoroughly tired of the starship and thoroughly tired of his shipmates. When he delivered this pronouncement, several of his colleagues around the table froze and stared at him.

Egg had maneuvered the seating so that he was seated beside Professor Deehring. He let the government officials on the other side of the aliens monopolize their attention as he chatted with Deborah.

He felt a warm, pleasant feeling as she talked to him. She asked about Adam Solo, the Big Pharma moguls and what he thought important about his latest adventure. Egg talked on and on. She watched him with those big blue eyes.

At the head of the table, the president and the starship captain were having a private conversation. At least the president assumed it was private, since he spoke in a low voice and she didn't speak at all, merely fired thoughts into his cranium.

"So how long did your voyage here take?"

A long time.

"How long, in earth years?"

Perhaps a hundred.

The president thought about that. A century ago this planet was convulsed by World War I. He shook his head to clear it. He decided to change the subject. "You seemed very charmed today by the children," he said.

Ah, yes. Children. It has been a long time since I saw a child.

"What with the length of your voyage and all, I understand that."

No. You couldn't. We have lost the ability to have children. We have sex, certainly, but for reasons we don't understand, the women do not become pregnant. We have come here to your planet to get DNA samples from successful parents so that we can properly research the problem and find answers. If we cannot solve this problem, the people of our planet will become extinct.

20

AFTER LUNCH THE PARTY ADJOURNED TO THE EAST Room, where the assembled American scientists awaited them. More wine, water and soft drinks were served by waiters with trays.

Professor Hans Soldi, the archaeologist who had helped Rip dig the Sahara saucer from the sandstone that entombed it, sought out a biologist from the starship and began questioning her. He wanted to know if the aliens had colonized earth 140,000 years ago when the Sahara saucer was abandoned. She didn't know.

"Surely," he said, "your DNA sampling of our population must indicate we are closely related to you?" He didn't know about the aliens' DNA sampling or storage activities, but he was making a leap to a rock he thought likely to be there.

The biologist was evasive. **If it happened,** she said, **it happened prior to the records I have access to.**

He couldn't budge her off that position, although he tried.

Then he noticed that there was a hair on her shirt, on her shoulder. When she sipped her drink, he picked it off. *Two can play the DNA game,* he thought.

Around them conversation swirled. "What is your home planet like?" "How many solar systems have you visited on this voyage?" "Tell me about your civilization." That was cocktail party chatter, intended to get acquainted, not solicit information.

Still, the Americans wanted all they could get. NASA officials asked questions about the problems of space flight. Anthropologists questioned them about conditions on other planets, creatures they had found, how life had evolved under different gravity, atmospheric chemical composition and radiation levels.

The captain and president mixed and mingled for a bit, then went off to the Oval office for private conversations. Petty Officer Hennessey accompanied them.

In the president's office, the elected one got down to it. "How can we help you with your problem?"

We would like DNA samples from a fairly representative group of successful earth parents, she said. **And we would like to meet and talk with the survivors of the saucer that crashed on earth during an electrical storm in 1947.**

"The Roswell saucer?" the president asked, his eyes narrowing.

I believe it is the large saucer parked outside on the lawn.

"The crew was never found. Nor any bodies. How many people were aboard it?"

Six. Three men and three women, all biologists engaged in genetic research.

The president's eyes registered his surprise. The American public had choked down the fact that Adam Solo had been marooned on earth for thirteen hundred years. Telling them six more aliens had been roaming around unsuspected since 1947 would ignite a political firestorm.

The captain read his thoughts. **We need make no announcement,** she said. **We have already summoned them. They and their families are outside now. All we ask is that you admit them to these grounds and we will meet with them secretly.**

The president caught Hennessey's gaze and said to him, "Ask Egg Cantrell to come in here. Tell O'Reilly to have the Secret Service admit anyone and their family who mentions that he or she was on the Roswell saucer."

That will be most appreciated, the captain said. **I will tell them now.**

An hour later the group was gathered. There were five families. One man had not lived to marry and have children, the others said. The women were mothers, and their children were in their fifties and early sixties. One of the surviving men was a father. Between them, they had nine children, who had so far produced eleven grandchildren and two great-grandchildren. Neither the grandchildren nor great-grandchildren were included in the group here today. Only the saucer survivors knew of their origin, and they had never told their children, who with their spouses learned the facts now with mouths agape.

Tears were shed, children hugged parents, and everyone talked at once.

When we were unable to rescue you immediately, the captain said, **we hoped you would continue your research into our genetic difficulties, find a mate here on this planet and conceive offspring. That you have done so fulfills our faith in you. I invite you now to return home with us on the starship, bringing your families if you wish, and help us solve our genetic problem.** Everyone in the room heard this speech, including Uncle Egg, the president and Hennessey.

More tears flowed. They had indeed continued doing biological research here on earth, and they produced digital thumb drives they handed to the captain. "Certainly you have the capability of reading these files," one man said.

As for leaving earth, the answer was universally no.

"This is our home," one woman explained to the starship commander with tears running down her face. "Certainly we faced all the problems of immigrants, learning the language, earning a living, getting an education here that would qualify us for professional positions, but somehow we all did it. We became Americans, citizens of this planet. Some of our children and grandchildren have served in the armed forces, and some have been elected to various government positions. A few have screwed up their lives before finally getting on the right track, and a couple have screwed up beyond redemption. We pay taxes and we vote. We are Americans and we don't want to leave. Ours is an American story. This is where our families are, this is where we built our lives, and this is where we hope to live the rest of our days."

Egg Cantrell clapped. Everyone looked at him. He kept clapping, and the survivors, their children and the president joined in.

When the hubbub died, the president had a few words to say. "I must caution you that making your secret public now might be harmful to our diplomatic efforts. While you can undoubtedly sell a book and make some money, you would be creating problems for your children and future generations. I urge you to continue to keep the secret you have so far kept so well. Thank you for coming."

The captain asked the survivors and their children for DNA samples, permission for which was freely given. O'Reilly was summoned and told what was wanted. After much handshaking and hugs all around for everyone, the survivors and their families were escorted away, to be driven to Bethesda Naval Hospital for DNA testing.

When the room once again contained only the captain, the president, Uncle Egg and Hennessey, the president told Egg of the captain's request for DNA samples of successful earth parents.

Before Egg could get a word in edgewise, the president

went after the starship captain. "We can certainly help you," he said, "but we want something in return. We want your research into the diseases aging—senescence—causes or enables, things like Alzheimer's disease, osteoporosis and cataracts. And we want what you know about the causes, prevention and cures for cancer."

The captain looked around the room, at the three men, at the paintings and decorations, looked out the window at the weak November sunshine. Finally she turned to face them. **Biology is not my field; I am a starship commander. I have my orders and diplomatic guidelines that my government expects me to follow. My orders are not to disrupt or interfere with the natural progression of a civilization, nor to take sides in planetary disputes.**

Still, I have a certain amount of discretion. We can give you everything you ask for about cancer. Senescence is a much more difficult problem according to the biologists in my crew. In my judgment, giving you thousands of years of research into senescence would revolutionize your society in ways it is probably not prepared to handle. However, I can ask my biologists to look at where your researchers are and suggest lines of inquiry that they believe will be of value to you and not violate the spirit of our orders.

"Mr. Cantrell?" the president said.

Egg already knew precisely what he thought. He spent a few seconds figuring out how to verbalize it, then said, "Too much too soon would turn the lives of the six billion people on this planet upside down. It might also cause hundreds, or thousands, of other species to become extinct, species for which we are moral guardians. Biological diversity is one of the miracles that sustain life on this planet. My advice is to accept her offer."

"Petty Officer Hennessey?"

"Mr. Cantrell offers wise advice, sir, in my opinion. Accept her offer."

"Captain, what can we offer you in the way of provisions to continue your journey?"

Water, sir. Recycling water inevitably leads to losses. And I am sure my first officer can go over available protein and vegetable matter and find some items that we can put into the starship's food supply system.

"I also wish you folks would take these two saucers with you. They contain computers full of information that our civilization is not yet ready to use wisely."

The captain smiled. **Your wisdom is commendable. My superiors ordered me to recover or destroy them, if possible. As it happens, we have no room for them on the starship. I suggest launching them into your star.**

The president lowered his head, then nodded.

"I accept your offer," he told the captain. "Give us what biological assistance you can consistent with your orders, and we will provide the DNA samples you asked for and all the provisions you wish. I am sure Mr. Cantrell can dispose of the saucers." He eyed Uncle Egg, who nodded.

They left it there.

As Egg left the room, he felt as if a great weight—eternal life in a pill bottle—had been lifted . . . from his shoulders and the shoulders of all mankind. Thank God, he thought, Harrison Douglas and Johnny Murkowsky were dead and the body of Adam Solo was beyond the reach of other greedy men.

SINCE THEY HAD FEASTED IN EARLY AFTERNOON, DINner for the space voyagers was snacks. Rip and Charley, Uncle Egg and Professor Deehring mingled for a bit, then thanked the president and departed for the Willard Hotel, where Egg had managed to obtain rooms. He had asked for the presidential suite and a penthouse—an extravagance—but if the four of them hoped to sleep in Washington under a roof in real beds and use showers with hot water, that was about it. Of course, Egg could have asked the White House staff for help, but he didn't want to owe them a favor. Better to pay the American Express bill when it came.

They walked to the Willard through dissipating crowds. None of the people in the streets recognized them, which was a blessing.

Egg signed his name and presented his credit card. The desk clerk certainly knew who they were and called Egg, Rip and Charley by name. Two bellhops almost came to blows over their overnight bags. Rip and Charley got the presidential suite. There was a balcony that overlooked the city, the Washington Monument and the White House.

The saucers and starship shuttle were just visible through the trees.

When the bellhop had departed with a tip, Rip locked the door and joined Charley on the balcony. "Uncle Egg said the aliens don't want the saucers. We are supposed to fuel them and launch them into the sun."

"It'll make great television," Charley said distractedly. Obviously she had something on her mind.

Rip did too. He decided the time was right, so he dived right in. "Will you marry me?" he asked Charley Pine.

She turned and looked at him, surprise written all over her face. "Say that again?"

"You heard me. Will you marry me?"

"You're proposing?"

"I certainly hope so. I think this is the way it's done. Will you marry me?"

"I thought you'd never ask."

"Well, I am asking. I don't know what the future holds, or where our lives will take us, but I want to share life with you. So will you marry me?"

"Yes," said Charley Pine.

Rip was not slow. He gathered the lady into his arms and kissed her deeply.

When they broke, Charley said, "With one tiny little proviso."

"Only one?"

"Only one, but I suppose it's not so tiny. I talked to the

captain of the starship this evening. They were hoping to take home some of the Roswell survivors and their families, but they all said no. They have some room on their starship. I volunteered us to go with them."

Rip stared at her. "*Us?*"

"*Us.* You and me. You know that they are having a baby problem on their planet. Genetics and such. They are going to get DNA samples from successful earth parents for research. And I thought, well, heck, Rip and I are going to be parents, so why don't we go with them and have a huge adventure?"

In the silence that followed, she added, "What do you think?"

"We've got to do something with our lives," Rip admitted.

"Right."

"But a hundred years? It would be really tough. Even if it's a luxury hotel—I doubt that it is—and we're busy as heck, spending a hundred years with just a dozen people? We'll go crazy or kill them."

"They made it," Charley shot back. "If they can do it, we can! And imagine what we'll learn! Not to mention the extraordinary adventures we'll have along the way and when the voyage is over."

That, in a nutshell, Rip reflected, was the life philosophy of Charley Pine. He scrutinized her face. That was the optimistic outlook and determination that had gotten her into tactical military aviation and through test pilot school. It was also, he realized, the philosophy of the millions of immigrants to America through the centuries, immigrants who left everything, endured untold traveling hardships, then started from scratch in a new world.

If he wanted this woman, he was going to have to sign the Pine manifesto. Of course, Rip had already done that once, when he dug the saucer from the Sahara sandstone, fueled it with water and climbed aboard to fly. That adventure worked out rather well, he thought. If he had taken counsel of his fears then, he wouldn't have gotten to know and fallen in love with Charley Pine.

Almost as if she were reading his thoughts, she said, "Remember the Sahara? We didn't know how the adventure would turn out, but we both climbed into that saucer and flew it away. And here we are."

Another thought occurred to Rip. "How do you know we'll be parents?"

"Rip. Ripper. How do you think women through the ages have known that their man was going to be a father?"

He goggled. Grabbed her arms and stared into her eyes. "You're pregnant?"

"Yes." She said it simply, but it was the most powerful word Rip had ever heard.

Joy flooded him. *Oh wow, Charley was going to have his baby!* Then he remembered the recent adventures with Adam Solo. "How long have you known this?"

"Oh, a while."

"And you were dancing on top of a saucer over the Grand Canyon?"

"The little Ripper is going to have to take life as it comes. You and I have had to. That's what life is, Rip! It's an *adventure*. It *must* be lived that way or it is worth nothing."

He gathered her into his arms and kissed her.

IN THE PENTHOUSE UNCLE EGG AND PROFESSOR DEBORAH Deehring were having a glass of wine on their balcony. As it happened, their balcony was immediately above the presidential suite balcony, and they heard every word that passed between Rip and Charley.

They slipped inside and closed the door.

"They're leaving your life, Arthur," Deborah said.

Uncle Egg merely nodded. He was smiling, and tears were leaking down his cheeks.

"Adam Solo said he would meet us on the other side," Egg said. "I'll see Rip and Charley there too. That will have to do."

21

THE NEXT FEW DAYS WERE HECTIC. DNA SAMPLES were taken from volunteer couples, an undertaking that fascinated the press and resulted in worldwide publicity.

Several of the starship crew toured the zoo and oohed and aahed at the extraordinary diversity they saw. Others toured the arboretum, where they took samples and recorded images of plants they found interesting.

The shuttle was loaded with tanks of water, over a ton, and a thousand pounds of carefully selected living plants, including wheat, rice, soybeans and corn, a flock of chickens and two pigs, a male and a pregnant female. Charley Pine wanted to take Amanda to the starship for a look, but with all the supplies, it wasn't to be. NASA wanted to send two senior engineers to explore, and that plus the first officer, who was flying the shuttle, took all the room in the cabin there was.

Amanda and Charley toured the shuttle when it returned that evening. The first officer answered every question that was asked. Amanda had a wonderful time. Hennessey took her to the White House Press Room, where she answered reporters' questions.

Through the good offices of Petty Officer Hennessey, who was here, there and everywhere, Rip and Charley got in to see the president.

"We're going with the aliens on their starship," they told him. "They said they have the room."

The president felt a great warmth come over him, much like that produced by a shot of really good bourbon. The saucer aces, Rip Cantrell and Charley Pine, were going to be out of his hair permanently. He beamed benignly. "Godspeed, children."

"Before we go, however," Rip said, "we'd like to ask a favor of you."

The president's grin vanished. *This was too good to be true,* he thought.

"We want to get married," Charley explained, "and were hoping you could marry us. Like tomorrow."

Relief flooded the Grand Poobah. "I never married anybody before. I don't know anything about District of Columbia marriage laws. For all I know, I don't have the authority. We can probably find you a judge or preacher, if you want."

"Oh, we don't care about the D.C. laws," Rip said, making a gesture that swept away all little difficulties. "We aren't going to get a license. It's the ceremony we want. We'll invite the family and the aliens and tie the knot."

"Oh," the president said blandly. He was not surprised. In his experience Rip and Charley pretty much ignored other people's rules and made their own. "In that case, why not? When?"

"Would tomorrow evening work?"

"Sure."

"Great. We'll go buy some rings." They scampered away holding hands.

"I hope my presiding over a marriage doesn't set a precedent," the president growled at Hennessey.

"Don't sweat it, sir. You might tell the press you'll marry anyone leaving the planet without dying first."

Charley called her mom and dad and sister, and Rip telephoned his mother in Minnesota. The next evening, as the families and aliens watched, the president read a ceremony Rip and Charley had found on the Internet. Amanda was maid of honor. Everyone wanted to kiss the bride, including the president, who laid one on her cheek.

Uncle Egg snapped a couple of photos of Rip, Charley and the president with Rip's camera; then the president snapped a few of Uncle Egg and the newlyweds.

The president gave Egg his camera back, then whispered to the White House photographer, "Get some of Rip, Charley and Egg. I want an eight-by-ten of the best one framed for my desk."

P. J. O'Reilly knew good PR when he saw it, so he had photos of the wedding and watching aliens on the street within an hour.

The next day Rip and Charley fueled the saucers with water from a hose.

While they were at it, Uncle Egg climbed into the Roswell saucer and donned the headset. He knew what he wanted, and he spent over an hour communing with the computer trying to get it. He made notes on a small pad. He wasn't a physicist, but he was a very competent engineer. Finally, satisfied he had all he could get, he turned off the power and closed the hatch behind him. The closest marine saluted him, and he smiled in reply.

When the saucer he had discovered in the Sahara was completely full of water, Rip sat in the pilot's seat and told the computer what he wanted. Then he reviewed the graphics to ensure the computer had it right.

Charley Pine did the same for the Roswell saucer. She found John-Paul Lalouette's bloodstains still on the floor and said a little prayer for him.

Then the saucers launched from the White House lawn. Rip's went out over the Potomac gaining height and airspeed; then the rocket engines ignited and the nose rose to the vertical. It soared away on a pillar of fire as the world watched on television.

Charley's Roswell saucer was next.

When the two were gone the starship crew and Rip and Charley said their good-byes. Rip cried, Uncle Egg cried, Charley's parents and sister cried, and Rip's mom cried. Even the president's eyes grew a little moist.

"Thanks for everything, Uncle Egg. You were like a father to me."

"And you were a son to me. I love you, Ripper."

Amanda clung to Charley and wouldn't let go. "I want to go with you," she said.

"You need to stay here with your family, grow up, get an education, fall in love," Charley whispered. "Have your own adventures. Live your life, savor it, live it to the hilt."

"I will, Charley! Oh, I will!"

The president gathered Amanda into his arms.

The aliens climbed aboard the shuttle first. Charley reluctantly released Uncle Egg's hand and followed her new husband up the little stairway. The door closed with a tiny hiss, and the crowd drew back behind the velvet ropes.

The shuttle flew away effortlessly, without the sound and fury and visual power of the saucers, almost as if it were a dream departing. The antigravity system repelled the earth and slingshotted it into orbit, where it rendezvoused with the starship. A few hours later the starship left orbit on another voyage across the universe.

LIFE IN THE WHITE HOUSE SOON RETURNED TO "NORmal." Congress resumed the eternal argument about the budget and addressed tax and immigration reform. The fall football wars once again became of serious interest to millions of Americans. Kids returned to classes all over the nation, and people began to think about the Thanksgiving holidays and fall hunting seasons.

A week after the shuttle left, the president called Petty

Officer Third Class Hennessey into his office and poured him a drink from his private bourbon bottle.

"What are you going to do with your life, son?" he asked.

"Well, sir, I have only two years of college. I thought when my hitch is up in May I'd go back to school, work part-time and try to qualify for naval aviation."

"You want to fly, do you?"

"Yes, sir. The F-35 is an awesome airplane. Maybe that will work out for me, maybe it won't, but I want to try."

The president took a sheet of paper from his desk and passed it over. "I thought it might be something like that," he said. "Here's a commission as an ensign in the United States Navy."

Hennessey looked at the document in surprise. There was his name. Orvul Allen Hennessey. At least they got that right.

The president kept talking. "I spoke to the CNO. He said the navy can send you to college to get your degree while you draw full pay and allowances, and from the looks of your last physical, you qualify for flight training. Congratulations."

Hennessey didn't know what to say. Finally he managed, "Thank you, sir."

"You have good sense," the president said, "which is a rare commodity. Your country needs you. Thank you for your help these last few weeks."

After Hennessey left, the president looked at the photo of Uncle Egg, Rip Cantrell and Charley Pine that sat framed on his desk. Looked, and smiled.

• • •

BACK IN MISSOURI, PROFESSOR DEBORAH DEEHRING and Uncle Egg let the dust settle while they really got to know each other. Uncle Egg downloaded the photos from Rip's camera onto his computer and spent a few minutes a day looking at them.

Professor Hans Soldi called Deborah and asked for her help. He had a hair from an alien, he said, and was awaiting a complete DNA analysis. He thought it might prove that she was related to the people on earth. Maybe. To a statistical probability. He wanted Deborah to help him explore the relationship.

Deborah Deehring objected. Biology was not her field.

"Nor mine," Soldi admitted, "but together we can learn it."

She talked it over with Egg, who urged her to go with it. They liked each other a lot and decided to see each other every weekend, when she wasn't tied up at the university or with Soldi.

"Are you going to look for more saucers?" she asked. "It seems impossible that the two that were found are the only ones on the planet."

Uncle Egg wasn't so sure. "The Roswell saucer crashed in an electrical storm. The crew of the Sahara saucer Rip found was unable to return to it for unknown reasons, but the saucer that delivered Solo to earth was flown away by a madman. Even if saucers came and went on some kind of regular basis, there are probably few that crashed or were abandoned that remain undiscovered."

"But in one hundred forty thousand years, there might be."

Uncle Egg begged off. "If I found one, without Rip and Charley to fly it, it wouldn't be the same."

"So what are you going to do, Arthur?"

"I'm going to live out the days God gives me and find interesting things to think about."

She seemed pleased with that answer.

"And maybe," Egg added, "in a year or two, if you are willing, we'll get married."

"Oh, Arthur! You are such a romantic!"

They left it there.

Still, about a week later, an Arizona sheriff's deputy showed up with a summons for Rip and Charley. "We want to question them about some bodies that were found in the Grand Canyon," he said.

"Don't you people read newspapers or watch television?" Egg asked. "They aren't here."

"This is a serious matter, Mr. Cantrell. Where are they?"

Egg jammed a thumb toward the sky. "Up there. They left with the aliens on their starship."

The deputy tore the summons in half, gave it to Egg and left.

Uncle Egg went inside and made himself a pot of coffee. As it dripped through, he found himself thinking about the antigravity devices on the saucer and on the alien starship, which had used a more advanced version of the gravity attraction and repulsion technology to propel itself around the universe.

How had that worked, anyway? What did they know about gravity that we don't? Rip had built an antigravity device for an airplane, but he never understood the physics. The aliens had indeed discovered the Grand Unified Theory, the holy grail of physics, the theory that combined all the known forces of the universe. Egg had actually seen the symbols and had written them in his notebook. He hadn't understood them when he wrote them. Perhaps with some research he could make sense of it.

When Uncle Egg had a hot cup of java in his hand, he turned on his computer and began researching the physics of gravity on the Internet. He read his notes again and began to think.